Hazel Bly
and the
Deep Blue Sea

Hazel Bly
and the
Deep Blue Sea

Ashley Herring Blake

LITTLE, BROWN AND COMPANY

New York   Boston

Little, Brown and Company
Hachette Book Group
1290 Avenue of the Americas, New York, NY 10104
Visit us at LBYR.com

First Edition: May 2021

Little, Brown and Company is a division of Hachette Book Group, Inc. The Little, Brown name and logo are trademarks of Hachette Book Group, Inc.

The publisher is not responsible for websites (or their content) that are not owned by the publisher.

Library of Congress Cataloging-in-Publication Data
Names: Blake, Ashley Herring, author.
Title: Hazel Bly and the deep blue sea / Ashley Herring Blake.
Description: First edition. | New York : Little, Brown and Company, 2021. | Audience: Ages 8–12. | Summary: For two years, twelve-year-old Hazel has coped with her Mum's accidental death by overprotecting her sister and Mama, but when Mama reconnects with her first love, roles begin to shift.
Identifiers: LCCN 2020023867 | ISBN 9780316535458 (hardcover) | ISBN 9780316535465 (ebook) | ISBN 9780316535502 (ebook other)
Subjects: CYAC: Mothers and daughters—Fiction. | Lesbian mothers—Fiction. | Sisters—Fiction. | Loss (Psychology)—Fiction. | Maine—Fiction.
Classification: LCC PZ7.1.B58 Haz 2021 | DDC [Fic]—dc23
LC record available at https://lccn.loc.gov/2020023867

ISBNs: 978-0-316-53545-8 (hardcover), 978-0-316-53546-5 (ebook)

Printed in the United States of America

LSC-C

Printing 1, 2021

For C, B, and W, who love me anyway

If nothing saves us from death,
may love at least save us from life.

—Javier Velaza

chapter one

I peer out the window at death.

Well, not death. But an ocean a few hundred feet from the front door of our new house might as well be death, all that fog-draped water just waiting for a fresh swimmer to devour, which would be exactly my luck. And don't even get me started on water beasts, all manner of fascinating yet deadly sharks and jellyfish and god-knows-what-else lurking in the deep. After two years of traveling around the country with Mama and Peach, keeping a keen eye all the while, I'd say I've probably saved us from at least a few catastrophes, dozens of minor injuries, and myriad everyday annoyances and mishaps. I'm not about to let this pesky Atlantic Ocean win now.

That's easier said than done, though.

Take my sister, Peach. Her real name is Penelope, but when she was born, according to my mothers, I was very into peaches. I ate them constantly, insisted on peach-patterned sheets for my bed, and let's just say a seven-year-old should never be allowed to paint her own nails. I looked like I'd dipped my fingertips in peach jelly. My moms left the polish on for a whole week because they thought it was just about the cutest thing they'd ever seen.

When *Penelope* was born, I kept calling her Peach, which I guess my moms thought was also pretty cute, because it ended up sticking, and it's the perfect name for my sister. A tender little fruit if ever there was one, the kid is constantly covered in bumps and bruises, despite my best efforts to keep her safe. I hate to think what disastrous circumstances she'd tumble into if it wasn't for me. Of course, Mama looks out for her too, but Mama needs plenty of looking after herself, which means on any given day, I've got a full schedule of maintaining order and sniffing out potential dangers.

And now here's this ocean, looking like a giant black hole under the cloudy sky, ready to swallow us all in one gulp.

"Hazel, let's go!" Peach yells from the cottage's open front door. She's five and her brown curls are a tangle around her face. I've begged Mama to cut her hair—less chance of accidental middle-of-the-night strangulation that way—but Peach refuses to let her. She loves that she and Mama have the same hair, loves that they match.

I keep my own wavy white-blond hair cut to my shoulders, just like Mum used to wear it, while Peach and Mama have dark, curly hair that cascades down their backs. They have the same eyes, too, chocolate brown, but mine are bright blue like Mum's. Back when she was alive, Mum used to joke how the four of us went together perfectly, two and two.

Now it's two and one, with me as the odd one out.

"Hazey!"

"I'm coming, Peach, one second." I hop down from the top bunk in the tiny bedroom Peach and I will share, where I've been glued to my phone for the past hour, poring over maps and tourist sites for Rose Harbor in southern Maine, which will be our home for the summer. The town is small, with wild roses growing all over the hills and dunes and an old myth about a mermaid in the harbor, in honor of whom they hold some big festival in July. And let's not forget the very angry-looking ocean full of rope-like seaweed and claw-clicking lobsters and bacteria galore.

Two days ago, while we packed up our rented apartment in Ohio, I asked Mama if we were going home. Back to California, where we lived with Mum, where we were a family. We haven't been there in two years, not since Mum died, and after our lease runs out in each new town, I hope.

I tell myself this town will be the last.

We'll be home in a matter of days.

But we never are. Mama just says we're not ready yet, which makes no sense to me. I've never *not* been ready. I hate traveling around, hate the rented apartments and houses full of god-knows-what left over from god-knows-who. How is a duplex in Colorado better than our *home*, our yellow house on Camelia Street, Berkeley bustling just down the sidewalk? Mama will never give me a straight answer, and I can't bear to beg her, to do anything more than nod.

It's my fault we're like this, after all. It's my fault we're three and not four.

So here we are now, teetering in a tiny cottage on the edge of the world. When it was clear we weren't heading home but toward the *sea*, my stomach wove itself into a tight knot and hasn't unwound since. Peach has learned to swim, but our family knows better than anyone that even the greatest swimmers can drown in a matter of minutes, especially in oceans or rivers where rocks and currents are like hidden water demons.

So I argued against Rose Harbor. Or rather, I *told* Mama I didn't think it was a good idea. Mama and I don't argue. We barely *anything* at all these days. And, as usual, Mama ignored my warnings and said Peach would be fine and that I used to love the ocean.

That's all she said.

You used to love the ocean, Hazel.

Then she sighed, like my *used to* was the most horrible thing that could've happened. No mention of *why*, no mention of Mum at all.

I can't remember the last time she even said Mum's name.

Now, from under the bottom bunk I pull out my heavy forest-green trunk, right next to Peach's smaller yellow one. I've already unpacked most of my clothes, slipping them into the top half of the plain wooden dresser that came with the furnished cottage, but some stuff I keep in my trunk all the time. I unzip my navy-blue fanny pack—which I've appropriately dubbed my Safety Pack—and start reloading it with supplies from my trunk, Band-Aids, Neosporin, sunblock, a travel pack of Clorox wipes, hand sanitizer, bug spray, hair elastics, tweezers, a mini-flashlight, an extra phone charger, a couple of granola bars, and a twenty-dollar bill.

"Hazel!" Peach calls, her voice traveling through the short hallway. "Nicholas and I are ready to explore."

I push my trunk back under the bed and walk into the living room. Peach is standing at the open front door, salty sea wind in her hair, with Nicholas, her stuffed purple narwhal, perched on her shoulder. He's the last thing Mum ever gave her, the morning Mum and I left for our kayaking trip on the Mendocino coast. Peach was three, so there was no way she could go kayaking, but she still pouted that she had to stay home. Mum brought home Nicholas from the local toy store to soften the blow, and Peach carries that thing everywhere now, clinging to it like it's Mum herself. Nicholas has turned ratty, loved so hard and so often the poor whale's fur has gone pilly and one of his beady black eyes is missing.

I give Peach a once-over, checking to make sure she's all buttoned and zipped and shoed.

She isn't.

"Peach, get some shoes on."

"But we're going to the beach!"

"So?" I look down at my snugly tied sneakers.

"Sooo," my sister drawls, rolling her eyes at me. This is a new thing. The rolling of the eyes. "I want to wiggle my toes in the sand."

I press my lips together and step out onto the front porch. The late afternoon is dreary and overcast, the clouds above swirling like they're getting ready to release some great fury. The ocean below, darkly blue and deep, foams like a wild animal. Even like that it's pretty, but pretty can be deceiving. Just look at a jellyfish.

There are a few steps from our porch leading down to a pebbly path, no doubt full of all manner of things to cut up tender bare feet. Still, despite the dangers all around, I have to admit the view is nice. Our house—dubbed Sea Rose Cottage by a wooden sign hanging next to the bright blue front door—is really old and small, with creamy stone and fresh white trim. All around us are hills and rocky paths, trees that are probably a brilliant green on a sunny day. And the cottage is pretty secluded—the nearest neighbor is a little seafoam-green house about a quarter mile down the beach that I can just barely see.

I breathe in the salty air and hook my thumbs through my Safety Pack, telling myself everything will be fine. I've gotten us this far. In two whole years, there've been no broken bones, no long hospital stays, nothing a Band-Aid and some antibacterial cream couldn't fix. Peach bounces around me, babbling about the sand and surf and how she wants to really experience it, except she says *experiment*, and it's so cute I can't even correct her.

"Hazel," Mama calls from the kitchen, where she's been sifting through the dishes the landlord provided with the house, figuring out what needs cleaning. I poke my head back through the door to see her standing by the big farm-house sink, drying one of the Mason jars we're supposed to use for drinking glasses, using a striped hand towel. "Let your sister have some fun on the beach, okay? She's not going to swim. It's still too cold this early in June."

I blow out a breath through puffed cheeks. "At least make her wear some flip-flops to get down there."

Mama smiles, but it doesn't reach her eyes. It never does these days. Not when it concerns me, at least. I guess I can't blame her, though.

"Fair enough," she says. "Hear that, Peach Fuzz?"

Peach releases a labored sigh. "Fine." Then she stomps back to our room and quickly emerges holding her bright green flip-flops. She walks right past me and out the door.

"On your feet, Peach."

She grumbles some more but finally slips the flimsy shoes on.

"I'll join you two in a few minutes, okay?" Mama says, sliding the jar into a cabinet.

I nod and follow my sister outside. As soon as she hits the top step, she lets out a squeal and zips down the rest of the stairs.

"Peach, hold up!" I yell over the wind. She either doesn't hear me or doesn't care to, because she doesn't hold up at all. I huff and puff behind her, but despite my long, twelve-year-old legs that *used to* be pretty great at cutting through the water, I can't catch up. My sister is lightning fast.

Peach bursts onto the sand, which is positively riddled with all sorts of pebbles and broken seashells. This doesn't deter my sister, however. She kicks off her flip-flops as soon as her feet hit the beach and keeps on running toward the water, splashing into the shallows, waves licking up her calves.

"Peach, get out of the water!" I call, halting before the sea can touch my shoes.

She giggles and yelps. "It's so cold!" She reaches down and scoops up a handful, Nicholas still tucked under her arm, and tosses it into the air in front of her. Droplets gather on the ends of her hair, and I try not to hyperventilate.

"Peach."

She doesn't get out, though. She kicks and twirls, and I follow her horizontally, careful to keep away from the foamy slide of the sea. I feel my nose start to tickle, a sure sign I'm about to cry. I inch forward, only to inch back again.

"This is fun!" she says.

"Yeah, a blast," I say, once my breathing calms down. "Come on out. We can build a sand castle or something."

"You come in."

"I'm not coming in."

"Because you're afraid of the ocean?"

She doesn't ask it to be mean—I know this. She turns to look at me, her eyes wide and curious as she swirls one foot through the sea. I wonder if she even remembers when I loved the water—six AM practices with my neighborhood swim team, day trips to Half Moon Bay and me diving deep into the water even though it was usually freezing, searching for any signs of life with my snorkeling mask, dreams of being a marine biologist constantly floating through my head. The tickle in my nose skitters up into my eyes, and I blink fast to get rid of the sudden sting. My fingertips twitch without my permission, as if they might rebel so they can feel that cold, salty water flow between them. Traitors. I knew this ocean was going to be bad news.

I look away from Peach and up the beach, just long enough to get my emotions back in check. Movement catches my eye, drawing my attention to the little green house. Someone stands on the porch—looks like a woman with bright red hair, but I can't really tell from this far away. She's watching us. She waves.

I turn away and focus on the task at hand—keeping my sister alive—which is exactly when I notice that Peach's lip is bleeding.

"What's wrong with your lip?" I ask, hand on my Safety Pack.

She sticks her tongue out and laps up the bit of blood. "I bit it."

"What? When?"

She shrugs. "When I was running around." Blood bubbles up on her lip again, and my stomach turns.

I smell that salty-metallic scent, see red spreading through the water.

I blink and the smell is gone, the water only blue gray. I shake my head, trying to clear the memories, but my breath stays caught between my ribs.

"Come on, we need to get some ice or something for that," I say.

"It's fine!" She scoops up some water and rubs it all over her mouth. I shudder, imagining a million microbes infesting her body through that one little cut.

"Gross, don't do that."

"What? It helps." She douses her mouth with water again. This time, her lip comes through clean, the blood gone for now. I breathe out a few lungfuls of air.

"What's going on, you two?" Mama asks, walking through the sand behind me. She's barefoot, her own sandals dangling from her fingers. On her arm are the beaded bracelets Peach made for her, all different colors. I've got five stacked up on my wrist too, and I'm pretty sure at least two of Peach's own bracelets are floating out into the open sea by now.

"She's swimming," I say, motioning to my sister.

"I'm not swimming," Peach says.

"And bleeding," I say.

"I am not, Hazey!" she screeches, fists clenched.

Mama splashes into the water before bending down to inspect the cut. "You're fine, Peach Fuzz. Don't go any deeper, though—this water is freezing."

Peach nods and continues skipping through the sea.

"Mama," I say.

She doesn't say anything. She just walks back toward me, her pale legs wet and goose-pimply, and settles on the sand.

"Calm down, Hazel," she says softly. "Sit down. Try to relax."

I sit down, but I definitely don't relax. Lately, it seems like *Calm down, Hazel* is constantly coming out of Mama's mouth. All those words do is make me feel even more keyed up, like something's wrong with me and I can't even do the most basic, easiest things.

"Did you finish?" I ask Mama to get my mind on other things.

In every new town, Mama sets up the kitchen while I make all the beds and start our laundry. Back in California, Mama and Mum shared all the housework, even though Mum taught visual art at the university and Mama worked from home as a writer. Now that Mum's gone, it's up to me to take up the slack. I taught Peach how to wipe down the bathroom sinks, though I won't let her touch a toilet.

"All finished," Mama says, brushing some sand off her knee. "You?"

"Yeah. Peach needs some new jeans. Both pairs have holes in the knee."

"How long did those last? A month?"

"Twenty-four days."

She laughs. "I'll pick some up in town this week."

"I can get them," I say. I always pick out Peach's clothes. At least I have for the past two years, usually on a trip to Target while Mama browses the books. "Just give me some money and I'll—"

"I'll do it, Hazel," Mama says. She tilts her head at me, eyes soft but narrowed. "Okay?"

I nod and look away, my throat feeling thicker by the minute.

"Whee!" Peach yells, splashing toward us. "I love this ocean, Mama!"

"I'm glad, baby girl. No swimming without me or Hazel, okay?"

Peach nods, and that is the extent of the water warnings. Mama stands up and swipes the sand from her cutoffs. "Ready to explore the town a little? I thought we'd go out to dinner and save the grocery shopping for tomorrow."

"Okay," I say, even though *exploring the town* is always my least-favorite part of moving to a new place. At least with grocery shopping, I have a purpose. *Exploring* leaves too many variables up to chance, too many people to deal with I wasn't expecting, too many obstacles. I stand and make sure my Safety Pack is tight around my waist.

"Let's go get you into some dry clothes, Peach Fuzz," Mama says, lifting Peach out of the surf. Her shorts are drenched up to the pockets. Mama reaches out her free hand to tuck my hair behind my ears. Her fingers skim over my scars, a thick silver explosion across my left cheek like the branches of a leafless tree. I've got little white marks on other parts of my face and left arm, too, grain-sized nicks here and there left over from the kayaking accident.

She doesn't say anything about them, though.

She never does.

When she touches them like this, I don't think it's on purpose. Every now and then, Peach counts my scars when we're snuggled in bed at night. She gets a different number every time. She was three when Mum died, so I don't know how much she even remembers. I barely remember anything from when I was three—hazy pictures in my head of me and Mum and Mama at the park near our house, Mum pushing me along on a yellow tricycle while Mama snapped pictures.

Still, it's a relief when Peach asks about my scars, when she *sees* them, whispering questions at night about the mom who looked like me, the mom who gave her Nicholas. I tell her things like how Mum could climb the rocky crags in Lassen National Park just like a spider. How she was allergic to strawberries and hated chocolate. How she used to stick baby Peach in a carrier on her back while we all hiked near Point Reyes by the coast. Some days, the fog would be so thick I couldn't even see right in front of me. I'll even tell her about Mama, the Mama I used to know, the one who couldn't walk by me without kissing the top of my head or giving me a quick hug, the one whose favorite Saturday activity was curling up with me on the couch wrapped in a big quilt and reading for hours.

Peach loves hearing stuff like this, but she'll eventually get a little pucker between her eyebrows and trace a finger over my scars, and that's exactly when I'll change the subject or tell her it's time to go to sleep.

I want her to remember Mum, the way our family was.

I don't want her to remember why Mum is gone forever, why our family is ruined, how it's all my fault.

We turn our backs to the ocean and start up the path to our little cottage. Mama carries Peach, and my sister rests her head on Mama's shoulder. Moving is always exhausting—the packing up of one life, traveling, then unpacking a whole new life in a whole new town, a new house with bare walls and zero memories. I feel heavy just looking up at Sea Rose Cottage, like I might disappear altogether in this house, forgotten like Mum.

Right before we reach our porch, though, I catch a flash of movement in the corner of my eye. Turning, I see the redheaded woman from the green house hurrying toward us, a redheaded girl who looks about my age running alongside her.

"Let's go, Mama, I'm hungry," I say, picking up my own pace. Mama always chooses pretty-secluded houses to rent, which is the only thing I like about all these new towns. Ever since the accident, I seem to lock up around other people, especially kids my age, who tend to rudely stare at my face. Plus, why make friends when we're just going to leave in three months anyway? Why make friends I'll just end up losing?

For the past two years, Mama's let me homeschool. We use an online curriculum, and she checks my work every afternoon. We've never talked about it, really. We've never talked about a lot of things, but ever since we left California, there hasn't been any mention of Peach or me going to an actual school in a building. We move around too much to go through the trouble, I think, but even when we eventually go home to California, I'll want to homeschool. Being around other kids my age who will just stare and ask questions I don't want to answer, not to mention the myriad dangers to be found in school, from a billion germs to playground terrors—no thanks. Peach and I will have our own little academy during the school year, where I can keep us both safe.

People are everywhere, though, and neighbors get nosy, especially when you're new in town. Some might call it welcoming, but not me. I glance back down the beach, and the woman is still in hot pursuit.

"Okay, Haze, calm down," Mama says when I push on her back, trying to speed her up the stairs.

"Hazey, cut it out," Peach says, swatting at me with Nicholas. She's getting cranky, which means she's hungry, too, which means all the more reason to hurry.

The woman is closer now, close enough that I can see she has short hair, shaved on one side and curling elegantly over her forehead on the other. The kid with her has long, wild crimson hair. I mean, totally wild. She looks a little bit like Merida from *Brave*, except this girl's hair is more wavy than curly, but it definitely has that bird's nest look about it. She's probably about an inch taller than me and is wearing a long-sleeved navy T-shirt with THE ROSE MAID LIVES written across the chest in a curling seafoam-green script, along with seersucker shorts. One of those instant cameras on a rainbow-colored strap is looped around her neck. She sees me watching and lifts a hand to wave, but I turn away before she can flutter the first finger.

"Evie?"

Mama freezes. I freeze. Even Peach freezes, although she sort of has to, since she's attached to Mama like a koala. We all turn toward the redheaded lady, who's close enough now that she stops, hands on her hips as she breathes heavily and stares straight at Mama. For a second, I'm hoping it's all a mistake. Mama's name is Evelyn, but she definitely doesn't go by Evie. Never has, as far as I know. Not even Mum called her that. But then I hear her suck in a breath, and the lady takes another step closer. I back up. Mama stays put.

"Evelyn," the lady says this time, crushing all my hope. She knows my mom.

And I don't know who in the world she is.

chapter two

"Claire?" Mama says. Her voice is a gauzy whisper.

The lady's whole face breaks out in a smile, and she speeds toward us, kicking up sand with her bare feet. "Oh my god, I knew it was you! I'd recognize that walk anywhere."

Mama makes a funny noise—halfway between a sob and a laugh—and moves forward. She sets Peach down. I pull my sister to my side and back up as far as possible, my spine smacking against the porch railing. Then the lady draws Mama into a hug, arms all the way around Mama's back. She even rests her pointy chin on Mama's shoulder. At first, Mama sort of locks up—I can't remember the last time she hugged anyone, really, other than Peach, who insists on regular snuggles and sleeps in Mama's bed half the time—but then it's like she's a stick of butter in the microwave, and she melts right into this total stranger's arms.

"Claire," she says again, like she really can't believe it's true.

The lady pulls back and nods. "Goodness, it's been—what? Twenty-five years?"

"Sounds about right," Mama says.

"What in the world are you doing here?" Claire asks.

"We just moved in. We're here for the summer."

"Amazing," Claire says, then juts her thumb toward the green house. I notice a dock near its back porch, a little boat bouncing in the waves. I shiver. "We live just down the beach—can you believe it?"

"I can't," Mama says, laughing and shaking her head. "I really can't."

"Lemon." The lady—*Claire*, I guess she's called—turns to the girl behind her, who is just lowering her light blue camera from her face. She pops her head up, brown eyes wide and guilty-looking and fixed right on me. I untuck my hair from behind my ear so it curtains around my scarred cheek.

"Put that thing away and meet my old friend," Claire says.

"Sorry, sorry," the girl says. She twists the light blue plastic lens and it clicks shut.

Her cheeks have gone bright red, and I'm almost positive

she was just about to snap a picture of all of us without our permission. Or rather, of *me*, as she was staring right at me. I press my hair against my cheek and grit my teeth.

"Hi, oh my gosh, hi!" the girl says. The wind whips her hair around her face and she flails to get it out of her eyes. Her nails are painted a bright turquoise. "Sorry. Wow, it's windy."

"Isn't it always windy on the beach?" I say, my voice as flat as a griddle cake.

Mama gives me *a look* over her shoulder.

"Yes, it is, actually!" the girl says. When she gets her hair under control, she stares at me again, her mouth hanging open a little. I feel my cheeks warm up, and I frown back at her.

"Lemon, this is Evelyn," Claire says.

The girl keeps staring at me. It's really weird. Claire nudges her elbow, and she seems to snap out of it. "Sorry, sorry, you just look..." She shakes her head while I glare down at my feet, my face a raging fire now. My scars feel like lightning bolts across my skin.

"Sorry, hi, it's so nice to meet you," the girl finally says, sticking out her arm and pumping Mama's hand like a grown-up.

"You too...Lemon, is it?" Mama says.

"Clementine," the girl says. "But when I was little, I couldn't say it, and Lemon just sort of stuck."

"Hey, I'm named for a fruit too!" Peach says, moving away from me and toward the fruit girl.

"You are?" Lemon says, leaning down with her hands on her knees so she's eye to eye with Peach. "Let me guess... Strawberry?"

Peach giggles. "No way!"

"Hmm... Mango?"

Peach shakes her head.

"Apricot? Plum? Dragon fruit?"

"Dragon fruit?" Peach says, covering her mouth and laughing. "That's so silly!"

Lemon straightens and taps her chin. "Well, I'm stumped."

"Peach! My name is Peach!"

"Of course it is!" Lemon says, popping her hands onto her hips. The two grown-ups laugh. "Pretty as a peach."

Peach practically glows. "My real name is Penelope Foster Bly, but Hazey named me Peach. Her middle name is Foster too, because—"

"And this is my older daughter, Hazel," Mama says, placing an airlike hand on my back for a second before removing it. I glance at her, a lump in my throat. Foster was Mum's last name—Nadine Elizabeth Foster. She grew up in England until she was eighteen and came to the United States for college, which is why I called her Mum. When she had me, she and Mama just wanted me to have a single last name, so they chose Foster as my middle name and Mama's surname, Bly, as my last. And when Mama had Peach, they did the same thing. "She's twelve."

"Hey, me too," Lemon says. I lift my mouth in an attempt to smile, but my stomach is in such knots, it might look more like a grimace. Lemon definitely manages a perfect-teeth smile, but I see her eyes roaming all over my face, then flicking down to my Safety Pack and away. When I glance back, she's staring at my face again. I know I'm blushing, which just makes my scars stand out even more.

"So wonderful to meet you, Hazel," Claire says. She starts to put out her hand, but when I keep mine clasped firmly behind my back, she drops it and keeps her smile. "You too, Peach. Goodness, Evie, she looks just like you."

"Doesn't she?" Mama says, smoothing Peach's curling hair.

I look down at my feet, eyes blurring on the pebbly sand.

Goodness, Nadine, she looks just like you.

Doesn't she?

"Girls," Mama says, "Claire here was my best friend growing up. Until we were—what? Twelve, thirteen?"

"Twelve," Claire says. "That's when my whole world ended and my family moved from California to Maine, remember?"

"Your world ended?" Lemon asks. "I thought you loved Maine."

Claire laughs. "I do, sweets, but losing your best friend and first love is the stuff of catastrophes when you're twelve."

Lemon's eyes go wide. Mine do too, stinging from the salty air. Even Peach's mouth drops open.

"What?" Lemon says, clicking the *t* sound so loudly I hear it even over the wind.

"Oh my god," Mama says, putting a hand over her eyes. She's smiling, though. "*Claire.*"

"Don't tell me you forgot," Claire says, fists popped playfully on her curvy waist.

Mama's eyes go gooey-looking. "Of course I didn't."

Then they stare at each other for ten whole seconds. Really, really stare. And let me tell you, ten seconds doesn't sound like a lot, but when your mother is gazing into the eyes of someone else who is most definitely not your mom, it feels like an eternity.

"Wait, wait, wait," Lemon says really fast. She holds up her palms all dramatically. "First *love*? As in...*first kiss*?"

"Mama!" Peach says, giggling. Then she shakes her hips from side to side, singing, "K-I-S-S-I-N-G!"

"Peach, cut it out," I say, watching Mama try to suppress a smile.

"Well?" Lemon asks. She's pretty much vibrating with excitement.

"Please excuse my daughter, Evie," Claire says, smoothing her hand over Lemon's hair. "She's recently discovered romance."

"It's been a long time since I've thought about all that," Mama says.

"Me too," Claire says.

"Tell us how it happened!" Lemon says, her hands literally clasped together and tucked under her chin. "Please. *Please.*"

This is getting out of hand. I've got to get Mama away from this family. My chest feels tight, my stomach swirls like the sea.

"Mama, Peach and I are hungry," I say. I take Peach's hand and start tugging her toward Sea Rose Cottage. She digs in her heels, but I don't let go.

Mama nods, but before she can make her polite goodbyes, which I'm sure she was just about to do, Claire pipes up.

"Hey, Lemon and I were just about to head into town for some dinner," she says, her brown eyes flitting between Mama and me. "How about we all go together? I'd love to catch up."

"Yes," Lemon says, stretching out the short *e* in the word, her voice all breathy. "Mom, we have to take them to your restaurant."

"Oh, honey, we don't need to go there tonight," Claire says.

"Mom. Come on, it's a special occasion."

Claire shakes her head. "I don't know, Lem."

"Hang on," Mama says. "You have a restaurant?"

Claire's cheeks go pink. "Yes. It's just a little place downtown, and I—"

"It's not a *little place*," Lemon says. "It's a big, wondrous, amazing place that's always packed, and we need to go there now."

"Lemon—" Claire starts, but Mama interrupts her.

"Absolutely, we have to go there," she says. "You *own* a restaurant? I mean, of course you do. You were always cooking up stuff when we were kids." Then Mama smiles this little knowing smile I've only ever seen on her face when she and Mum were talking about something that happened before I was born. My stomach coils up.

"Do you remember when we almost burned down your kitchen?" Mama goes on.

"Oh my god," Claire says, covering her face. "The butterscotch cookies."

"Hey, we were kids. Who knew you're supposed to turn off an oven when you're done using it? But those cookies"—she reaches out and grabs Lemon's arm— "Lemon, those cookies, I'm telling you, were *delicious*."

Then Mama goes on to describe the cookies in intimate detail. I watch her talk, hands fluttering, smile on her face, words flowing and flowing and flowing from her mouth like a river. I haven't heard her talk this much in two years. Not since before Mum died.

"And she was only seven years old," Mama says, shaking her head. "She's so talented."

Claire shakes her head, but she's smiling, her eyes locked on Mama's.

"Butterscotch chocolate chip cookies," Lemon says. "They're my absolute favorite cookie in the whole wide world."

"You still make them?" Mama asks.

"She sells them with homemade whipped cream at the Rose Maid Café. That's the name of the restaurant." Lemon pops her hands onto her hips. "So we have to go. And where else can you get rose ice cream?"

"Rose ice cream?" Mama asks.

"Rose ice cream," Lemon says. "My mom's own recipe." Then she bends down so she's eye level with my sister again. "Also, Peach, my fruit-named friend"—Peach giggles—"how do you feel about mermaids?"

Peach's eyes go wide. "I love mermaids. You look like Ariel!"

Lemon laughs. "Well, I can tell you that I did not trade my voice to a sea witch for legs, *but*..."

"Lemon," Claire says.

"What? They'll hear about her eventually," Lemon says. "Your restaurant is named after her."

"Named after who?" Peach asks, her mouth open a little in wonder.

Claire shakes her head and gives Mama a *look*. It's one of those looks grown-ups don't think we notice—those looks that say, *I'll tell you later, my kid is a mess*—but we *do* notice.

I notice everything.

Mama tosses the same *look* right back. Things are getting dire. My mind whirls for a way to get out of this. I try to catch Mama's eye, pouring as much desperation as I can into my expression, but she doesn't even glance at me. She's too busy with the *look*.

"What if I told you," Lemon continues, "that mermaids are real and Rose Harbor has one living in our waters. Right. Out. There." She straightens her arm and moves it across the horizon, fingers slicing between sky and sea.

"Really?" Peach whispers, her mouth hanging open.

"Really," Lemon says.

"Local myth," Claire says to Mama. "There's a mermaid in the harbor, didn't you know?"

Mama laughs.

"The whole town's a little obsessed," Claire says, then heaves a huge sigh, eyes a bit sad. "Lemon...well, she's a believer."

"Because it's a beautiful, magical story," Lemon says.

"Honey, can we not?" Claire says, that warning back in her voice. Lemon looks away, her eyes on the ocean. The wind whips her hair into her face, blocking her expression from view.

"It's a fun myth," Claire says, laying a hand on Lemon's shoulder. "But it is a *myth*. Though very good for business, I'll admit."

"Well, I'm intrigued," Mama says.

"Me too!" Peach says.

I wait for Lemon to squeal with excitement or something, but she's gazing out at the water, her camera pressed to her eye. She snaps the button, and out shoots a tiny rectangular photo. She waves it through the air for a second, then puts it in her pocket. For a moment, I wonder what the picture showed, if there really is a mermaid swirling under the gray ocean, but then Peach starts jumping up and down about rose ice cream and butterscotch cookies and before I can say another word to Mama, she's walking with Claire up our porch steps, arm in arm, without another backward glance at me.

chapter three

Rose Harbor's town center is only about a mile from our cottage, just down the pebbly beach. I *could* be enjoying a very nice walk, Peach between Mama and me, holding our hands while we breathe in the salty sea air and pick some wild pink roses that pop up along the dunes and rocks. *Sea roses*, the tourist sites call them, which I have to admit is a nice term. Certainly sheds more light on our cottage's name. We had wild roses in California, too, right in our backyard, but they were a paler pink than these, which are a bright fuchsia.

So, yes, this could be a lovely and calming evening, and my heart could be beating nice and slow and steady.

Instead, Mama is a few feet ahead of me, talking to

Claire, laughing every now and then, their arms still linked like they're teenagers on their way to school.

Instead, Peach is holding on to Lemon's hand while Lemon chatters nonstop.

Instead, my heart feels like a wild animal caught behind my rib cage. Any second it'll bust right out.

"...Rose Maid Café is so great," Lemon is saying. "Mom's worked so hard on it and you can learn all about the Rose Maid and the rose ice cream is really, really unique. They make it from actual rose petals, so it tastes a bit like perfume, but I still like it."

"Oh." I try to think of something more interesting to say, but my mind is nothing but white noise, my mouth so dry I'm worried I might choke on my tongue. I'm way out of practice talking to kids my age. Talking to anyone, really, other than Peach and Mama and the occasional retail personnel. Even then, though, I limit it to *please* and *thank you*. My scars are really obvious, marks that will never, ever go away. Sometimes, if a person's feeling really bold, they'll even ask about them, how I got them, which isn't something I ever want to talk about.

I look down at my feet as we walk. The ocean is far too close. We're on dry sand, a good hundred feet from the water, but surely there's a normal road or sidewalk that could've taken us into town. It hasn't rained yet, but the water is still angry. Or sad.

Maybe it's both.

I glance at Peach, but Lemon still has a firm grip on her—but then I look right back to the water, like it's a magnet pulling on my eyes. Way out past the larger rocks, something flits in the waves, a fish reaching for the sky.

"How can something taste like perfume?" Peach asks.

I open my mouth to answer her, but Lemon dives in before I can get a word out. She gives the exact answer I would—that our mouths and noses are connected and all that, so sometimes smells can remind us how things taste and vice versa—but still. I feel her watch me even as she talks to my sister, eyes flitting between my Safety Pack and my face, which I'm trying to hide with my hair, but the ocean wind is making it hard. Sweat pools under my arms and on my upper lip. For real, even though it's pretty cool out here, I think I'm starting to stink.

Up ahead, Mama and Claire keep talking and laughing, laughing and talking.

"Amazing, isn't it?" Lemon asks. She's right next to me, her shoulder pressing against mine.

"What?"

"Them." She motions to our moms, then aims her camera at them, twists a few things on the big lens, and snaps a picture. The thing zips and zings and then spits out another rectangular piece of paper, almost completely dark except for a white border. She holds it out to me as color begins to seep into the center, shapes forming, then people. I take it, watching our moms come to life. Their backs are to us, of course, but Lemon has captured their faces at the perfect moment, the two of them turned toward each other so you can see their profiles. The twilight glow washes them a little purple, a little silver.

It's a pretty picture, and it makes my stomach twist and turn.

"Now we'll always remember this night, exactly like it is," Lemon says, taking the photo back and tucking it into her pocket. "It's miraculous that you moved here, don't you think? Right down the beach from us? Totally meant to be."

"Um..."

"Do you think they still like each other? We need the full story, don't you think?"

"Full story of...what?" I swallow hard, wishing I hadn't asked, hoping she won't even answer me. Except, of course, she does.

"How they met. How they *kissed*." She digs the photo out of her pocket again and waves it around. "I mean, look at—" She stops walking and pulls on my arm. "Hold up. Oh my god."

"What?" I swear this girl is making me dizzy. I jerk my arm away, but she doesn't even notice.

Lemon leans close and whispers, "She's not married, right?"

"What?"

"Married. I mean, I know no one else was with you

today, but I didn't even think. Do you have a dad? Or maybe another mom? My mom is bisexual, so she likes guys or girls or anyone."

Her eyes are so wide, I would worry that they might pop right out of their sockets, but I'm too busy swallowing hard and trying to breathe. Mum was bisexual, so I know what it means, and Mama told me a long time ago that she prefers the term *gay* and that she's really only attracted to people who identify as women. None of that is what makes my heart feel like a scooped-out cavern in my chest, though.

Is Mama still married?

She still wears the platinum band Mum gave her at their wedding, hand-engraved with a pattern of flowers, a pale green diamond inlaid into the middle. Mum's was similar, but she had a blue diamond. Other than all that, I don't know the answer to Lemon's question. I never even thought about it. Now, thanks to Lemon, I can't think of anything else.

"My parents are divorced," Lemon says when I don't answer. "My dad moved to Georgia after that. Atlanta. He said it was too hard after she..." Her voice trails off, and now her eyes have gone back to normal size. In fact, she's not even looking at me. She's staring straight ahead, her gaze all glazed over.

Something sad tinges her voice, and I think, just for a second, that maybe I should ask more about her dad, but

I don't. Peach and I don't have a dad. Mama and Mum both used the same sperm donor to get pregnant with us, but it was totally anonymous. I've barely ever thought about the guy. I have two moms, two parents. I don't need anyone else.

My mind autocorrects itself—I *had* two parents.

"Girls, look how beautiful," Mama says. She and Claire have stopped at a rosebush, bright pink flowers blooming so thickly there's hardly any green. Lemon seems to snap out of it and, before I can stop her, loops her arm with mine and starts running to catch up with our moms. My feet follow smoothly, but my mind stumbles behind, tripping on Lemon's question about Mama and marriage.

I watch Mama as she picks a flower and smells it. "I can't believe these grow right here by the water."

"Sea roses," I say, but Claire says it too, at the exact same time as me, making our voices sound almost like a song. She smiles at me, her gaze darting down to my scars, then up to my eyes again. I don't smile back.

"Sea roses," Peach whispers to herself, trying out the words in her mouth like she does sometimes. Then she stoops down to pluck one of the pink flowers.

"Peach, hang on, I'll get you one," I say, but she's already closing her whole hand around a stem and pulling as hard as she can. I wince, phantom pain zinging through my fingers as she yelps and drops the flower on the sandy path. Nicholas takes a dive too as Peach looks down at her hand, which is marred with several smears of blood.

My heart jumps into my throat and stays there, pounding like a bass drum.

"Oh, baby girl," Mama says.

"The flower bit me!" Peach wails.

"Thorns," Lemon says, nodding. "Gotta watch out for those."

I ignore her ridiculous calmness and unzip my Safety Pack.

"Ow, ow, it hurts!" Peach says. Big tears well up in her eyes and trickle down her cheeks.

"It's okay, you're okay," I say, then repeat it a few more times in my head. I take her hand and inspect it. Tiny orbs of blood swell on three fingertips and on her palm. She grabbed that rose like she was strangling it.

"Just a tiny prick," Mama says.

"She's bleeding," I say. "For the second time today and we've been here—what? Seven hours?" I can't even keep her safe for seven hours. I can't even keep a tiny thorn out of her skin.

"She's barely bleeding. She's okay, Haze," Mama says, so quietly I hope only I can hear her. But one glance at Lemon proves otherwise. She watches me and Mama, watches as I sift through my Safety Pack. Heat springs to my cheeks, which just makes my scars stand out even more, but I push all that from my mind.

I concentrate on action. Fixing. Saving. Antiseptic wipe. Neosporin. Band-Aid. Peach wails even louder when I clean her injuries, but I keep on moving, keep on doing until there's no more blood, until her wounds are covered up and her tears have stopped. She sniffs and I breathe, my heart so loud I'm sure everyone hears it.

"Okay, she's fine, honey," Mama says. The words sound comforting, but her voice doesn't. Her voice sounds annoyed. I don't look at her, instead pressing gently at the Band-Aid on Peach's palm, making sure it'll stay.

"That's enough, Hazel," Mama says. Then she takes my arm, moving it away from my sister. She grabs Peach's hand and starts up the beach with her.

"Everything all right?" I hear Claire ask, walking alongside them. Mama just nods. Doesn't say anything else about it. Lemon is still standing nearby. I can feel her watching me. I don't look up at her. I tuck the Band-Aid wrappers and the cleaning wipe into the front pocket of my Safety Pack. Zip it up. Then I start walking without another word. Downtown twinkles up ahead, and I try to keep my eyes fixed on it, ignoring the pull of the sea.

chapter four

The Rose Maid Café is right in the middle of down-town, snuggled in between a bakery that sells differ-ent kinds of whoopie pies and a shop called Rosemary's Wishes. The store has all sorts of things in the window, everything from lamps with a curvy mermaid as the base to sea rose candles and soap and room spray. Streetlights that look like old-fashioned gas lamps line the streets, and peo-ple mill around licking ice cream cones and holding hands and sipping on paper cups filled with steaming drinks. The air smells salty and herby, like the ocean wind picked up a bit of spearmint.

Mama and Peach are still ahead of me with Claire. Lemon's up there now too, while I trudge behind them, which is just fine with me. The solitude gives me a second to check my Safety Pack supplies again, to think through how the rest of the night might go. We're just eating in a restaurant, so it's not like all that much can happen. Then again, you wouldn't think picking a rose would end in skin lacerations, but it did.

I glance up at the sky. The clouds have started to clear off, the first stars blinking through, so it probably won't rain or storm. One less thing to worry about. Still, I jog to catch up with Peach, who seems to have forgotten all about her wounded fingers, showing Nicholas the sights around us and whispering secrets no one else can hear into the spot on his faded purple head where I assume his ears would be if he had any.

When we reach the Rose Maid Café, Lemon pulls open the front door, which is a dark and heavy oak, a tarnished brass anchor for its handle.

"You're going to love it so much in here, I just know it," she says to me after Mama, Peach, and Claire pass through. "I can't wait to see what you think. I'm so nervous."

"Why? I thought you said I'd *love it so much*," I say. I'm being snarky, I know, possibly bordering on mean, but it feels like there's a snake coiled up in my belly and Lemon keeps poking at it, making it rear up and hiss.

Her smile dips, but only barely. "Yeah. Right. You will. But, I mean..." She shakes her head. "Never mind."

I shrug and walk inside, which is all smooth driftwood booths and tables with glass orbs hanging from the ceilings, amber lights flickering inside. The walls are white wooden slats and are lined with different kinds of artwork in matching driftwood frames—sketches and paintings, watercolors and collages—every single one of them depicting a mermaid, in all sizes and shapes. They're pretty amazing, actually. They look like the kind of drawings Mum would've done for me, or at least bought me if she'd spied them in some local shop. We would've hung them in my room, next to the other artwork she'd gotten for me over the years—watercolor sea turtles and moon jellies floating through a sea so dark blue it was almost black, a pod of narwhals against the white Antarctic ice.

Something almost happy springs into my chest as I look at these mermaid paintings. Just for a second, and then it's gone. I'd never tell Lemon that, though. I gaze coolly at the art. Each piece is done only in shades of blue, from deep navy to the lightest sky, which gives the whole café a gauzy, underwater feel. Some of the art looks like little kids did it and some of it looks professional, which just makes it all that much more amazing.

"Hazey," Peach says in a breathy voice as she takes my hand, so I know she agrees with me. Together we weave through people waiting for a table and gaze at the art hanging in the entryway.

Mum would've loved this, I think.

She taught college-level visual art, helping students paint their inner feelings or whatever, but she was an artist herself, too. If we weren't out hiking or kayaking, she was working on some project at home. Acrylics were her specialty and she always, always created something to do with nature. But her pieces weren't just boring old sunset pictures. They made you feel you were really there, out in the wild, and there was a bit of magic in her paintings too. Some dreamy quality, something only she could do that made you think that anything was possible out there on the flat plain or on a mountain or looking down on a river. She even sold some of her art at a local gallery. She kept the best pieces, though, and hung them all over our house. She'd display Peach's art too. Peach loved to sit with her at the kitchen table and make what looked to me like a giant mess. But Mum would take two- and three-year-old Peach's splotchy watercolor picture of a flower or the sun or a cat and let it dry. Then she'd put it in a white matted frame and hang it in the hallway, turning it into the prettiest picture in the house.

My favorite art she did was the piece she painted for me when I was born. It wasn't of my face or anything. It's an abstract. She told me, years later when I could understand it and asked about the small rectangular canvas hanging over my toddler bed, that she had painted how I made her feel the first time she held me. My painting is turquoise and navy and sea green and aqua and sky. It's peace and quiet. But sort of fierce, too, parts of the painting writhing up like an ocean wave before rolling back down into calm.

You feel like this to me, Mum had said. *All the blues, calm and adventure at the same time. Like you're the deepest, most beautiful, most mysterious sea.*

Back when water was my whole life—posters of dolphins and blue whales and sea lions all over my room's walls, swim practice every morning before school, websites for college marine biology programs bookmarked on our family's computer even when I was an eight-year-old—Mum's words, her art, meant everything to me.

She painted a picture for Peach, too, but my sister's is brighter, bolder, a desert sunset with colors so vibrant you can almost taste them. Pinks and golds, red and orange and plum. And then, like a cool breeze on a hot day, a little river of kelly green right through the middle. Perfectly Peach.

My sister never got to ask Mum about her painting. I'm not even sure if she remembers it exists. Mama put most of Mum's art in storage back in California, but she kept a few pieces, her favorites, and packed them away in a big trunk we take with us everywhere. Peach's and my paintings are in there. I remember when Mama took them off our bedroom walls. She carried them both into the room she used to share with Mum and sat on the floor, staring at them for hours before she packed them into the trunk. Now Mama keeps that trunk locked and tucked away under her bed in whatever house we're living in. I haven't seen a single one of Mum's paintings since the day we packed up our house, a few weeks after the memorial service.

I feel Mama come up behind me. I wonder—I *hope*—she's thinking about Mum's art too. I wait for her to put her arm around me, or at least touch my shoulder, but she doesn't.

She never does.

Don't they remind you of Mum?

The words gather on my tongue, but I can't seem to get them to come out. We never talk about Mum. Not in two whole years. I don't know who decided that talking about her was too hard, too sad. At first, it really was too painful, especially when I was still in the hospital and going through skin grafts to fix my face. But then the silence became a habit, and I'd be too scared to break it. Sometimes, I get so mad about Mama's quiet I want to scream. But then, just when I think I'm going to talk to her about it, tell her how I *need* to talk about Mum, that Peach needs to hear about her, the guilt rushes in like the ocean filling up a tiny bucket, and I'll remember that it was all my fault Mum died and I won't be able to look at Mama again for hours.

"Hey, there you are," Claire says, coming up next to Mama. "I got our best table. Lemon's already over there."

"Claire, this is amazing," Mama says. Her voice sounds gauzy, awestruck. I turn to look at her. Her arms are folded, but her face is soft. The dim light glints off her wedding ring.

I'd seen all the pictures from my moms' wedding.

Mama wore a lacy lavender dress, and Mum had on an ivory suit that looked so amazing with her blond hair. It was in our backyard, and every single person who'd ever been important to Mum or Mama was there.

Claire wasn't.

And she definitely wasn't at Mum's memorial service. How good of friends could Mama and Claire really have been if she wasn't even at the two single most important moments in Mama's life?

Not very good, in my opinion, even if she does have a cool café.

"Thank you," Claire says, looking around and smiling. "I do like it. And now I've trained my sous chef well enough that I can have a night off here and there. I bought it about three years ago, right after..." She trails off, eyes all distant for a split second before she clears her throat and looks at Mama again and smiles. "Well, Lemon and I made it what it is. All the décor is one hundred percent Lemon—the colors, the driftwood."

"Even the art?" I ask, then snap my mouth shut. Pesky question just slipped right out.

Claire nods and looks around at all the frames for a second. "She commissioned most of it. Went around the entire summer before we opened, getting people to draw their versions of the Rose Maid. Only one rule"—she sweeps her arm through the room—"shades of blue."

"It's beautiful. Right, Haze?" Mama says.

I don't answer.

"Hopefully, you'll feel the same way about the food," Claire says.

"I have no doubt we will," Mama says, a smile in her voice. Then she turns and walks off, following Claire through the crowd. I sway a little, feeling suddenly like a boat that just got pushed out to sea by a storm. My chest goes tight and I can feel it coming on—the Sadness. It happens every now and then. It's like, I'll be going along just fine, playing with Peach or cleaning or just lying in bed reading a book, and then, suddenly, it's like I fall into the coldest water in all the world and I'm sinking, sinking, sinking. Now I squeeze my eyes shut, the crowd noise fading to a dull hum, and when I open them again, I'm staring right into the eyes of a watercolor mermaid in her driftwood frame.

She's got white-blond hair like mine, except hers is long and flowy and slightly blue tinted. She's got pale skin like mine. She's got ice-blue eyes like mine, except you can only see one of them, because the other is covered up with her hair, only the tip of her dark eyebrow visible. In fact, the whole left side of her face is covered, just like I try to do all the time, and her other eye is big and wide and sad-looking, like she's holding the whole weight of the ocean and all its mysteries and dangers inside her.

I look for a signature in the bottom left or right corner

of the piece, like Mum used to put on her art, but there isn't one.

"Come on, Hazey," Peach says, tugging on my arm. I blink and let my sister pull me through the crowd, but I glance back at that mermaid, locking my eye with hers one more time.

I notice the same illustrated mermaid all over the restaurant.

I mean, yes, there are painted, sketched, collaged mermaids in frames on every single wall, but they're all different faces, different styles, different bodies and skin colors, except this one with her white-blond hair and cool blue eyes. Her clothes are different from the others too. She's still blue hued, turquoise and navy and aqua all swirling together, but she doesn't have on a shell bra or anything like that. Instead, she's wearing what looks like an old-fashioned dress. It has long sleeves with lace circling her wrists and a high-necked lace collar. But then, at her hips, instead of a smooth-scaled mermaid tail like the rest of the art pieces have, her dress continues flowing down. It's in tatters, though, patches here and there and golf-ball-sized holes, through which you can see glimpses of those blue scales. Her mermaid tail flicks out of the bottom hem of the dress, big and beautiful and graceful.

That's how I know whoever did these paintings is really

good—you can *feel* that mermaid tail gliding through the water. Her hair, too. Fingers and arms. Mum used to say capturing movement was one of the hardest things to do in drawing or painting, and this mermaid is nothing but movement. Slow, sad, graceful movement.

She doesn't look magical or mythical at all.

She looks like me.

"Do you like her?" Lemon asks me.

We're sitting in the back of the restaurant, in a corner booth that curves around the table so we're all able to see each other. I'm smooshed in between Lemon and Mama. Peach wanted to sit with her *fruit friend*, so she's way over on Lemon's other side. The same blond mermaid hangs on the wall right above Claire, who, of course, is sitting next to Mama.

"Who?" I say. My voice comes out all wispy, like the faintest cloud on a sunny day.

"The mermaid."

I can't help it. My gaze goes right back to the blond mermaid, and I feel myself nodding. I think my mouth might even be hanging open, and my nose feels a little tingly. I clear my throat and look down at the menu, which is full of fancy stuff like *blackened harbor shrimp and mush-room risotto. Maine lobster bisque. Grilled free-range chicken with fresh rose crema.* I really want to look at that mermaid again, though. Mum used to say one of the purposes of art was to make us feel things, sometimes things we didn't even understand. I guess whoever drew that mermaid did a pretty good job fulfilling that purpose, because my chest is achy and my nose prickles, but there's also this pressure in the back of my throat, like a scream is caught in there and wants out.

I shake my head to try to clear it. The menu below me blurs and then sharpens. I need to read the kids' section for something Peach will eat, but I can't seem to get past *coconut chicken tenders*. I've finally moved on to *noodles with rose cream butter* when Lemon flips my menu to the back page. She doesn't even say anything. When I start to flip it back—hello, rude—she holds down one corner with her finger and then *tap-tap-tap*s with her turquoise fingernail. I sigh and look down to see that *The Rose Maid* is written at the top in curly script. Underneath it, a poem in five stanzas.

Deep in the ocean
where the current slips free,
there lives the Rose Maid,
our Rosemary Lee.

She's beauty and sadness,
she's love and she's loss.
She's a memory you hold dear,
she's the treasure and the cost.

Her tears are the ocean,
her heartbreak the wind.
Her eyes are like jewels,
her arms like a friend.

If you find her, beware.
If you find her, be keen.
She'll sing you into madness
or grant you one dream.

Secrets she knows,
sorrow she sees,
alone under the waves,
our Rosemary Lee.

When I finish, I breathe out like I've been holding in all my air. Maybe I have been. Then I read it again, slower. The rhythm feels like ocean currents. The Sadness swells in my chest. I try to swallow it down, but it's like there's an itch deep inside me, and these words almost scratch it.

Almost.

"What do you think?" Lemon asks. Her gaze flicks to my scars, then down to my Safety Pack, then finally back up to my eyes. "It's beautiful, right? Me and my best friends, Kiko and Jules? We're obsessed with her."

"With ... who?"

"The Rose Maid. Her." She points up at the pale blond mermaid above her mother's head. "Don't you think you sort of…" She trails off, head tilted as her eyes wander my face. I feel like a specimen in an aquarium. Still, though, my arms break out in goose bumps, and the hair on the back of my neck sticks straight up. I swear my scars even tingle.

Before Lemon can say anything else, the server comes to take our order. Claire chitchats with the guy—dark-haired with a lip piercing—before ordering for all five of us, which Mama doesn't seem to have a problem with but I think is just plain rude. What if I was a vegetarian? Vegan? A sufferer from celiac disease and couldn't touch even a pinch of wheat?

After the server leaves, I sip my water and try not to glance at the mermaid on the wall, and then Lemon starts asking Mama and Claire for stories from when they were growing up in California. I slink down into the booth as Claire babbles on about how they met when they were in kindergarten and Mama stole Claire's aquamarine crayon on the first day.

"I needed it for my unicorn," Mama says, laughing. "My pack of crayons only had sixteen boring colors. Yours had forty-eight."

"Yeah, well. I never saw that crayon again."

"Mama!" Peach says. "Stealing is wrong!"

Mama spreads her hands out. "I *borrowed* it."

"Which meant I had to partner with you for every art activity, just to use my own aquamarine crayon," Claire says, then holds up one finger. "Hang on. That was your plan all along, wasn't it? To ensnare me into best-friendship."

Mama throws her head back and laughs. "Yep, that was it. My diabolical plan."

"Clearly it worked."

Mama laughs even harder, her eyes gleaming and locked on Claire's.

Our food comes, and the shrimp and grits Claire ordered for me actually smells really good, but my appetite curdles like old yogurt. I can't remember the last time Mama laughed like this. Between her and Mum, she was always the quieter one, but, oh boy, could Mum make her laugh. One time, years ago, Mum made Mama laugh so hard she peed her pants a little. It was just a normal night. We were having vegetable pot pie. I don't even remember what was so funny, but Peach was in her high chair clapping, with mashed sweet potato all over her chubby cheeks, and Mama's face was red, her hands covering her mouth while Mum roared with laughter at the ceiling. Then suddenly, Mama shot out of her chair and ran for the bathroom, which only made Mum laugh harder. From then on, it was this running family joke, anytime Mama would release the tiniest giggle.

Watch out, Evelyn, better cross your legs!

She'd roll her eyes and smack Mum's shoulder, but she'd be smiling. She'd be laughing, just like she's laughing now.

"Are you still writing, Evie?" Claire says when her infernal laughter finally dies down.

Mama's smile dips a little, but she nods. "I am. Though I'm between projects right now."

Mama writes romance novels, a few of which have done really well and none of which I'm allowed to read yet. When Mum died, though, Mama missed a deadline and then decided to scrap the whole project she'd been working on. She hasn't finished a story in two years, and her editor wants a new book pretty much yesterday. I guess it's hard to write romance, about people being all happy and in love, when your wife is gone forever.

"You're a real published author," Claire says, stirring her risotto. "I'm so impressed."

"You've read my books?"

Claire tilts her head at Mama. "Every one. I love them. And I'm completely unsurprised by your success. You were always writing stories in that notebook of yours."

"With your aquamarine crayon."

Claire laughs so hard she slaps the table. I notice that Lemon's eyes follow her mom with a kind of awe, a little smile lifting the corners of her mouth.

"You're an author?" she asks Mama.

"Romance," Claire says. "And no, you're not old enough to read them."

Mama grins. "I tell Hazel the same thing."

"K–I–S–S–I–N–G!" Peach chants, and everyone laughs except me and Lemon, who elbows me so hard I have to glance at her. She widens her eyes and purses her lips, and I feel like she's trying to communicate some message, but whatever it is, I'm not getting it. Nor do I care to.

"So tell me," Claire says, "how long are you three staying in Rose Harbor?"

"Oh, just for the summer," Mama says. "We've been traveling around for a while now."

"Really?" Lemon says. "That sounds so adventurous."

"It does," Claire says. Then she glances at Mama and back down to her food, super quick. "So you're not...I mean, I don't want to assume..." She takes a deep breath, and I feel it coming before it does, like that electric zip in the air right before lightning strikes.

Claire lets out this nervous little laugh and runs a hand through her short hair. "I'm trying to ask whether or not you're married, or with a partner, or..."

I go very still.

I think Peach does too.

Even Lemon is a statue next to me.

I stare down at my shrimp. I don't want to see Mama's expression, see her smile and shake her head and say *no*. I hold my breath, wishing I could stuff cotton into my ears, but when I don't hear Mama say anything, I finally look up.

She's very still too. Her mouth is open a little, like she's trying to answer Claire's nosy question but it's stuck on her tongue. Claire's eyebrows dip in the middle. I see realization spill over her face—not the truth about Mum, necessarily, but *something*. Something horrible and sad. I don't even dare look at Lemon.

"Evie," Claire says, then word-vomits everywhere, talking so fast I can barely keep up. "I'm sorry. We don't have to talk about it. Look, I get it. I really do. And I—"

"Mama, I'm really tired," I say, way louder than I should, probably. But someone has to put an end to this horrendous night, and it looks like it's going to be me.

Mama finally closes her mouth and nods. "It's been a long day." Then she picks up her bag and digs around inside. "This has been lovely, Claire, but if you don't mind, I think we'll call it a night."

"Of course," Claire says, a frown still puckering her forehead. "Are you okay?"

Mama pulls three twenties from her wallet, handing them to Claire. "Yeah. Move-in is always exhausting. Is this enough to cover our meals?"

Claire waves away the money, and while Mama protests, I scoot my hip against Lemon's. At first she doesn't get it and I'm worried I'm going to have to literally bump her out of the booth, but then Peach scurries out and Lemon finally follows. As soon as I'm free, I grab Peach's hand and start walking. She comes with me without protest, which means she's ready to go too.

"We'll see you soon, right?" I hear Claire say behind me.

"Hazel, wait," Lemon says, but I don't.

I don't hear what Mama says to Claire, either. I don't let my eyes go back to that blond mermaid in her driftwood frames. I just keep walking until I'm out the door.

chapter five

We pause under the restaurant's awning to get our bearings. It's nearly dark, just a little bit of lavender light left in the sky. We spot the ocean, a deep blue swath to our left. Then we walk fast. The speed feels good, like we're outrunning something terrible.

Peach, as it turns out, really is super tired. We only get about a block away from the restaurant before she starts crying, whining that she wants to sleep at Lemon's house but rubbing her eyes like she does when she's exhausted. Mama picks her up, and Peach immediately passes out on her shoulder.

Mama and I walk in silence. I don't dare interrupt it, even though there are a million things I want to say.

We should leave tomorrow.

We don't need the ocean.

We don't need them.

We don't need this.

We only need us.

I walk close to Mama's side, trying to press the three of us together. Her warmth almost pushes out the cold crackle in my chest, that hollow feeling I got as soon as Lemon asked me if Mama was still married. Claire clearly didn't know about Mum at all. I can't decide how I feel about that—on the one hand, it means Mama didn't tell Claire anything about Mum on the walk into town, when they were strolling by themselves and laughing and smiling, so she can't trust or care about Claire that much. Who doesn't tell a childhood best friend about their *wife*? On the other hand, it's like Mum doesn't exist. Like she's just a memory who interrupted Mama's fun. Claire and Lemon didn't know what to think about our abrupt departure, I could tell. But they had to know it was something bad, and I couldn't even look at them. I know exactly what I would've seen if I had.

Pity.

I've seen it a million times. Not that we've ever told anyone we've met on the road about Mum—you don't tell complete strangers about how all the color seemed to disappear from the whole world—but I remember that look at Mum's memorial service. Dozens and dozens of eyes, all red-rimmed and wide and sad, their owners whispering about how terrible they felt for us, how grief was a heavy burden for someone as young as me.

Grief doesn't feel heavy, though. It never did. Maybe that's why I couldn't seem to cry at all at the service. I tried. I wanted to, but I felt all dried up. If anything, I think grief feels too light. I always feel like I'm about to float away, like there's nothing to hold me to the earth anymore. I hate that word, too—*grief.* It's terrible. Wrong. It makes me think of tiny packages of Kleenex and droopy carnations and frozen casseroles with too much cheese. Grief is a section in the greeting card aisle. It doesn't feel like anything to do with me or Mama or Peach.

Hollowing. Now that's a good word. *Emptying.* That's what it really felt like when Mum died, like a piece of me got scooped right out.

That's how other people look at us too—that's how I know Claire and Lemon would've looked at us in the restaurant if we told them about Mum. Like we're missing something.

And the way Mama is staring into space, her eyes misty and sad, I know she's thinking all the same things. I just know it. By morning, I'm sure, we'll be packing up and heading somewhere new.

The next morning, I wake up before the sun, my heart already pounding in anticipation. It'll be sort of a pain, repacking after we just unpacked yesterday, but totally worth it, in my opinion. We don't have a ton of stuff. Mama always rents places that are furnished and have the basic kitchen supplies, so really all we have to do is clean out the closets and toss everything into our trunks. Then Mama and I will load them into our truck and we can get out of here, away from that infernal ocean and our nosy neighbors.

Where we'll be going is the real question. Surely, Mama sees now how we just need to go home, back to California, back to our house on Camelia Street. We don't need nosy childhood friends asking her about her spouse or her partner, reminding her of everything she lost—we just need to go where we're safe, where everyone around us already knows and will leave us alone about it, where we won't risk all sorts of unknown dangers and strangers and possibly friends and attachments who will just hurt us in the long run.

Friends and attachments Mum will never know, never get to experience.

No, it's time to go home. Mama sees that—I know she does.

When the sky starts to lighten, I toss my covers back and climb down from my bunk. Peach is still completely out, but she'll be up soon, so I get dressed quickly and go to find Mama. I want to talk to her alone about going home. Peach is always in on our decisions about where to move to next, and I have a feeling that this time she's going to put up a fight about leaving her *fruit friend*.

The house is still quiet, the first shades of lavender-gray light peeking in through the windows. Outside, it's cloudy again and the wind swirls, whipping through the waves and the surrounding evergreens like a ghost.

"Mama?" I call, but she doesn't answer.

I head to her room at the other end of the house, but her door is open, her bed empty and neatly made. Mama is a big believer in making beds every morning, so they're ready to sleep in that night and you don't have to fuss with them when you're good and tired. You can just slip right in between the sheets. It would be a good strategy if we weren't leaving today. I figured Mama would be up earlier than even me, like she always is on moving days, already packing up linens and folding her clothes, stacking her books into her trunk.

"Mama?" I call again, wandering into the kitchen, but she's definitely not in the house. In the living room, I notice the front door is open, sea wind slipping in through the screen door, filling the room with salt and chill. I go to close everything up, but then I see a flash of blue on the porch. I go out, screen door creaking as I fling it wide, and there's Mama, sitting in one of the Adirondack chairs with her laptop open and on her legs. She's wrapped in the quilt she made for Mum the Christmas before Mum died. She called it the Sister Quilt, because it was sewn out of all of Peach's and my baby clothes, with a soft border of aqua blue, Mum's favorite color.

"Mama?"

She startles, fingers flying up from her laptop keyboard.

"Hey," she says, then looks back at her computer screen. "I didn't even hear you come out. Did you sleep okay?"

"What are you doing?" I ask instead of answering.

She releases one of those exhausted but happy kind of sighs and keeps on typing. "I'm writing. Can you believe it? I've been up half the night."

"You . . . you're writing a book? A new one?"

She wiggles one hand back and forth before attacking the keys again. "Getting there. That's the plan, at least." She smiles at the screen, eyes wild and bright, exactly the way I remember her looking years ago when she'd get caught up in writing, like she was lost in a whole other world and she was happy to be there. Mum called it *The Zone*, and we both knew better than to try to interrupt Mama when she was in *The Zone*.

"But aren't we—"

Leaving is what I want to say, but she looks up at me sharply, eyes soft but her mouth pressed into a tight line, like she knows exactly what I'm thinking and is begging me not to say it.

"Why don't you go get some breakfast started?" she asks. "I'll be in soon."

Then she turns back to her computer, lost in her brand-new romance.

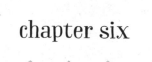

chapter six

We don't leave that day.

We don't leave the next day either. Or the day after that. In fact, Mama never even brings it up, which means I don't either.

After Mama came in from writing and Peach woke up, we all sat down to eat the French toast I made. I kept waiting for Mama to tell us we were moving on so I could bring up going home. I kept waiting for her to say anything about the previous night, but she just gazed at me over her tea mug and asked Peach what she wanted to do that day.

Thankfully, a storm rolled in while we were eating, all blustering winds and angry sea, so Peach's excited declaration that she wanted to go to the beach and swim was quickly put off for another day.

That's what Mama said—*We'll have to save that for another day, Peach Fuzz.*

Now, three days later, Mama still hasn't mentioned a thing about leaving, and the storm that kept us locked up safe in Sea Rose Cottage is clearing out. We wake up this morning to a sun fighting its way through the thinning clouds, pushing all the dreary away until there's nothing left but blue and bright.

"Beach day, beach day!" Peach chants in the kitchen, the remnants of her avocado toast still all over her mouth.

Mama laughs—*laughs*—while she rinses her plate. She peers out the window over the sink. Then she dries her hands on a tea towel. "It's certainly a good day for it."

My toast gets stuck in my throat. I try to envision what a *beach day* might look like. Sand castles and sunscreen, fizzy drinks in a cooler, paperback books dappled with seawater. A pretty picture if it didn't end with Peach drowning in the ocean every single time.

Before I have a chance to come up with some alternate plan, though, there's a knock at the front door. Then, while Mama hangs the towel by the stove and heads to the living room to answer it, there's another knock. Then another.

I know who it is before Mama even opens the door.

"Hi!" Lemon says.

There she is, Claire right next to her, their red hair like flames in the sun.

"Fruit friend!" Peach yells, leaping out of her chair and running to wrap her arms around Lemon's middle.

"Hey, you two," Mama says.

"Sorry to just drop by," Claire says. She's watching Mama nervously, her smile barely there.

Mama waves a hand. "Totally fine. I was just thinking of walking down to say hi myself. I guess we forgot to exchange numbers the other night."

Claire visibly relaxes, her shoulders dropping. "Well, let's fix that right now, shall we?"

Mama nods and takes out her phone, handing it over to Claire as Claire does the same with hers. I watch it all happen, like I'm watching a car accident in slow motion.

"We came over because I had the greatest, most wonderful idea," Lemon says. She's looking right at me, Peach still attached to her like a barnacle. I have a feeling her greatest, most wonderful idea is actually the complete opposite.

"And what's that?" Mama asks.

I get up from the kitchen table and take my plate to the sink.

"Well, you see, every summer—"

I turn the water on and run it at full blast. The white noise fills my ears, Lemon's voice nothing but a dull mumble.

"Really?" I hear Mama say loudly. "That's actually—"

I flip on the garbage disposal. It eats up my bread crusts with a rumbling gurgle. I stare into the white porcelain sink, resting my fingers on the faucet, wondering how long it'll take for Lemon to tire out and move on. A slender hand whips into my vision, slapping the faucet off. I look up at Mama, her eyes tight as she looks back at me.

"You're being rude," she says quietly so only I can hear her.

"I'm cleaning my plate," I say.

"It's clean."

She wraps her arm around my shoulders and turns me so I'm facing the living room, walking me over until I'm in front of Lemon. She's got that stupid camera around her neck again, wild hair like a bird's nest, a short-sleeved blush-colored tee with a mermaid printed on it over jean shorts, and a backpack on her shoulders.

"Lemon, can you say that again?" Mama says, keeping her arm around me.

"Um...well...," Lemon says. "Every summer, the library has all these programs for kids. Reading clubs and art clubs, some sports and drama clubs. This year, they're doing an Ocean Club every weekday from nine to one, and it's really fun. We just started last week, but I'm sure you can still join. I thought...I thought maybe you'd like to go with me?"

"Me?" I say.

"Yeah, you," Lemon says. "It's just for kids our age, and you can meet some new friends. A real oceanographer teaches it. Her name is Amira and she's awesome. We learn all sorts of ocean facts, do some arts and crafts. We'll have a few field trips too, like to the aquarium. And of course, we go to the beach every day for lunch, then do some exploring and digging and looking at stuff under magnifying glasses."

I blink at her, my mind snagging on words like *oceanographer* and *facts* and *aquarium*. Words that used to make my heart beat faster with curiosity, even happiness. I think about the other posters that used to hang on the walls in my room, among all of Mum's ocean paintings and sketches. Fact-filled infographics about the sea and sea life, full-color drawings of mollusks and shells, cetaceans and sharks, complete with labels and diagrams. I'd spend hours soaking up all the information, then even more hours diving deeper, days devouring my favorite book, the *Ultimate Oceanpedia* by National Geographic, which Mum got me the Christmas before she died.

A swell of something that feels like interest fills my chest, but it deflates just as quick, because my mind gets caught on other words too. *Beach* and *ocean* and *kids*.

Friends.

"No thanks," I say.

Lemon's smile drops. She fiddles with her camera strap. "Oh. Um."

"I want to go, I want to go!" Peach says. She gazes up at Lemon like she's the goddess of the sea herself.

"Oh, man, I wish you could, Grapefruit," Lemon says, smoothing Peach's hair. "It's only for middle schoolers, though."

"Well, I think it sounds lovely," Mama says. "Hazel, you go ahead." She pushes on my shoulder, just a little. Just enough.

I glare up at her. "I said no thank you."

"And I said it's a lovely idea."

We stare at each other. I fill my eyes with desperation, but if Mama notices it, she's totally unmoved. Tears start to tickle my nose. "But Peach—"

"I'll take care of your sister," Mama says. "We'll go to the beach, won't we, Peach Fuzz? Maybe Claire can join us?"

"I'd love to," Claire says, ruffling Peach's hair but gazing at Mama. "Sounds like a perfect day. I have to work tonight, but I'm yours until six."

Mama smiles. No, she *grins*. "Wonderful. It's settled, then." She finds my shoes by the front door and pushes them into my arms. "We'll see you this afternoon, okay?"

"Wait, my Safe—"

"You don't need it, sweetie," Mama says softly, still trying to maneuver me toward Lemon, toward the door.

"Yes, I do!" I yank my arm out of hers, and the room goes quiet. There's just my breathing. Loud, panicked breathing.

"Okay, honey," Mama says gently, calmly. "All right, we'll get it."

I look up at her one more time. Don't dare look at anyone else. Even Peach has gone silent. "Mama, please."

Her eyes go soft, but her mouth is still a firm line. She reaches over and plucks my Safety Pack from where I left it on the couch and loops it over my shoulder. As she pulls back, her fingertips graze my scars. "This will be good for you. You'll be fine. I promise."

And then she's making plans to meet Claire on the beach in ten minutes, telling Lemon thank you so much for inviting me, instructing Peach to go get her swimsuit on, chattering on and on while I just stand there, Mama's words echoing between my ears.

Because if there's anything I know for sure, it's that promising someone they're going to be fine is never a promise you can keep.

chapter seven

The Ocean Club meets in the library, which is a huge redbrick building in downtown Rose Harbor. It's set right on the water and, according to Lemon's incessant chattering, used to be some rich person's summer house back in the 1800s.

I offer up a *hmm* every now and then, but mostly, I'm thinking up a new plan. Clearly, leaving for home is out of the question.

Or at least, it's out of the question for now.

Mama has booked Sea Rose Cottage until the end of August, and we've never left a town after only a few days anyway. I've survived three-month stays in towns before. Seven times before this, in fact. I can do it again.

And I can do it perfectly. Calmly, just like Mama

wants. I can grit my teeth through Ocean Club, tune it all out, tune Lemon out, and then, in August, Mama will have to listen to me about going home. She'll have to, because I will have done everything right, been the calm, serene daughter she clearly wants. I won't bring up Mum. I won't freak out over Peach and the ocean. I'll keep it all to myself.

And then I'll tell her—with my voice and not just my thoughts—that I want to go home. No, I'll demand it.

I nod to myself as we enter the Rose Harbor Library, my plan taking shape. I take a deep breath in, let it out slowly, just to calm down my roiling thoughts. Best start now, this new worry-free Hazel. I can do it. It's just a matter of deciding to, right?

Inside, everything is dark wood shelving and furniture and high ceilings. Stained-glass windows cover the back of the building, refracting the morning light into a million colors. It's beautiful in here—I'll admit it.

But only to myself.

I follow Lemon up a set of stairs and then down a hall lined with what look like meeting rooms.

"I can't wait for you to meet Kiko and Jules," Lemon says, coming to a stop in front of the last door on the left. I peek through the window, catch a glimpse of at least twenty kids sitting at several round tables. My heart leaps into my throat. Other plans whirl through my thoughts.

Faking a headache.

Faking getting a text—oops, family emergency!

Faking vomiting.

Actually vomiting, because my stomach feels like it might rear up at any second and try to exit my body.

"My friends are really amazing," she says.

Friends. I crane my neck, watching everyone inside the room talking and laughing. Lemon has friends in there. Meaning kids my age. Meaning several sets of eyes staring at me, wondering about my scars, eventually asking. I'll just have to make absolutely sure they never get that curious. I roll my shoulders back, fix my hair against my face. Calm. Cool. Uninterested.

Then she pushes the door open, grabs my hand, and yanks me into the room.

We spill inside and every head turns our way.

No one is talking.

No one is hanging around, laughing, waiting for the class or club or whatever this is to start.

It's already started.

"...five zones in the ocean," a woman at the front of the room is saying.

"Crap, we're late," Lemon says, barely whispering as she pulls me to a table in the middle of the room with two other kids sitting at it.

"Let's call it barely on time, Ms. Calloway," the woman says, crinkled smile directed at Lemon. "As usual."

Everyone laughs, but not in a mean way. Still, I know it pulls every single eye in the room toward Lemon and me, and my face goes right on ahead and flames up. I press my hair against my warm cheek and slide into the chair next to Lemon, slink down as much as I can without it looking super obvious that I'm, well, slinking down.

"It's about time," a girl whispers to Lemon from across the table. She's Asian, with long dark hair and sleek bangs, purple-framed glasses, and braces on her teeth. She's wearing a fitted T-shirt that, now that I look closely at it, matches Lemon's exactly. It's blush pink with a white mermaid printed on it. But instead of shorts like Lemon has on, this girl has her tee tucked into a high-waisted skirt with orange, navy, pink, and light blue stripes. I glance down at my own ratty cutoff shorts and plain gray T-shirt—both of which are in need of washing—and my knockoff black-and-white Skechers I got at a Target for twenty bucks back in Ohio.

"Sorry, hey," Lemon whispers back as she digs a notebook and pen out of her backpack. The notebook is blue and has tiny silver mermaids printed all over the cover, because of course it does.

"Ocean zones today," the other kid at the table says. "She already said."

"Ooh, fun," Lemon says, then glances at me. Opens her mouth. I brace myself. "This is Hazel. Hazel, this is Kiko Masuda"—the girl—"and Jules Renleigh"—ocean zones kid.

"Hey," Jules says, waving at me, which is when I notice a button on their shirt that says ASK ME ABOUT MY PRONOUNS.

I've seen the button before. Lots of times, back in California. It's blue and pink and white, and Mum's good friend Sidney, who worked at the university with her, used to wear the same one a lot. They were nonbinary and preferred the pronouns *they* and *them*. I'd talked to them enough to know that when they wore the button, they really did want people to ask.

"Plus, it just makes people think," Sidney had said the first time I saw their button. "It makes them pause, stop thinking so much in terms of only *he* and *she* and girls and boys."

Now, I press my hair against my cheek, clear my throat, and try to make Sidney proud. Make Mum proud too. "So, um, what . . . what are your pronouns?"

Jules grins. "Oh. Wow, awesome. Yeah, thanks for asking."

I nod. "So . . ."

"Oh, sorry! I use *they* and *them*." They laugh, and Kiko pats them on the shoulder. They've got pale skin and dark hair, short on the sides and longer on top so that it swoops over their forehead and curls at the ends. Their eyes are so deep blue they look like sapphires.

"See?" Kiko says. "I told you people would ask."

"Yeah. She's the third person in two whole weeks," Jules says.

"That's more people than none," Lemon says.

"What about you?" Jules asks me. "What are your pronouns?"

"Oh," I say. "Um, *she* and *her*."

Jules nods and smiles at me again. I feel something warm in my chest, knowing from Sidney how much asking meant to them, but then it's sort of like I remember where I am and start shrinking in on myself. The lady at the front keeps talking, and Lemon and Jules and Kiko tune in, so I use the time to take a deep breath and study my tablemates a bit more. They just seem like normal kids, but the odd thing is that Jules is also wearing the same mermaid-printed blush tee as Kiko and Lemon, like the three of them are in some sort of weird club. A quick glance around tells me that no one else is in matching T-shirts, so there's that, at least.

Kiko catches my eye and offers a smile. I try to smile back, try to act as normal as possible, nice and flat and boring, but it's hard, with my hair covering half my face, which isn't exactly a normal look. Plus, my hair is pretty fine, so it doesn't want to stay in place. It wants to flit around, little wisps reaching for any part of my face it can find so that, before I know it, a tickle starts in my nose and shoots up between my eyes. I try to think of strawberries, look up at the light, but it's no use. I let out the loudest sneeze the world has ever heard. On instinct, I cover my mouth, pushing my hair out of my face, so when I drop my hands, my scars are *right there* for all the world to see. Kiko's eyes go round behind her glasses, and Jules says what sounds a lot like *whoa* under their breath.

I fix my hair over my cheek again fast.

"Bless you," the teacher says. "I see we've got a new friend with us today. Lemon? Care to make an introduction?"

"Um, yeah, totally," Lemon says, then proceeds to tell everyone else in the room that I'm Hazel and I'm here for the summer and our moms are BFFs from when they were kids, which makes several people say *Awww*, and I just want Lemon to shut up so everyone will stop looking at me.

"Welcome, Hazel," the woman says. She's got nearly black hair and brown skin, dark eyes that sparkle in the fluorescent lighting. "I'm Dr. Amira Khoury and I work at the aquarium just outside of town. You can call me Amira, though, and I hope you've brought a sense of adventure with you today."

I blink at her.

She tilts her head at me. Smiles. "Okay, then. So, like I said, we're talking about ocean zones today. Just like Earth has layers, so does the ocean. Does anyone know how many?"

"Five."

My eyes go wide as I hear my own voice echo through the room. Lemon shoots me a thumbs-up, but I look down. I hadn't meant to answer. I hadn't meant to even remember that tiny little ocean fact.

"Very good," Amira says. "Anyone know their names?"

Sunlight zone.

Twilight zone.

Midnight zone.

Abyss.

Trenches.

The words float through my head, but I keep my mouth shut this time. A boy in the back gets sunlight and midnight but can't remember the others. Amira goes over all five with a diagram on the big screen at the front of the room, then gestures to several jars on the table there, holding up the only one with five layers of colored liquid, ranging from the lightest blue, at the top, to black. The liquid undulates just like an ocean current, but the colors don't mix together.

"You're each going to make your own ocean," she says, "with all five zones accurately represented. Then we'll observe each other's creations, talk a little more about each zone's characteristics."

A girl sitting in the very front shoots her hand up.

"Yes, Vanessa," Amira says, "you can take it home with you today."

The girl's hand goes down and a few people laugh.

Amira explains the directions, how we're going to use food coloring, vegetable oil, Dawn dish soap, corn syrup, water, and rubbing alcohol to create liquids with different densities so the layers don't mix. I watch as she demonstrates making a new jar, using black food coloring and corn syrup to create the trenches layer, the darkest, coldest, most mysterious part of the ocean. Oceanographers and marine biologists keep learning more about it, but nearly eighty percent of Earth's oceans is still unexplored. And a lot of the sea life we do know about is wild and strange. Some of it seems impossible. Like the frilled shark, which looks like something right out of the dinosaur era. Or the red-lipped batfish, which looks like a nightmarish combination of a frog and a crab but which is, in fact, a fish.

"Cool, huh?" Jules asks me.

I hadn't realized I was perched on the edge of my chair, my elbows on the table and my mouth hanging open a little as I listened to Amira. The ocean is vast and weird and used to fascinate me no end. Now, though, the sea just feels like fear. Like cold and blood and loss.

I snap my mouth shut. "I guess."

Jules lifts a skeptical eyebrow, but they're smiling at me, like maybe they're trying to get me to smile back. I almost do, too, but then Jules edges forward, looking at me with softly narrowed eyes like I'm some creature newly discovered in the ocean's trenches. "Wow."

"I know," Kiko says. She leans toward me too, so far it's like she's trying to crawl across the table. "It's wild."

I lean away. My face goes end-of-the-world red and I can't decide if I'm humiliated or furious. Who just *stares* like this at someone's scars and then talks about them to their friends right in front of the scarred person? Who does that? Apparently, Lemon's rude friends do that. Looks like I won't have any trouble staying uninterested in this club, in this whole stupid town.

"I told you," Lemon says, sitting back and smiling at me proudly.

I glare at her, then push my chair back. Most of the other kids are diving into the materials Amira is placing at their tables. They won't notice if I just walk out, which is exactly what I plan to do, without a single word of explanation to Lemon and her imbecilic friends.

"I mean, you really do look just like her," Jules says. "I didn't believe Lemon at first, but it's true."

Lemon and Kiko both nod.

"Wait, what?" I ask, shoulders relaxing just a little. But then a whole other set of questions and worries fills my head. Before I can ask, though, Amira comes by with jars for all four of us, then sets a big tub on the table full of the materials we need to make our zones.

"You didn't tell her?" Kiko asks Lemon.

"Well...no. I didn't really know how," Lemon says.

"Tell me what?" I ask.

"I guess it is a weird conversation," Jules says.

"Yeah, but still. She needs to know—"

"Hello?" I sort of yell it. A few kids' heads snap toward our table, and Kiko's eyes go wide. "*She* is right here," I say, quieter.

"Sorry," Lemon says, wincing.

"Whatever," I say, and notice Kiko's eyes narrowing, her mouth dipping into a frown. "Who are you talking about?"

"Um, Rosemary Lee," Lemon says as she passes around the jars. I close my hands around mine, feeling the cool glass under my fingers.

"You ever heard of her?" Kiko asks. She squints up at the directions Amira posted on the screen at the front of the room, then reaches for the corn syrup.

The pale-haired mermaid in the drawings from the Rose Maid Café flashes through my head, along with words that gave me goose bumps.

Her tears are the ocean,
her heartbreak the wind...

"The mermaid from that poem?" I ask, rubbing my arms.

"Yes!" Lemon says.

"Well, Rosemary Lee is the *girl*," Jules says, swirling the trenches layer in their jar, black oozing up the sides. "The Rose Maid is the mermaid."

"Aren't they the same?" I ask.

Jules peers at me through the jar, the glass magnifying their eyes. "One's a girl. And one's a mermaid."

"Yes, they're the same in essence," Lemon says, shoving Jules's shoulder. "Rosemary Lee became the Rose Maid."

"You really believe that?" I ask, finishing up my own trenches layer and grabbing the blue dish soap for the abyss.

Kiko stops, her measuring cup frozen in midair. "You don't?"

"Um. Mermaids aren't real."

Jules makes a sound like they're in pain. Kiko rubs her forehead.

"It's okay, she doesn't know the story yet," Lemon says.

"Then tell her," Jules says. "No way can someone who looks like Rosemary Lee's doppelgänger *not* believe in the Rose Maid."

"I really look that much like her?" I ask. "I mean, I saw the drawings in the café, but still. Those are drawings."

"So you noticed them?" Lemon says. "I knew it. I knew you liked the drawings."

"I didn't say I liked them."

Lemon's wide-eyed-wonder look drops. Something like hurt flashes across her face.

"Okay," Kiko says, slamming her jar onto the table and glaring at me. "Who are you, again? Lemon, who *is* she and why is she here?"

Lemon looks miserable. A tiny flare of regret blooms in my chest, but I squash it quickly. I didn't say anything wrong. I simply stated an opinion.

"Easy, Kik," Jules says, but keeps their eyes on their own jar.

"What did I say?" I ask, glaring right back at Kiko. "Did one of you draw those pictures or something?"

Lemon's mouth opens, but nothing comes out. The other two share another look, one of those looks that clearly say I'm missing something.

"Our friend did," Jules says.

"Who?" I ask.

Lemon sets her jar to one side and dives into her backpack so deep, her entire head disappears.

"Immy," Kiko says. "She...she's our best friend. She's not around anymore, though."

"And this *Immy* is an artist?" I ask, getting tired of hunting for every little detail. It's not like I actually care.

Jules nods, a soft smile on their lips. "The best. I wish I was half as good as her."

"You draw too?"

They nod. "Mostly pencil sketches. Immy does watercolors." They frown, glance at Lemon, who's still buried in her bag. "I mean, she...she *did* watercolor."

"She *does*," Lemon says, bursting out of her bag, bringing out a glossy paperback called *Coastal Lore*. It's thick but small, about the size of one of those travel guides that you can fit into your jacket pocket. She opens the book and flips furiously until she lands somewhere in the middle.

"Here. Read this." She shoves the book into my hands and taps her finger on the heading at the top of a two-page spread.

Below that, there's a bunch of text, but what catches my eye is the large sepia-toned photograph in the middle of the first page. It's of a family—a mom, dad, a girl who looks around our age, and a smaller girl who looks around Peach's age. In the photo, no one is smiling. They all just stare out at the camera, dead-eyed, stiff hands on shoulders and ruffly collars no doubt scratching at their necks. I remember hearing that, a long time ago, people wouldn't smile in pictures. It was the style, I guess, but the style is beyond creepy.

But what's even creepier is that the older girl looks like a long-haired me. Not just a resemblance, but *exactly* like me. I can't tell what color her eyes are, but they look light—green or blue for sure—and her nose turns up at the end just a little bit, like mine does. Her eyebrows are straight and thick—*like tiny caterpillars*, Mum used to say— and I wonder, if the girl did smile, whether or not she'd have a tiny dimple on the right side of her mouth but not her left, just like I do.

Below the picture, there's a caption.

The Lee Family, 1882: Aurelia (33), Jacob (39), Rosemary (12), and Nell (6).

·I can't seem to drag my eyes away from the photo. And it's not just because she looks like me or I look like her or whatever. It's the family. The parents, the little sister. Even though they're unsmiling, my chest aches with a familiar feeling, a *surrounding*. A fullness I haven't felt since Mum died. My eyes cloud over and I keep my head down, eyes on the photo, hair curtained around my face, until Lemon slides a finger into my vision, her brightly painted nail jabbing at the text.

"Read it," she whispers, not unkindly but firmly enough to jolt me back into the room, remember where I am. Without looking up, I do what she says, knowing she'll never let it go until I do. A sinking feeling settles into my stomach, though. Happy stories don't make it into books like *Coastal Lore*. Only the sad ones do that.

Spend a mere hour in the sleepy coastal town of Rose Harbor, Maine, and you'll no doubt hear about the famous Rose Maid, the purported mermaid who lurks in the cold harbor waters, intriguing lore-lovers for nearly one hundred and fifty years. But unlike the Loch Ness Monster or the kraken, this mythical creature is based on a real girl, a teenager who lived in Rose Harbor in the late 1800s, which is perhaps what makes the story so enticing to tourists and locals alike.

Rosemary Elizabeth Lee was born in Rose Harbor on May 1, 1870, on the heels of the Civil War. Rosemary was the elder daughter of Jacob Lee, a ship captain, and Aurelia Lee, a homemaker and seamstress. Very little is known about Rosemary's early life. What we do know is that the family routinely accompanied Captain Lee on his maritime travels during the summer months. On July 22, 1882, Aurelia, Rosemary, and little Nell boarded Jacob's ship, the *Skylark*, a small steam-powered ocean liner that ferried wealthy families to and from Southampton in England twice a month. On this particular trip, however, the vessel never made it to its destination. In the early-morning hours of July 26, a storm—which most historians now concur was a Category 3 hurricane—waylaid the ship, capsizing the vessel and killing nearly everyone on board.

Rosemary Lee was among the few rescued from the cold Atlantic waters. Tragically, she was also the only member of her family who survived the wreck. She returned with a broken arm and several fractured ribs to Rose Harbor, where she found herself orphaned and without any other family to call her own. For the next two years, she lived with a widow named Anne Lancaster at the north end of town. Anne was kind, and her house was comfortable and boasted ocean views, but Rosemary Lee returned from her ordeal at sea a troubled soul. According to Anne's journal, which now resides under glass at the Lancaster House Museum and attracts thousands of visitors a year,

Rosemary was quiet, seldom speaking more than a few words a day, and would often spend hours frantically walking up and down the beach, eyes on the ocean, as though searching for her lost family.

"Her loneliness is a constant chill in my bones," Anne wrote in her journal on December 15, 1882. "I try to help her, but she seems lost, a ghost in a girl's skin."

Anne wasn't the only one who noticed the change in Rosemary. There are several written accounts of strange behavior by the girl, including splashing into the ocean fully clothed, losing her temper with classmates over trivial matters during school hours, and even disappearing for days at a time, only to return to Anne's house as though nothing had happened.

On July 26, 1884, exactly two years after her family perished at sea, she told Anne she was going for a walk on the beach after dinner, which wasn't unusual for the girl. "I thought nothing of it, nor did I offer to accompany her," Anne wrote a few days later. "She often rebuffed my attempts at comfort and companionship. Now I wish I had insisted."

As do those intrigued by the story of Rosemary Lee, for the girl never returned to Anne's house that night. For a while, the town assumed she had run away or that some evil fate had befallen her. Anne, however, knew better.

"I looked for her just before darkness fell," Anne's journal recounts. "Of course I did. I followed her footprints across the sand, but as far as I could tell, she never left the beach. She simply walked and paced as was her custom, toward the water and then away and back again, until the tide swallowed any trace she'd left behind."

Not long after Rosemary vanished, strange reports began to surface. Sightings. Whispers. Fishermen returned with their daily catch clearly spooked, rambling about iridescent flukes sliding through the water and blue eyes as big as the ocean itself. One or two wild stories might have been shrugged off, but soon tales of a mermaid in the harbor—a mermaid with swirling blond hair and a tattered blue dress, which was what Rosemary was wearing when she was last seen—were numerous, filling the town with both unease and excitement. Moreover, the sightings only increased as the years passed until Rosemary became the Rose Maid. Storms, shipwrecks, illness at sea, madness, unfruitful fishing trips, and pretty much any misfortune on the waves were soon attributed to her, as well as dozens of sailors' accounts of experiencing "unearthly comfort and peace" upon making eye contact with the mermaid.

Now the Rose Maid is a local legend. Poems have been penned about her, beguiling drawings and paintings rendered. Sightings of a strangely beautiful fishtail, a flash of blond hair, or a hauntingly sad human face under the waves are still reported yearly. And every July 26, the town celebrates the mermaid with the Rose Maid Festival, a bacchanal of sea-green beverages, mermaid costumes, golden spyglasses, and sighting parties on one of the many boats in town. The Rose Maid, it seems, isn't leaving Rose Harbor anytime soon.

Two days before the girl disappeared, Anne wrote these chilling—prophetic?—words in her journal: "She has the sea in her soul now. I fear one day it will claim her completely."

Did the sea claim Rosemary Lee as Anne feared? Visit Rose Harbor today and decide for yourself.

At the bottom of the second page, there's a painting of the sea. The view is from under the water, looking up to a fisherman standing on what's left of his boat, barely more than a ragged plank of wood. Wreckage surrounds him and he gazes out, hand to his brow, as though looking for rescue. Below him, a mermaid drifts, reaching a hand toward his ruined vessel.

"Well?" Lemon says. "What do you think?"

I shiver. Goose bumps are everywhere now.

She has the sea in her soul now.

"Hazel?"

I fear one day it will claim her completely.

"Hazel!"

I jolt back into the room, so startled I drop the book on the floor.

"Oh, yeah," Jules says, grinning and clapping their hands together, then points at me. "We got her. Total believer right there."

I pick up the book. "It's a tourist guide. Not fact."

"Facts are boring," Kiko says as she mixes water with dark blue food coloring for her midnight layer.

"You're holding a *fact* in your hands right now," I say.

"She's got you there, Kik," Jules says.

Kiko sticks her tongue out at them and holds her three-layered jar up to the light, swirls it around. "Okay, fine, but I'm not here for the facts. I'm here for the arts and crafts and the magic."

"The magic," I say.

"The ocean is full of magic," Kiko says, lifting one eyebrow at me like a challenge.

"I never thought about it like that before," I say.

"Kiko is a fantasy nerd," Jules says. "She'll have you sprouting fairy wings and riding on a dragon in no time."

Kiko sighs, gets a dreamy look in her eyes. "Wouldn't that be amazing?"

"More like terrifying," I say.

She lifts her eyebrows. "You wouldn't want to ride on a dragon?"

I visibly shudder at the thought, which I hope is answer enough.

Lemon laughs, a shiny glint in her eye as she looks at her friends. It makes my throat go a little thick. But then I notice Kiko studying me for another beat before glancing down at her work, unsmiling. I feel a tug in my chest, embarrassment or worry or confusion over Kiko's coldness, but then I breathe through it, remind myself that's exactly what I wanted.

Thankfully, we all fall into our work for a few minutes. These three talk so fast and seem to know each other so well, they make me dizzy, and I need a second to shake off whatever Kiko thinks about me. The quiet settles around me, and my mind clears while I concentrate on my ocean zone jar. It's beautiful, really, the way all the different liquids keep their own space, each blue just barely blurring into the next shade.

I hold my completed jar up. This project is actually really accurate. Daylight from the window gleams through the sunlight layer, dappling blue onto the table in front of me. A little gets through the twilight layer, just like it should. But the light can't work its way through the midnight layer. And the abyss and trenches layers are so dark I shiver in my chair, all those mysteries pinging around in my brain just like they used to.

The ocean is full of magic.

"We think the Rose Maid lives somewhere around in here," Lemon says, tapping the twilight layer on my jar. "And if we're really lucky, like when all those sightings are reported, she's here." She taps the sunlight layer.

"If she lived in the twilight layer," I say, "someone definitely would've spotted her already."

"Who's to say they haven't?" Kiko says. "There are tons of sightings documented. And not just the Rose Maid either. My grandma? She swears she saw a mermaid in Japan when she was a kid, before she moved to America. She told me all about it, how she was in Ishigaki with her family and the water is super clear there. She was swimming with her brother and saw this creature with the body of a fish and the head of a girl. They call them ningyo."

I shiver but shake my head. "I mean oceanographers. People like Amira."

"Who's like Amira?"

I look up to see the woman herself standing by our table, arms clasped behind her back.

"Oceanographers," Kiko says. "*Hazel* here"—she says my name like it's a swearword—"was saying that if the Rose Maid lived in the twilight zone, you would've found her already."

"Oh, not necessarily," Amira says. "The twilight zone can get pretty dark, and the ocean is vast. Lots of mysteries out there still to solve or discover."

"Wait," I say, ignoring how her words mirror my own

thoughts from only a moment ago. "You believe in the Rose Maid?"

She smiles. "Well, oceanographers do like evidence, I'll give you that. Facts, numbers, sure. But oceanographers also believe in *possibility*. If we don't, what are we looking for when we go out to sea? What drives us?"

And with that proclamation, she walks back to the front of the room.

"See?" Jules says.

"Magic," Kiko says, nearly squealing with excitement.

"I prefer the term *mysteries*," says Jules, "but fine, have your fun."

Kiko and Jules continue to banter, but I look down at my jar, run my finger over the darkest three zones. My mind spins, circles, rushes back to that last day with Mum on our kayak trip. We weren't out that deep. The sunlight zone glimmered beneath us and still, it took her. Just like that. From life to death in a blink, like it was . . . like it was some sort of magic.

"Okay, it looks like everyone is finishing up their ocean zones," Amira says from the front of the room, snapping me out of my memory. "Carefully seal them and place all the materials back in the tub. It's time for lunch!"

The class cheers and everyone starts scrambling to clean up. I help, my limbs moving automatically, but my mind is far away, lost out at sea with Mum.

chapter eight

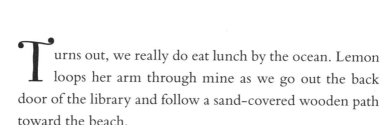

Turns out, we really do eat lunch by the ocean. Lemon loops her arm through mine as we go out the back door of the library and follow a sand-covered wooden path toward the beach.

"I don't have any food with me," I say.

"I packed you a sandwich this morning," Lemon says. "Just in case."

"Of course you did," Jules and Kiko say together.

Lemon laughs and hugs my arm tighter. I let her, if only because my stomach is growling. Breakfast seems like ages ago. With my free hand, I take my phone from my back pocket and text Mama.

How's it going?

She doesn't answer right away, so I type another question.

Did you remember to put sunscreen on Peach?

Other questions fill me up—*Did she actually swim? You went with her, right? Watch out for the rocks. Jellyfish. Shallow-swimming sharks*—but before I can tap any of them into my phone, her response buzzes.

We're fine. Just go have fun.

And that's all she says.

I'm about to ask for more details, when the sea oats rising up on either side of us break, revealing the sprawling shore. The sun glimmers into the sunlight zone, turning the water a rare-for-Maine aquamarine color. Tiny evergreen-covered islands rise up in the distance, and rocks lie across parts of the shallows like beached sea lions.

It's beautiful. So beautiful, tears sting my nose. Something pulls at my chest, some kind of longing or memory or I don't even know what. The rocks send a spike of fear through my heart, which tangles up with everything else so tightly I almost can't breathe.

"You okay?" Jules asks from next to me.

I nod. Can't speak. I just follow the group down to a wider patch of dry sand. Lemon releases my arm and sits in the sand, unpacking her lunch—and mine, I guess—onto her lap. Kiko does the same. Only Jules stays standing with me. I can feel them watching me, wondering about me, but I can't seem to sit, to settle, to look away from the water.

That's when I see it.

A cut of bright yellow to my left, leaning against one of the larger groups of rocks.

A double kayak.

Two paddles.

Two red helmets and two bright orange life jackets.

The waves crash on the shore, smacking against the rocks over and over and over...

Suddenly, it's too hot out here. Sweat beads on my upper lip, on the back of my neck, under my arms. I feel a flash of cold, then heat again, like I've got a fever. My heart grows three sizes, just like the Grinch's, but not in a good way. In a my-body-is-one-giant-heartbeat kind of way.

"Hazel?" Jules asks. They turn to face me, a frown pushing their thick eyebrows together. I try to smile, shake my head, nod, shrug, anything, but I can't do much except focus on breathing in and out. If I stop concentrating, my lungs will shut down, I'm sure of it.

"Hey, you okay?" they ask.

"What's wrong?" Lemon calls. Her voice sounds far away.

"I don't know," Jules says. "She just looks...weird."

I'm fine, I try to say, but I can't get it out. Not enough air. Not enough anything.

Lemon's face swims into view. Too close. Eyes looking for mine. My bones feel like rubber, as flexible as raw clay.

"Are you having a panic attack?" Lemon asks. "You are, aren't you?"

I shake my head, but she's right. I am. I know all the signs, and these are the signs.

"For real?" I hear Kiko say.

I had these attacks a lot, right after Mum's and my accident. I'd wake up sweating in the middle of the night. Or my lungs would feel like they were shrinking every time I caught Mama lying on the couch by herself when she thought Peach and I were asleep, sobbing into the Sister Quilt. I went to a counselor for about a month, right after. But then we left California, and the attacks stopped. Or at least, I learned how to control them. Like when Peach got sick or cut herself or hurt her ankle, the panic was always *right there*, like water just about to boil over. I figured out how to stop it, though.

My Safety Pack.

Staying alert, being prepared for anything.

Taking care of my sister.

Just Mama and Peach and me.

No heartache.

No risks.

I've done everything right, but still, here I am, crumpling into the sand in the middle of Ocean Club lunch. Other kids start to notice now. Over Jules's shoulder I see Amira walking this way. I try to tell them all that it's okay, but all I hear is this horrible gasping sound and then I realize it's me. I'm the horrible gasper.

"Is she all right?" Amira asks.

"I don't know," Lemon says. "I think she's having a panic attack."

"Are you sure?" Amira says, taking out her phone. "Does she have any medical conditions?"

I shake my head, the world tips on its axis. I sink down onto the sand.

"Just give her a second," Lemon says, then turns back to me. "Okay, breathe."

I want to scream at her that I'm trying, that if it was just that easy, I wouldn't be in this situation in the first place. I shake my head, try to glare at her.

Everyone's looking now. They're looking at me. My scars. *My fault, my fault, my fault.*

I squeeze my eyes closed as tight as they'll go, so tight my head starts to hurt.

"Breathe," Lemon says again. When I open my eyes again, she's right there, squatting down so we're eye level, her hands gently resting on my knees. "Focus on my face. See those five freckles on my left cheek that are bigger than all the others? Focus on them. Connect the dots. They form that constellation Cassiopeia. Like a weird-looking *W*. Do you see it?"

I wrinkle my nose, wishing I had enough air in my lungs to yell at her to stop babbling, but then... I see it. The freckles on her face, soft brown dots, five of them that stand out. I trace them with my eyes and they really do make a wonky kind of *W*. Cassiopeia's throne. I remember, in fourth grade, we did a unit on Greek mythology and we talked about Cassiopeia, the vain queen in the northern sky.

"Good," Lemon says, squeezing my knees. "Good, keep breathing. Feel your feet on the sand, the sun on your back. Check out my awesome constellation face."

Jules is kneeling next to Lemon, concern all over their face. Kiko paces behind them. Amira stares at me, phone poised, no doubt to call an ambulance.

But then...my lungs slow down. Open up. I'm sort of light-headed, but I'm not horrible-gasping anymore. I'm still breathing kind of loud, but it's a good loud. I trace Lemon's face constellation a few more times, and soon, I can get one whole lungful of air. Soon after that, I get three.

"Lemon, is she okay?" Amira says, her voice tight.

"Yeah, I think so," Lemon says.

I give a small nod without looking up. Oxygen flows pretty easily now, but it won't if everyone keeps hovering nearby like they're sea gulls and I'm a piece of bread.

"You're sure?" Amira says, then looks at me. "I don't need to call anyone? Hazel?"

"No," I manage to croak out. "I'm okay." I start to stand, my legs still wobbly, and Lemon and Jules each grab one of my arms and pull me up the rest of the way.

"She just needs some food," Lemon says, patting my arm. "Low blood sugar, right?"

I blink at her. At everyone hovering around, watching me like I'm about to drop dead.

"I need to go," I say, but it's low, quiet, and Lemon starts pulling me over to where she's set up our lunch on the ground.

"I need to go," I say again, louder.

"What?" Lemon asks.

I work my way out of her grip, my fingertips still tingling. "I just need to go home."

"I don't think you should go anywhere on your own," Jules says.

"I'm not sick," I say. "I'm fine."

"Let her go," Kiko says, earning a glare from Lemon.

"Still," Jules says, "maybe you should—"

"I'm fine!"

I yell it. Jules snaps their mouth shut. Kiko chews on her thumbnail, an *I told you so* look on her face. Amira starts heading toward me again, that adult, take-control-of-the-situation gleam in her eyes.

I back up, turn around, and start running, ignoring Lemon's voice as she calls after me.

chapter nine

I run all the way back to the cottage. By the time I burst through the door, I'm a sweaty mess and what feels like an ocean of tears is on the edge of spilling over. Mama and Peach are both on the couch with their laptops on their legs—Mama's real one and Peach's little LeapFrog computer that teaches her letter sounds and words. She's in her bathing suit and there's a little sand still dusting the bottoms of her feet, but I'm so relieved I didn't come back to find her in the sea—or worse—I don't even care about the dirt.

"Hazel," Mama says, looking up from her screen as I spill into the room. She glances at her phone on the table next to her. "I didn't expect you back for another hour. Doesn't the club go until one?"

"It did."

Mama lifts an eyebrow. "So what happened?"

"Did you get scared in the ocean, Hazey?" Peach asks.

"No. I just—"

"I went in the ocean! All the way up to here!" She pokes her belly button with one finger. My chest goes tight again, thinking of my sister waist-deep in the sea, unknown depths swirling around her. "Then I got too cold and Mama made me get out."

"Good, Peach," I say, managing a smile for her.

"So now I'm braver than you!" She doesn't say it to be mean, but it hurts anyway.

"Peach," Mama says, closing her laptop. "Go change for me, okay, Fuzzy? And rinse your feet in the bathtub."

My sister nods and slips off the couch, leaving little sandy footprints on the hardwood floor as she skips toward the bathroom.

Mama taps the spot on the couch next to her. Relief fills me up and I all but run to get near her. I want to lay my head down in her lap, have her smooth my hair, rub my back. As I sink next to her, though, she doesn't do any of those things. She pats my leg and then places her hands back on her laptop.

"So tell me," she says. "How was it?"

"It was…" I swallow a few times, trying to remember my plan to be calm, to be *fine*, but I feel the tears tipping and spilling. Tears very rarely mean you're *fine*, and these

99

are hot as they run down my cheeks. I wipe them away just as fast, but Mama sees them.

She sighs and I feel myself lock up, bracing for *Calm down, Hazel,* for all the wrong that's inside me to push her farther and farther away.

Or.

Maybe she'll see now. She'll see that this place isn't good for me. For *us.*

"It was horrible," I say through tearful gasps, because she already knows it.

"What was horrible about it?" Mama asks. Her voice is soft, gentle, but she still doesn't touch me, doesn't even offer to get me a tissue.

"Just…just everything. I don't fit in with the kids. They stare at me like I'm some exhibit at the zoo."

Her eyes go to my scars, but she just nods like she wants me to keep talking. Like other kids staring at her daughter's face-marring scars isn't enough.

"And then…then we went out to the beach and there…" I don't want to say it. I can already feel the sweat forming again on the back of my neck, my lungs tightening up, but maybe it's the only way to get Mama's attention. "There was a kayak."

Mama stiffens. "Oh."

"And I just…I had a panic attack. Like I used to. Except this time, it was right in front of everyone. Lemon helped me, but…it was bad."

I stop talking, let it all sink in. My tears stop and I get a deep, shuddering breath. I wait for her to pull me into her arms, to tell me she understands. She remembers the panic attacks. After Mum died, Mama barely slept for weeks. She heard me in the mornings, gasping for air, saw my sweat-soaked sheets. She came and picked me up the first day back at school, when I couldn't even walk into my classroom. I sank to the tile floor right there outside room 208, my heart skittering around inside my body and my lungs full of barbed wire.

Mama places her hand on my back, carefully, like she's afraid she might scare me. Then she rubs in slow, soothing circles. I close my eyes, let the soft motion soak into my bones. She hasn't touched me in so long. Decades, it feels like. It worked. It actually worked.

"Sweetheart," she says.

Then she leans her head against mine.

I grab her other hand, lace our fingers together.

I can't remember the last time we sat like this. I breathe in and out normally, like a regular kid sitting with her mom.

"Kayaks are everywhere, honey," she says.

I lift my head from hers. "What?"

"And kids . . . well, kids can be mean."

"Yeah, I know," I say, even though no one at Ocean Club was necessarily *mean*.

"But you're strong," she says. "You can handle this."

I pull my hand from hers. "Handle . . . what?"

She gestures toward the window to where the sea stretches out forever and ever. "This. Being here. Going to the Ocean Club."

"Wait. I don't—"

"It'll be better tomorrow."

"I have to go *back*?"

She frowns at me. "Hazel, we don't quit something because it's a little hard. *Life* is hard."

"Yeah, I know all about life being *hard*, Mama."

She flinches at my tone, her eyes growing sad.

Say it, I think. *Say Mum's name.*

Say why life is so hard.

Say why I have these scars.

Say she's gone.

Say she even existed.

Say it, say it, say it.

But Mama doesn't. Just like I knew, deep down inside, that she wouldn't. But her eyes go shiny, and I think I see her bottom lip tremble. Just a little.

"You'll try again tomorrow," she says as she closes her laptop, then stands and walks toward her bedroom, her back to me. "We all will."

chapter ten

The best thing I can say about the next two weeks is that they pass quickly, getting me that much closer to the end of summer. Mama makes me go to Ocean Club every weekday. There's no way I can even leave the house and then skip out on the club and spend the day reading on a beanbag chair in the library's kid section instead, because Lemon knocks on our door at what feels like the crack of dawn every single morning, ready to escort me like I'm four years old.

And every day I have to leave Peach with Mama—and *Claire*, who seems to be with Mama anytime she's not at her restaurant, even if it's just to sit on our porch or on the beach while Mama taps away at her laptop—trusting that my sister won't drown or break a bone while I'm gone.

Which gets even harder when Mama enrolls her in a ballet class.

Ballet.

As in jumping and pirouetting and spinning on her little five-year-old legs, with other equally clumsy and spindly five-year-old legs, which, in my opinion, has all the makings of a disaster. The only good thing I can say about it is that it meets every afternoon from twelve to one thirty, so that's one less hour and a half Peach spends frolicking in the treacherous Atlantic.

I can't say the same for me. At Ocean Club, we go to the beach every day for lunch. Sometimes we just sit and eat and watch the surf. Other times, Amira brings along buckets and magnifying glasses and we—and by *we*, I mean everyone but me—walk along the edge of the sea, barefoot, searching for shells and tiny crabs to examine before setting them free again. Lemon and Jules try to get me to join, but they don't push too much.

I think they're afraid to, like I might break. I don't like feeling weak, but at least it makes them leave me alone, for the most part.

When Lemon showed up at our front door the day after my panic attack, she didn't say anything about it. Neither did Kiko or Jules when we got to the library, although Kiko kept shooting me looks like I was about to sprout tentacles and strangle everyone. Even Amira simply asked if I was feeling well, to which I offered some unclear combination of a nod and a shrug. She seemed to take it as a *yes*, though, because she asked everyone to settle down and launched into an in-depth presentation about the sunlight zone and the marine life found there. Sharks and tuna and mackerel, stingrays and sea turtles, jellyfish and seals and sea lions. Manatees in Florida. Atlantic white-sided dolphins in the Gulf of Maine.

It wasn't at all interesting.

Nope, not one bit.

Since then, she's covered all five zones and the kinds of life we might find there. I guess, because we're living in mermaid central, someone asks about the Rose Maid every single day. And every single time someone asks about the Rose Maid, Lemon's, Kiko's, and Jules's gazes float over to me, just for a second. And not only them—apparently, the pale, ghostly visage of Rosemary Lee is well known, so now more and more kids are glancing at me all the time, whispering.

Just yesterday, this one kid named Jackson asked me outright if I was *her*.

"Who?" I asked. We were on the beach. The kayak was gone, but the whole ocean was still there, and I was sitting as far up on the dry sand as possible. I was practically in the sea oats.

"You know, *her*," he said again. His friends chuckled around him. Stared at me.

I wasn't going to give him an inch. "You'll have to be more specific."

"If it is her, she's having some memory problems," another kid, Huntley, said.

"Maybe if we dump some salt water on her legs, she'll sprout fins." This from a genius named Nate.

"If mermaids were real," I said, "they'd have flukes on the end of their tails, not fins."

Jackson wrinkled his nose at me. "What's the difference?"

The facts flooded into my brain and straight out of my mouth, completely without my permission. "Ocean mammals have flukes, which are two lobes that come together in the middle. Whales, dolphins, and porpoises move their tail up and down instead of side to side like a shark, which has fins, not flukes. And each set of flukes is unique, like a fingerprint. It's how researchers identify certain whales when they see them out in the water."

"Yeah, but you're not a whale," Nate said.

"Well spotted," I said.

"Shut up, you idiots," a new voice piped up.

The boys turned around, revealing Lemon with Kiko and Jules flanking her.

"Oh, it's the MerSquad," Huntley said, lifting his hands like he was surrendering. "Don't want to piss them off—they might aim a spyglass at you!" Then the boys laughed like hyenas and scattered.

Lemon, Kiko, and Jules sat down next to me.

Lemon handed me a turkey sandwich.

"They've got a point," I said, gesturing to Lemon's T-shirt, which, as usual, matched Jules's and Kiko's. So far, the three of them have worn a different one every day. That day's flavor was hunter green with a mermaid in the center. The words *Seas the Day* curled around her head in white script.

"You know you want one," Jules said before biting a huge hunk out of their pimento-cheese-on-wheat sandwich, the same kind they've eaten every day for the past nine club sessions.

I snorted, ignoring the strange feeling fluttering in my chest.

Today, two weeks into Ocean Club, we're finally going to the Gulf of Maine Aquarium. It's not huge, not like the Georgia Aquarium, which is the largest in the United States and has 10 million gallons of fresh and salt water and over 100,000 animals. Used to be, I'd pull up images of the Georgia Aquarium online, salivating over their whale shark exhibit—they have four, named Trixie, Alice, Yushan, and Taroko—and the beluga whales, whose population they're trying to preserve. It's a marvel.

Gulf of Maine is dinky in comparison, but one thing it has that even the Georgia one doesn't is direct ocean viewing. Yesterday, before we went to the beach and Jackson and his friends tried to turn me into a sea creature,

Amira told us all about the observation level. The top floor is the main level of the aquarium and houses their jellyfish exhibit, crustaceans, and all sorts of other small ocean life. But if you go below, there's an entire wall of thick glass, a window into the sea's depths.

I shivered just thinking about it.

Now, as Lemon rings the doorbell and Peach runs to answer it in the purple tutu Mama bought her a few days ago, my stomach feels like it's full of moths. I can't tell if it's from excitement or dread. Funny how those emotions feel the same sometimes.

I hook my Safety Pack around my waist and follow my sister to the door. She flings it open, then spins on her tiptoes with her hands above her head so Lemon can see all she's learned in the past few days since she started her dance class. We both wait for Lemon to squeal and tell Peach how awesome she is, but there's nothing but the roar of the sea, a few gulls squawking in the sky.

Lemon stands in the doorway, her eyes red-rimmed, her hair a mess—I mean, more of a mess than usual—and her gaze is inward, like she's staring at a whole world happening in her mind and doesn't even see us.

She looks terrible.

Peach lowers her arms and looks up at me, frowning.

I shrug. "Lemon?"

Nothing.

"Lemon!"

She startles, bleary eyes focusing on me. "Oh. Hey."

"'Oh. Hey'? You did ring the doorbell, didn't you?"

She swallows and smiles, this weird bend to her lips that doesn't reach her eyes. "Yeah, totally. You ready to go?" She looks down at my sister. "Hey, Peach, I like your tutu."

Peach glances at me again. Lemon's never called her by her regular nickname. It's always Guava or Mango or Nectarine, which Peach thinks is the funniest thing in the world.

"Hey, is that Lemon and—" Mama comes out from the back hall into the living room, hand fiddling with a large gold hoop she just put in her ear. She's got on makeup and she's actually wearing her hair down instead of her usual sloppy bun. "Oh, hey, Lemon. Your mom's not with you?" She comes closer and cranes her neck toward the porch, like she's hoping Claire is hiding behind her daughter.

Lemon shakes her head. "Not today."

Mama nods but then frowns at Lemon. "You okay, honey?"

Lemon nods. "Yeah. Yeah, fine. I'm just fine. Totally fine. You ready, Hazel?"

"Um. Yeah. I guess."

Lemon nods again, fake smiles, then takes off toward the stairs that will lead us to the path into town without another word.

I glance at Mama, but she's busy staring after Lemon, her eyebrows pushed together. She takes out her phone and starts typing. When she's done, she waits for a second, eyes on the screen, but I guess there's no response, because her frown stays put and she tucks her phone into her pocket.

"Go on, Hazel," she says when she notices me watching her. "Make sure she's okay, all right?"

I'm already out the door and halfway down the stairs when I realize I have no idea in the world how to do that.

"Um...are you okay?" I ask Lemon when I catch up to her.

"Yeah, fine," she says.

I try to think of something else to say, something to *make sure she's okay*, but the only thing I can think of is "It's warm today."

She just nods.

"First official day of summer," I say, the fact that it's June twenty-first popping into my mind. I grab on to it. "So I guess that makes sense."

Her mouth tightens and I don't even get a nod out of that one. She speeds up her already fast walking. She's got long legs, longer than mine, and I nearly have to run to keep up with her.

"What's the hurry?" I ask.

"Nothing. I just want to get there."

After that, we lapse into silence, which almost never happens. Usually, she babbles about I don't even know what the entire walk to the library, so I should be welcoming this bit of quiet. Instead, I feel unsettled, like I've left home without my Safety Pack, even though I can feel it bumping against my hip.

When the library comes into view, the rest of the kids from Ocean Club are already gathered outside the front doors near a big white van with the words GULF OF MAINE AQUARIUM on the sides. Amira stands nearby, a clipboard in her hand.

Relief washes over me when I spot Jules and Kiko near the back of the group in their usual matching tees. These are heather gray with a navy mermaid in profile, her body and hair formed from swirls and stars. Lemon doesn't walk over to them, though. She weaves her way through all the other kids and stands near Amira. I follow her, because I don't know what else to do. I lock eyes with Jules as they and Kiko make their way over to us.

"Hey," Lemon says when they reach us, like everything is totally normal.

"Hey," Kiko says softly. "How...how are you?"

"I'm fine, okay?" Lemon says, her voice so tight it's a wonder it doesn't snap in two.

Jules just nods, reaches out and squeezes Lemon's shoulder once, and leaves it at that. I know I'm missing something, but I don't know what to ask to find out what. I remind myself that I don't really care, that Lemon says she's fine, so that means she's fine, but then I think of the times that I say I'm fine. To Mama, to Peach, to a cashier at a gas station who I guess thought I looked particularly sour as I paid for some travel snacks. I say I'm fine a lot, thinking maybe if I say it enough it'll be true, I'll *deserve* for it to be true.

I'm not always fine, though.

Now that I think about it, I'm not sure I ever am.

"Okay, let's get going," Amira says, and a cheer goes up from everyone except the four of us. "There are seat belts for all of you, so buckle up and keep your butt on the seat. No horsing around. You hear that, Nate?"

"Yes, ma'am!" Nate calls back, then socks his friend Max in the shoulder.

We file into the van. There are five rows and each row can fit about four kids, so Lemon, Kiko, Jules, and I all squeeze into the front. I'm the last to join, which is when I notice that Lemon is wearing a plain green tee, no gray mermaid shirt in sight.

chapter eleven

Once we reach the aquarium, Amira sets us loose.

"You're free to look at whatever exhibits you want," she says as we all gather around her in the front atrium, "but meet back here at twelve o'clock sharp. We'll eat lunch and then head back to the library at exactly twelve thirty. We don't want to get caught in all the Solstice Fire traffic."

Everyone scatters.

Everyone except for Lemon, Kiko, and Jules, who just stand there looking awkward. I stand with them, mostly because I'm not sure I even want to venture any farther. Arched hallways break off from the atrium, signs announcing the treasures to be found within, like NEW ENGLAND RIVERS and OCEANS AND SEAS.

"What's a Solstice Fire?" I ask. Sounds dangerous.

No one answers. They all just stand there like I'm invisible. Not that I'm all that eager for their attention, but it's still not a great feeling.

"Hello?" I say.

Jules clears their throat. "It's, uh, just this thing Rose Harbor does every year for the first day of summer."

"There's a big bonfire on the beach," Kiko says. "Plus food and flower crowns and arts and crafts, s'mores and suncatchers and things like that."

It sounds like the sort of thing Peach would love, so I'm hoping she doesn't get wind of it—bonfires and s'mores? How about raging fires, flammable clothing all over the place, and sharp pokers in the dark? Yeah, sounds like a top-notch idea.

"Do you guys usually go?" I ask.

Jules and Kiko glance at each other. Lemon says nothing, just picks at a loose thread on her backpack strap. Eventually, the two of them sort of shrug.

"Um, so, where should we start?" Jules says.

"How about the moon jellies?" Kiko says. "I love those. They're so beautiful, the way they move. Like magic."

"They're not magic," I say. "They're organic beings." And they're beautiful, but I'm not going to admit that and feed Kiko's fire. Plus, moon jellies are relaxing to watch. Their tentacles are really short, so they don't give me nightmares of getting tangled up and stung to death. And even if you do brush up against one, their sting is really mild, like a little zap of static electricity. Or so I've read.

"Thanks for that bit of enlightening information," Kiko says, clasping her hands to her chest sarcastically.

"Easy, Kik," Jules says.

"What?" Kiko says. "I'm just—"

"I want to go there," Lemon says, and Kiko shuts up, thankfully. Lemon's voice is thick, like she just woke up from a nap, but I'm done trying to figure out what's wrong with her. I follow her finger and see that she's pointing to the very last hallway on the right.

MYSTERIES OF THE DEEP.

I shiver and rub my arms, which are suddenly full of goose bumps.

"Yes," Kiko says, drawing out the short *e* sound.

"Perfect," Jules says.

"Wait, what mysteries?" I ask.

But Jules just hooks their arm through mine and says, "Exactly." Before I know it, Lemon's charging ahead toward a passageway that plunges us into darkness as soon as we enter it. I stumble along, torn between pulling back and going to wait in the atrium for the next two hours and this tiny itty-bitty flare of curiosity right next to my heart.

There are a lot of other people in the passage with us and several kids from Ocean Club, and I tighten my arm around Jules's just to keep from feeling like I'm about to disappear. The smooth tile floor slopes downward, like we're heading into some sort of dungeon, but then a soft blue glow begins to edge out the dark. It grows brighter and brighter until the passage opens up into a huge circular room and I finally see what's been lighting our way.

The ocean.

The real one, not a tank, right there in front of me, a whole wall of thick glass the only thing separating us from the deep blue sea. And it's so deep, so blue, I feel dizzy trying to take it all in. Tiny fish drift by, lots of little bits of things that could be anything from microorganisms to krill to dust. Other than that, it's just blue. But it goes on and on, like at any moment, anything could swim into view. Anything at all.

Around the glass there are smaller exhibits giving all sorts of information about the strange things found in the ocean's depths. There's a display on the angler fish, a classic favorite, the scary fanged fish from *Finding Nemo*, which is, admittedly, completely petrifying. Next to that, there's some information on the goblin shark. With its sharp teeth and pointed head, it looks like something that should star in a horror movie.

No one looks at any of those displays, though. If they're not pressed up against the glass, they're looking at another display, the largest one by far, complete with all sorts of photographs and captions. There are so many people crowding around it, it takes me a second to realize it's a display about the Rose Maid.

ROSE HARBOR'S MERMAID MYSTERY, it's called.

"Come on, you've gotta see this," Jules says, tugging me through the crowd. Kiko leads the way and soon we're at the front, the huge display rising up above us, lit by a few tiny amber-colored lights lining the top of the display's glass case.

It's mostly old photographs, sepia-toned and full of unsmiling faces in odd hairstyles and uncomfortable-looking clothes. I see that same picture of the Lee family that was in *Coastal Lore*, though I suppose this is the original, along with the same story about the Rose Maid's origins. There are also a lot more pictures, all of them of Rosemary Lee. There are shots of her as a toddler, a little kid, a girl just my age right before her world fell apart. They're mostly family portraits. I guess way back in the 1800s, people couldn't just take a candid snapshot super quick like we can today, and all the photos are so posed and stiff, it's hard to see what she might have been like.

But then I notice Jules staring up at one photo in particular. It's of a group of girls standing in what looks like a schoolyard. I find Rosemary immediately. She's maybe ten in the photo, smooth ringlets around her face, a long apron-looking thing over her dress that I think might be called a pinafore. She's holding hands with the dark-haired girl standing next to her, their shoulders pressed close. Friends. Maybe best friends. Both of them are even smiling a little.

"It's you," Jules whispers.

I don't answer them, but a chill picks up all the hairs on the back of my neck. It is me. Long-haired and in different clothes and with a smooth cheek instead of the pocked one I have, but the resemblance is...freaky. I thought maybe that picture of the Lee family was a coincidence, a trick of the light, the angle Rosemary was looking at the camera from, but no. She really does look exactly like me. And in this picture, she's smiling, she's happy. She's a normal kid, just like I was.

Before.

"Whoa," says Kiko, who's come up next to me and is staring openmouthed at the photo. "That's..."

I swallow hard. "Yeah."

Other kids whisper around me. I hear *just like her* and *face* and *scars*.

I force myself to ignore them, to look away from the photo like I don't see it, even though I sort of want to keep staring at Rosemary all day long. And I never want to see it again. I feel twisty, restless, like I'm trying to find an answer but I don't know the question.

Then I find Rosemary's *after*.

It's a photo of fifteen or so people on the beach, the ocean a gray blur at their side. A family portrait, but not Rosemary's. Still, I find her quickly, standing at the edge of the group. She's not facing the camera. Instead, she's looking toward the left, toward the water, but I can still see enough of her expression to know she doesn't look anything like that girl in the schoolyard picture. Her mouth is slack, her eyes dim. True, no one is really smiling in the portrait, but Rosemary stands out for some reason. It's her lank hair. The way she's the only one turned away from the camera, her whole body leaning toward the sea, a magnet searching for its other pole.

Under the photo, there's a caption.

The Anne Lancaster family and Rosemary Lee,
July 21, 1884

I think back to the *Coastal Lore* story I've read a million times by now and the date that Rosemary disappeared—July 26, 1884. So the photo was taken five days before she went into the water. Or wherever she went.

I look back at Rosemary in her school picture.

Then back to the Lancaster family picture.

Before . . . and after.

It's like two different girls. Two different lives.

Is that me? Am I that different now than I was before? Who would I be if Mum and I had never decided to go kayaking? If we hadn't gone on that exact day. If we hadn't gone that exact route. And who am I now, *after*? I look back at Rosemary with the Lancaster family.

A ghost in a girl's skin.

That's what Anne Lancaster wrote about her. And that's exactly what she looks like.

Lost. Alone.

My body washes cold, then hot. Sweat starts to pool under my arms, nausea crashing over me in waves. I can feel it happening again, a panic attack, just like that first day of Ocean Club.

"You okay?" Jules asks.

I ignore them, desperate for invisibility right now. I look away from the photos, away from Rosemary's *before* and *after*, looking for something, anything to distract me.

But when I turn around, there's only the ocean.

Only endless blue.

Only more mysteries, more questions.

Somehow, though, it works. The sea, at least this one behind glass, settles my breath into my lungs, soothes my wild heart behind my ribs. I stand there for a few seconds, letting the blue glow fill me up like a warm drink, but soon it's not enough. I want to be closer.

I spot Lemon off to one side. I guess she's been there the whole time, her palms pressed against the glass. Before I even decide, my feet walk me next to her. She doesn't acknowledge me but touches her forehead to the glass. A tear slips down her cheek. She wipes it away quick, but I saw it. I don't ask about it. It doesn't seem like she wants me to. Plus, my own heart and mind feel so full right now, so overloaded, I'm not sure what I'd say if she answered me.

Instead I lean close to the glass too, let the blue take up my whole field of vision. Is this what Rosemary wanted? Is this the only place that felt like home after her family died, the place where she was last with them?

Another shiver goes through me as I think of being out there on the ocean with Mum. I press my palms to the glass and for one wild moment, I wish I was out there. I wish I *could* go out there, just to be with Mum again. Just to remember that perfect hour with her on the water before everything went wrong. Just to feel normal again.

The longing turns into an achy throat, a stinging nose, and I sniff to clear it. I feel Lemon turn to glance at me, but I don't look at her. I keep my eyes on the blue, the mysteries, the last place—

A flash of color interrupts my thoughts.

Out there in the deep.

I smoosh my nose to the glass, trying to get closer, squint so hard my eyes ache.

There.

Something pale, like a spark of moonlight, which makes absolutely no sense.

"What is it?" Lemon asks.

I shake my head.

"Do you see something?"

"No," I say.

"You did. What is it?"

"Lemon, I didn't—"

But she grabs my hand and presses close to me, flattens her palm on the glass. "Where? Where is she?"

"Where's who?"

She looks at me, eyes puffy, eyebrows dipping in the middle, like the answer should be totally obvious. "The Rose Maid. If anyone will see her, it's you."

She looks so hopeful, so desperate. I glance back at the glass, something that feels like hope pulling at my chest. But that flash of color is gone. There's nothing but ocean. Nothing but water that takes and takes and takes.

"Why?" I ask, my voice coming out hard. "Because I look like her?"

"Well—" Lemon starts, but I don't let her finish. The hope is gone, replaced with something hard and mean and reckless.

"Because we're both sad and lonely?" I say, gesturing toward those pictures in the Rose Maid display. "Because neither one of us fits with anyone? Because we both lost our family?"

Her face falls. "Wh-what?"

I shake my head. "Nothing. Never mind."

"Hazel, wait—"

"I didn't see anything," I say, turning away from her. I ram straight into Jules, who I hadn't realized was standing behind us with Kiko, probably hearing everything. Jules grabs my arms to steady me. My eyes meet theirs and for a second, I want to stop, let them hold on to me. Keep me from floating away. Jules's fingers squeeze, their gaze soft and concerned, like maybe, just maybe, they might not mind keeping me from floating away.

But then I see the mermaid on their shirt. I remember the magic isn't real. There is no mermaid in the harbor. Mum isn't ever coming back. And no amount of dumb matching tees will change that.

I shake out of Jules's grasp and walk away, not stopping until I reach the atrium and that wall of deep blue is far behind me.

chapter twelve

fter we get back to the library, I don't wait around
for Lemon. I don't talk to anyone. Lemon doesn't
call out to me as I start walking. Neither do Jules or Kiko,
which is just fine with me. Except I feel itchy the entire
way back. Unsettled. I tell myself it's the ocean, it's being
away from Peach for this long during the day, it's those
stupid T-shirts Lemon wears.

It's this whole town.

I need a quiet night at home, just Mama and Peach
and me.

But before I even walk into Sea Rose Cottage, I know
that's not going to happen.

Mama's laughing.

As I climb the steps to the porch, her laughter spills out

the screen door like a gentle wave, calm and happy and so *Mama* that it makes my chest grow tight again. I close my eyes, shut out the ocean roar and the sand that always seems to find its way into my sneakers, and it feels as though I'm back in California, coming home from school or swim practice to find Mama and Mum together in the kitchen making lunch or dinner, their happiness burbling out like a little brook through the open windows. A smile almost slips onto my mouth, when I nearly trip over the top step, causing my eyes to fly open and Rose Harbor, Maine, to come swirling back into my already-exhausted heart.

The ocean.

Lemon.

Jules's sapphire-blue eyes.

The cottage Mum never set foot in.

And Claire Calloway sitting on the couch next to Mama, her shoes off and her knees tucked to her chest like she's been here for a while. There's a picnic basket on the floor, along with three plates covered in the remnants of what looks like chicken salad, crescent rolls, fresh strawberries, and chocolate chip cookies. No. Butterscotch chocolate chip cookies.

My traitor stomach grumbles against my will, remembering that I didn't feed it lunch. While everyone else got food from the little food court at the aquarium, I hid in the bathroom until it was time to leave. I press my hands against my gut and try to breathe.

"Hazey!" Peach says, leaping up from where she's coloring on the floor and running to me. She wraps her arms around my middle and I lift her into my arms, hugging her tight. The tutu she seems to wear incessantly scratches at my arms.

"Hey, Peach Fuzz," I say. "You okay?"

"Of course she's okay," Mama says. For a split second, she looks irritated, but then she smooths out her expression and smiles at me. "Have fun today?"

I don't answer but put Peach down and gesture to the carpet picnic happening in our living room. "What's all this?" Peach plops back down on the floor with her favorite baby-farm-animals coloring book.

"Oh, I crashed your mom's writing session," Claire says.

She smiles at me, but her eyes are sort of puffy and red-rimmed, just like Lemon's were. She's not wearing any makeup, and her hair looks like she just woke up. Plus, she's in yoga pants and a tank top and, seriously, I don't see her shoes anywhere, like she just might have walked over here totally barefoot.

"I needed some company, and your mom kindly obliged," she says.

Mama reaches out and squeezes Claire's hand, which makes Claire's eyes go all shiny for some reason. She turns her head toward the couch cushions and wipes at her cheek before smiling back at me.

126

"How's Lemon?" she asks. "Did she seem okay today?"

Her hand is still in Mama's. Or Mama's hand is still in hers.

"Hazel?" Mama asks. "Did you hear Claire's question?"

I blink at her. Hand still there. "Um...what?"

"Lemon?" Mama asks, that irritation back in her voice. "Did she have an okay day?"

"Why?"

Claire opens her mouth, glances at Mama, then shakes her head. "No reason. Just wondering. She didn't come back with you?"

"No."

"Oh," Claire says, frowning. "Let me text her, then."

Mama sighs and finally—*finally*—removes her hand from Claire's as Claire stands up and walks outside.

"You couldn't wait for her?" Mama asks me.

"Why?"

"Because she..." Mama's mouth snaps closed and she shakes her head. "Because she comes over here, every single morning, to walk with *you* to Ocean Club."

Something like guilt pricks my chest. "I didn't ask her to do all that."

Mama frowns. "Hazel. I didn't raise you to be ungrateful and cruel."

I feel all the color drain out of my face. *Cruel?* That's a harsh word. A word I never would've associated with myself. A word I can't even imagine being. A word I—

But then I think of how I snapped at Lemon about the Rose Maid, practically biting her head off when she was clearly having a rough day, for whatever reason. A new wave of guilt rushes in, linking up with all the old familiar guilt already sitting in my gut.

"She's fine," I say. "She's with Kiko and Jules."

Mama shakes her head again and says nothing else. Claire comes back inside and settles on the couch.

"She's already at home," she says to Mama. "She's going to take a nap. She didn't sleep much last night."

Mama nods and squeezes Claire's hand.

Again.

"Did you eat?" Mama asks me when she finally lets go of Claire and picks up her water glass, taking a sip.

"No," I say.

"You're welcome to have some," Claire says, waving at the food on the floor. "Goodness knows, I made a ton."

Mama gives me a stern look and I mumble out a *Thank you*, my stomach rumbling. Still, I can't seem to make myself move to join them. Mama and Claire have been together, alone and laughing and talking, for who knows how long. Their voices blur together as they start chatting again, nothing but gobbledygook to my ears, but it doesn't matter anyway because all that matters is that Mama isn't looking at me as I just stand there, frozen. She's looking at Claire, smiling, eyes shining, laughing, leaning toward the space between them with her legs tucked underneath her just like she used to do when she and Mum would sit on the couch after Mum got home from work and make a cup of tea and talk about every little thing that had happened in their day. It never mattered what they talked about. I'd watch them from where I always did homework at the kitchen table, and it looked just like this. Just like Claire and Mama. Smile for smile. Laugh for laugh. Lean for lean.

Except it's not Mum.

And Mama doesn't even seem to care.

Water spills into my eyes before I can stop it, like a river released from a dam. I turn and head to my room, closing the door and locking it behind me. I press my back against the wood, waiting for Mama to come after me.

I wait.

And I wait.

And I wait.

Mama doesn't come.

I hear them laughing out in the living room, even Peach, all their voices muddling together in one big kaleidoscope of happy. It sounds too much like home, like something that fits perfectly inside everyone's chest except mine.

I grab my earbuds from my Safety Pack and plug them into my phone before opening up my music app. I don't even stop at most of the music I've been listening to lately. I keep scrolling until I land on *Blue Planet II*, the soundtrack for this documentary all about the oceans. Mum and I watched it constantly when it came out a few years ago. Over and over, Mama laughing at us in the background while she followed a toddling Peach around the den.

A bubble of Mama's laughter reaches me from the living room, digging under the watery music. I squeeze my eyes closed, try to imagine I'm drifting in the ocean with Mum. A safe ocean. A tame ocean. One made just for me.

My eyes pop open.

I sit up and pull out my earbuds.

Voices rush in, but I leave my phone and music on Peach's bed, get up, and tiptoe to the door. Cracking it open, I peer out. I can't see the living room from here. The cottage's two bedrooms and the bathroom Peach and I share are in the back of the house, tucked away from the main living area.

I can't see Mama and Claire and Peach.

And they can't see me.

I creep down the hallway toward Mama's bedroom. It's clean and bright, her bed neatly made with her fluffy white down comforter, the Sister Quilt folded at the foot of the mattress. There's a dresser. A nightstand with a lamp. But other than the Sister Quilt and the faint smell of Mama's meadowy perfume, it could be any bedroom in the world.

Pausing to make sure Mama and Claire are still talking,

I kneel down by her bed and slip my head under the frame. There, pushed all the way against the wall, is a big trunk with a brass latch. It's just like the trunks we use to pack all our stuff in when we move, but this one is navy blue, while Mama's clothes trunk is a deep maroon.

And this one hasn't been opened in two years.

At least not by me.

I get down on my stomach and push myself under the bed until I can get ahold of the handle on the end of the trunk. I pull it out slowly, an inch at a time, trying not to make too much noise. When it clears the bed frame, I sit up and inspect the front latch, which is just like mine.

Except for the padlock hanging from the latch's loop.

I jiggle the lock a few times, just to make sure it's actually locked, but it won't budge. Turning it over, I see a tiny keyhole. The key is probably small and a tarnished brass color, just like the lock. I crawl over to Mama's nightstand and start to open up the drawer.

I stop. A warning goes off in my head, a prickle of guilt, but I ignore it. This trunk is Mum's. It has all Mum's stuff, her art that she made for me, for Peach, for her family. The memories Mama wanted to keep but won't talk about, won't share, won't let me see and remember, laugh over and even cry over if I need to.

This trunk is just as much mine as it is Mama's.

I open up the drawer all the way, scanning the contents quickly. But there's hardly anything in there. Just an old pack of playing cards with mermaids all over them that must've been left over from the last tenant or the cottage's owner.

I sit back on my heels, trying to think where else Mama might keep the key. I'm about to get up and check her bathroom when the dull hum of conversation in the living room shifts, grows louder. I hear *Goodbye, Thank you,* more laughter, and then *See you in a bit.* The screen door creaks open and closes again.

Scrambling back to the trunk, I push it under the bed until it smacks against the back wall, and then I worm my way back out and leap to my feet.

I reach Mama's bedroom door at the exact same time she does.

"Hazel," she says. Her laptop is tucked under her arm. "What are you doing?"

I'm out of breath, but I hide it with a sigh. "Just... looking for some medicine. I have a little headache."

"You do?"

I nod, swallowing the lying lump in my throat.

She frowns but takes my chin in her hand, tilting my face this way and that. Her touch is so soft, so rare, I want to wrap my arms around her waist and never let go.

"I'll get you some Tylenol," she says, then walks around me, setting her laptop on the bed before going into her bathroom. I wait as she rummages in a drawer, then comes back out with two red gel capsules in her palm. I keep my eyes on her as she tips the medicine into my hand.

"Take them with some water and then go lie down, okay?" she says. "We're going out later."

"What? Where?"

Mama sighs, then straightens the Sister Quilt on her bed. "I want you to be nice."

I frown. "Um. Okay."

"She needs a friend. So do you."

"Who?"

Mama straightens and folds her arms. "Lemon."

I almost laugh at that. "Lemon has friends. And I..."

But I'm not sure how to finish that sentence, so I just stop talking and press my thumb into one of the gelcaps in my hand.

"Go lie down," Mama says again. "Peach is taking a nap too. We might be out late."

"Where are we going?"

She meets my eyes for a split second before sitting down on the bed and opening up her laptop. She starts typing before she even says it.

"The Solstice Fire."

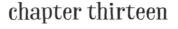

chapter thirteen

People are everywhere.

I hold tight to Peach's hand as we follow Mama onto the pebbly sand of Sterling Cove, this curl of beach at the north end of town where most of the tourists hang out—there are just enough rocks and evergreens in the distance to make it feel like you're in Maine, just enough wide-open sand to run around and splash in the cold surf.

And, apparently, build gigantic bonfires that the entire town can crowd around, wielding sharp pokers with flammable sugar puffs on the ends. Almost everyone is barefoot and it's nearly dark, just a hint of golden light left in the western sky and the dark gray ocean roiling in the east. It's a disaster waiting to happen, if you ask me.

"Happy Solstice!"

A white lady in a yellow sundress with jet-black hair down to her waist smiles and dances past us. Literally, she dances, removing three circles of flowers from her arms and dropping them into Mama's hands as she twirls by.

"Thank you!" Mama calls back, smiling as she places one on Peach's head, then one on her own. The third she simply holds out to me. I pinch it between my thumb and forefinger like it's a smelly dead fish.

"Put it on, Hazey!" Peach says, holding out her mint-green sundress and swirling around me like she's at a ball. I have to admit the white flowers in her hair are pretty. She looks like an adorable little fairy. I plop the flowers onto my head and promptly sneeze, which makes my sister laugh.

"Oh, you think that's funny, do you?" I ask, picking Peach up and twirling her around, which makes her laugh harder.

I feel Mama watching us for a second, a soft smile in her eyes. The flowers look beautiful in her hair too. She and Peach are in nearly matching green sundresses. And Mama's got on some makeup—mascara and a little blush that makes her cheeks sparkle. Some coral-colored lip gloss. Perfume. I try not to think about why, tell myself that she doesn't need a reason to put on makeup and scent and dress up. She can do it for her, just like I'm wearing cutoff jean shorts and a navy-blue Wonder Woman T-shirt for me.

"Let's find Claire and Lemon, huh?" she says, taking Peach's hand.

"My fruit friend!" Peach says, happily going with Mama into the fray.

I follow and we weave through the revelers, dodging costume mermaid tails and sparklers creating shimmering trails through the darkening sky.

I see them before Mama does. Lemon and Claire. They're standing by the water, alone. Claire is in a sundress too, though it's too dark now to tell what color from this distance. Something light and airy and summery, no doubt. But Lemon is dressed just like me, a cream-colored tote bag hanging from her shoulder. She's talking a mile a minute, which is no huge surprise, but she doesn't look happy. She looks...upset. Her shoulders are tense around her neck, and her eyebrows are smooshed together in a frown. Claire bends down so they're eye level and cradles Lemon's face between her hands, swiping at Lemon's cheeks with her thumbs as though wiping away tears. She says something, pressing her forehead to Lemon's. Lemon folds her arms and nods, but she still looks about as miserable as I feel.

"Oh, there they are," Mama says, spotting them just as Claire straightens up and tries to pull Lemon into a hug. Lemon's not having it, though. She steps back, shaking her head in a way that makes Mama stop in her tracks. Her eyes narrow on the scene, and she glances around like she's looking for somewhere else to go—our cottage would be good, if you ask me—when Claire sees her and waves.

"Hey, happy Solstice!" Claire calls, her voice artificially bright. Lemon turns her head in our direction super fast, her eyes wide and startled, then starts wiping at her face.

"Same to you," Mama says, but she doesn't move. "Everything all right?"

Claire nods. "Fine, fine. We were just—"

But before she can finish her sentence, Lemon starts walking away down the beach so fast her bare feet kick up the already-foamy water, tote bag bouncing against her hip.

Claire watches her for a second, shoulders drooping, and Mama hurries toward her.

"I'm sorry," Claire says, swiping her red fringe out of her face.

"What happened?" Mama asks.

Claire's eyes fill then. She shakes her head, then laughs in that way that means it's not funny at all, like she's holding back a sob. "The cake. I messed it up."

"The cake?" I ask.

"I shouldn't have made it at all," Claire says. "I knew she didn't want one. She never does, but I thought... it's been three years, and she's thirteen today. It's special. But she just..."

Claire trails off, a fresh wave of tears rivering down her cheeks.

A sinking feeling pulls my stomach toward my feet.

"It's her birthday?" I ask.

Claire nods while Mama rubs her back, unsurprised.

They must've talked about it today while they were together. Of course they did.

She needs a friend. So do you.

"She didn't tell you, did she?" Claire asks.

I shake my head, gazing off down the beach, where Lemon's form is getting smaller and smaller.

"Hazel, why don't you and Peach go check on Lemon?" Mama says, her eyes still glued to Claire, her hand still on her back.

"What?"

"You heard me. Take Peach and go. We'll meet up with you later, okay?"

I'd really rather not leave Mama and Claire alone again, but before I can think of what to say to get Mama to let me stay—maybe that, for whatever reason, Lemon probably just wants to be alone—Peach takes off down the shore.

"I'll save Lemon for you, Mama!" she calls over her shoulder, making Claire sob-laugh again before sinking down onto the sand.

"Peach, wait!" I say, but of course, she doesn't. "Mama, I—" I start, *but of course*, Mama's already sitting next to Claire. Their shoulders press together as they gaze at the sea. They start talking, low and quiet so I can't hear them over the noise of the party, and I feel like I've been dumped onto an island while they row away in a boat for two.

I turn from them and start running. I'm careful not to touch the water as I rush to catch up with my sister, who's splashing at full speed through the shallows. I squint into the growing dark and spot Lemon's form still walking, still edging the ocean and the land. It's a weird scene—the nearly black ocean to her right, firelight and laughter and celebration to her left, the three of us stuck somewhere in the middle.

Lemon walks fast. By the time I catch up with her and Peach, the party is at least a quarter mile behind me, a soft quiet closing in all around me as the noise and firelight fade. She's sitting in the sand, Peach smooshed up against her side, facing the calm sea. It's completely dark now, the only light a full moon glazing silver over the water. It's pretty secluded here. I only see one house, an old two-story Victorian with a wraparound porch and a widow's walk set up on the rocks right behind where Lemon's sitting, all its windows dark, like no one's lived there in decades.

"Hey," I say.

Peach is the only one who glances at me. Even in the dim moonlight, I can tell she's got the single most pitiful look on her face, and she pets Lemon's arm like she would a cat and then leans on her shoulder. Lemon just sits there, but every now and then, she wipes at her face and sniffs. It should be a sweet scene—my little five-year-old sister trying to soothe some unknown wound in this near stranger—but something in my gut clenches.

I back up a few feet, as though Lemon's sadness was something I could catch. Except looking at her in the moon's dim glow—the way her tears are pouring down her cheeks and she looks furious about it, her eyebrows all wrinkled up and her mouth curved into a frown, like she's held her sadness in for so long and can't believe it's bursting out now—I'm pretty sure I already have it.

I take a step closer.

Then another.

Finally I sit down on Lemon's other side and tuck my legs up to my chest, dropping my flower crown into the sand while I try to think of something to say.

Happy birthday is the first thing that comes to mind, but the *happy* doesn't fit. It doesn't fit at all. So instead I look out at the dark swath of calm sea, Lemon quiet and sad beside me. I wait for my own Sadness to well up, and it does, but it's more like a gentle current, a soft *hush-hush* sound in my head, rather than the ice-cold tidal wave I usually feel.

"I guess you heard," Lemon says after a few minutes. She presses the heels of both hands to her eyes, releases them with a huge sigh.

"Yeah," I say.

"It's weird, I know. Not wanting to celebrate your birthday."

I shrug. "I won't leave the house without this nerdy fanny pack around my waist. Doesn't seem all that weird to me."

Lemon laughs, just like I hoped she would. "Good point. What's the deal with that thing, anyway?"

I brought it up, so I should've known she'd ask about it. I wait for some panic to flare, the Sadness to swell up like a tsunami, but none of that happens. Instead, I look Lemon right in the eye and I tell her a kind of truth. "Just makes me feel safe."

She stares at me for a few seconds but doesn't say anything else. Finally, she looks out at the sea. "I hate my birthday. The only thing good about today is your mom and my mom."

I frown, a pinch in my heart. "What about them?"

She shrugs and waves toward where Peach and I just came from. "That they're hanging out. That...your mom's here. She makes my mom smile. A lot. Even on bad days. Have you noticed that?"

I look away, look at the water, the rolling waves and the moon spreading silver over the currents. I have noticed. Or at least I've noticed Mama's smiles. Smiles I haven't seen in two years. Even when Claire's not around, Mama's smiling. Unlike Lemon, though, I don't feel a *good thing* rise up in my chest.

I just feel scared. For Mama. And for me, for Peach. For Mum and our family.

I feel...*hollow*.

I don't say any of this, though. I can't say it to Lemon, not tonight, so I just *hmm* and keep looking at the water.

"She made me a mermaid cake," Lemon says. "My mom. That's why we were fighting back there."

"You don't like mermaid cakes?"

A few more tears drip from her eyes. "No, I do. I love them. It's really beautiful, too. Three tiers and different shades of blue icing. Dark on the bottom and then lighter and lighter as you go up."

"Like the ocean zones," I say.

"Yeah. Exactly. Then there's this really pretty mermaid, all made out of icing, on the middle layer. She's swimming, other little icing fish all around her, her hair bright red like ours. Like we're the mermaid."

"We...?"

Her face crumples up again and Peach pats her arm some more. I just wait, figuring she'll keep talking if she really wants to. When I'm in the middle of the Sadness, quiet works best. Some things, there just aren't any words for. Some things are too big to pin down with a sentence.

"Remember Immy?" Lemon asks.

I search my brain for the name. "Um..."

"The girl who did the mermaid paintings? The ones that look just like you?"

A memory flares from the first day at Ocean Club, Kiko saying Immy was their best friend. "Oh. Right. Your friend who's—"

Not around anymore is what I almost say. That's what

Kiko said about Immy. *She's not around anymore.* But she never said what that meant exactly—did she move away or drop Lemon and Kiko and Jules as her friends?—and I never asked.

But suddenly I know. I know with one hundred percent certainty. It's so obvious now, the Sadness hanging on Lemon like a heavy winter coat in summer. Jules fumbling over saying Immy *was* an artist and then saying she *is*, that weird past-and-present question when you talk about someone who's died. Immy's not around just like Mum's not around. She's gone and nothing will ever make her come back.

"The four of us were best friends, me and Immy and Kiko and Jules," Lemon says. "We'd always come to the Solstice Fire, every single year since we were kids. I mean, Immy and me came to the Fire every year of our lives, but then we met Kiko in kindergarten and Jules in second grade and ever since then, it's been the four of us."

She smiles, her eyes distant, like she's remembering.

"That last year," she goes on, "we sneaked away from the Fire and came here." She juts her thumb back toward the Victorian behind us. "Immy always loved this place, always wanted to explore it at night. It's locked up tight, but Kiko has this weird ability to pick any lock she comes across, so we went through the back door and into the kitchen, because it's the only door that doesn't have a dead bolt, then walked all around with our flashlights and looked at all the old stuff and hunted for ghosts."

I glance back at the house, its windows like dark maws gaping at us. "Doesn't anyone live there?"

She shakes her head. "The historical society took it over forever ago. That's the Lancaster House."

"The Lancaster..."

Lemon nods. "Anne Lancaster. Where Rosemary Lee lived before she..." She waves her hand at the ocean.

A chill crackles in my chest. I turn all the way around and gaze up at the house with new eyes. I press my palms into the sand on either side of me, close my fists around the cool grains. She walked here. Right here, maybe even on this very spot. Paced up and down this beach, searching for her family. This is where she was right before she...

I gaze back out at the water, that chill pulling up goose bumps all over my body.

"It's pretty freaky inside," Lemon says. "I mean, at night with flashlights, sure, but I've been there during the day, too, and it's like you can feel her. Or feel *something*, at least. A lot of people think it's haunted."

"By Rosemary?"

Lemon snorts a laugh. "How can she be a ghost and a mermaid at the same time?"

"I don't know, it's your weird town."

She smiles, just a little. "The ghost is Anne. Story is, she could never forgive herself for letting Rosemary go out alone that night, so she stays in the house, waiting for her to come home."

144

"God, that's creepy."

"Right? Immy loved it, though. The ghost, the mermaid. All of it. We all did."

"Do," I say.

"Huh?"

"You *do* love it. Right?"

Lemon's eyebrows dip into her eyes, but she nods. She sniffs and a tear drips down her cheek. "She's my sister."

I blink at her. "Wait, what? Who?"

"Immy. Imogene."

Peach perks up at that. "Like me and Hazey are sisters?"

Lemon wipes at her face. "Yeah. I mean, sort of. Except me and Immy? We have the exact same birthday."

My eyebrows pop up into my hair. "You mean..."

"Yeah," Lemon says. "She's my twin. I'm older. Born four and a half minutes before she was. Now I'm even older. Every year, I just get older."

I watch her, eyes glazed over a little like she's not even really talking to me, just saying stuff that's true, stuff that's hard. A cold, clammy feeling settles in my stomach. Her weird behavior all day makes even more sense. The awkward dance between her and Kiko and Jules at the aquarium.

"What happened to her?" I ask quietly. So quietly, I'm not sure Lemon even hears me. So quietly, I'm not sure I want her to hear me.

But I know she does, because her eyes narrow a little

and her lower lip wobbles. "Brain aneurysm," she says, just as quietly.

My heart trips, my breath coming in little, insufficient wisps.

"One minute she was there," Lemon says. "And the next she wasn't. She just...*stopped*."

"You weren't...you weren't with her, were you?"

Part of me hopes she was, just so someone else gets it, but then a fresh wave of watery guilt fills up my lungs, because what a horrible thing to wish. I wouldn't wish that on anyone, being *right there* when the person you love most in the world leaves it forever.

Lemon's eyes narrow and she breathes in really slowly, lets it out even slower. "No," she finally says. "She died in her sleep. I was in the room right next to hers, probably dreaming about something stupid, totally clueless that my sister was..."

I reach out and squeeze her arm. I do it without thinking, because I need to do *something*.

"After about a year," she says, "my dad left and moved to Georgia. He and Mom...they just weren't..." She shrugs and picks at a thread on the hem of her T-shirt. "Plus, Mom said he felt a lot of guilt. He's a doctor. Did I tell you that?"

I shake my head.

"A gastroenterologist, a stomach and digestive doctor, so it's not like he specialized in brain stuff. Plus, aneurysms don't show a lot of obvious symptoms. She'd had a headache for a couple of days before, but headaches, most of the time, are just headaches, you know?"

I nod, thinking of all the headaches I've had. Mama's had, Peach.

"Anyway," she says. "My dad, he didn't know how to handle it living here. But I think I reminded him too much of my sister, of everything that happened, so..."

"So he just *left* you?"

Lemon shrugs again, but a tear slips down her cheek. "It's okay. I see him at Thanksgiving and I go down there and stay with him and his new wife for two weeks every August."

Anger clouds into my chest. Anger and a little fear. But Mama would never do that. She'd never do that to me. Ever.

Would she?

She left California, just like Lemon's dad left Maine. And half the time, I feel like she doesn't really want me around, like *I* remind *her* too much of what happened. Fear spikes through me.

"He called this morning," Lemon goes on. "Sent me a check in the mail. It's fine. The worst part is that I'm a teenager and Immy's not. She never will be. She'll always be ten. But I'll just get older and older, having all this... this *life* that she never will."

I swallow hard, tears pooling in my eyes. I don't bother

to wipe them away. The Sadness is too big, too much. I can't stop it from spilling over, reaching for the Sadness in Lemon. Because how many times have I felt this exact same thing? Every birthday I have, every holiday, every time I eat something I know Mum loved, every time pink streaks through a sunset, there's this little prick of misery.

Every time I think that I might want a friend, I'm hit by this feeling that, if I'm happy, that must mean that Mum didn't matter. It must mean I'm fine without her and how can you ever be *fine* without your favorite person, the person who loved you most, accepted you most, made you laugh and think and feel brave?

"My mum," I say, and that's all I can get out before my throat goes thick and I have to breathe, breathe, breathe to keep from losing it right here and now.

Lemon lifts her head to look at me. "Your mum?"

Peach gets up and then crawls into my lap, wrapping her arms around my neck and her legs around my waist, her belly pressed to mine. Her flower crown tickles my face, so I slip it off and lay it carefully in the sand. Then I hold her close, rubbing her back and resting my chin on her shoulder. My sister knows and notices so much more than she talks about. I forget that.

"*Our* mum," I say, then I swallow some more. Breathe some more. Finally, the Sadness works its way out again, but there's this...release, too. Just saying her name out loud.

Mum.

Mum.

Mum.

"She'll always be thirty-seven," I say.

Mum will never see Peach grow up—or me, for that matter—and she'll never paint again and she'll never kiss Mama again or make her laugh or hike in Claremont Canyon or eat a fresh avocado from the tree in our backyard. She'll never do any of that ever again. Mama will never have her wife back and Peach will never have her mum.

Because of me. Because I couldn't save her.

"Hazel," Lemon says, and that's it. Just my name, softly spoken through a sigh. But it's enough. She reaches out her hand and grabs mine, laces our fingers together to rest on Peach's back. I look at her, look at my sister, and I feel all our Sadness mingle together like tides from different lands meeting in the middle of the deep blue sea. And before I know it, it's all spilling out of me, everything Mama and I never once talked about.

"You were meant for this," Mum said, waving her arm at all the blue, both sea and sky.

We'd just set off from the Mendocino shore in Mum's navy-blue double kayak. The Mendocino coast is beautiful, all blue Pacific and rocky arches stretching over the water, little coves and wide-open sea. It's about a four-hour drive from Berkeley. We'd driven all morning and planned on staying in a little inn in the town after our kayaking adventure.

Adventure. That's what Mum called it. That's what she always called these trips she and I'd been taking for the last year and a half, ever since I'd become pretty obsessed with marine biology. The Mendocino coast hosted lots of marine life throughout the year—blue whales, orca, California sea lions. You were almost guaranteed to see something. The first time we ever went, we kayaked through a pod of harbor seals. Literally paddled right through them as they all lay on their backs, tiny whiskered faces lifted to the sun.

I was never happier than I was right there, with Mum, floating on the sea.

"Tell me the story again," I said as we paddled out into the sunlight zone, the sun shimmering in and out of the water. An hour ago, when we'd first come down to the beach, the sky had been completely clear, but now, clouds started to drift over the sky, playing peekaboo with the sun. The wind was calm, but every now and then, it would stir the waves and cause our little kayak to undulate up and then down, like it was traveling over a hill. I wasn't scared. There was no reason to be scared with Mum.

"Again?" she asked, navigating us from the front of the kayak. "Don't you ever get sick of hearing about your triumphant entrance into the world?"

"No way," I said, and she laughed.

"All right, fine, I never get sick of telling you about it, either."

"See? It's good for us both."

She smiled at me over her shoulder, then rested her paddle on her lap. I did the same. I always took my cue with paddling from Mum. For safety, she'd told me more than once.

"Once upon a time," she started as we bobbed on the water, "there was an extremely pregnant lady in a warm October who just had to go swimming in the sea."

"Because you were so hot?"

"So hot. Like, center-of-the-sun hot. And pools grossed me out for some reason. All that bacteria and toddler pee."

I laughed at that point, like I always did.

"So Mama took you to Santa Cruz."

"That she did, even though I was about to pop and it was an hour away from home." Mum picked up her paddle again and steered us toward a rocky arch. I paddled too, the current resisting my efforts so much, my biceps ached with the effort.

"It was glorious, though," Mum said. "So cold. I'd never normally swim in that freezing water, but with you, it was like you were pulling me in. And then—"

"I got jealous and wanted to see the ocean too."

"That you did, my darling. The moment I ducked under that water, you decided you just had to show up so you could be in the sea with me. Take in all that beauty, wonder all those wonders. Just like you were meant for the sea."

I smiled at this, like I always did. I wasn't actually born in the sea. Mum started feeling weird in the water, some small contractions, and she and Mum made it back to Berkeley so I could be safely born in the Berkeley Medical Center. Still, the way Mum told the story, it felt like I was born in the sea, or at least like it called me into the world.

We went quiet after that, paddling toward the arches and rock formations where the waves were always a little rougher. Never too rough, though. Mum could always handle it. She'd been kayaking since she was just a little older than me. That day, though, the clouds swept over the sky so fast, whipping the current into swirls and figure eights. It wasn't supposed to rain—Mum always checked the weather—so I didn't think much about it while Mum paddled this way and that around the foaming ocean, directing me left and right, letting out a laughing whoop every now and then.

I laughed with her.

For a while, it was just fun, an adventure, periods of wild waves and then little moments of calm. We looked for sea lions and whale flukes peeking out of the deeper waters. We talked about how we were both craving fish and chips for dinner and there was a place in downtown Mendocino called Fiddleheads Café that made the best Mum had ever had.

But then, when we got on the other side of the cove, rock formations rising up out of the water like giants, it was like the ocean shifted.

Grew restless.

Or angry.

At what, I didn't know. But suddenly, Mum's shoulders grew tight. White water foamed around the rocks, wind whirring through our hair and ears. A huge wave swelled in front of us, rising up and up and up . . .

"Get your paddle out of the water, Hazel!" Mum called back to me.

I hesitated, the wind stealing her words and mixing them up. When I finally realized what she'd said, it was too late. The water yanked my paddle right out of my hands. The kayak veered left, tipping the whole world on its side.

"Hang on, baby!" Mum yelled. Her paddle worked furiously, dipping over the right side of the kayak, then the left, but nothing seemed to help. It felt like we were in the center of a whirlpool.

And right there, just behind me, I could still see the shore.

Mum yelled something else. I couldn't hear it, whatever it was. And she never got a chance to say it again. Our kayak tipped . . . tipped . . . and finally dumped us into the sea. The water was cold—freezing—shock blasting through my whole body like I'd stuck my fingers into an electrical socket. I flipped and somer-saulted, then pain like I've never known ripped across my face. I tasted blood, saw red, my shoulder slamming into the rocks that had just moments ago seemed so gentle, so quiet.

I spluttered to the surface, trying to yell for Mum, trying to find her, trying to find a paddle, anything.

But there was nothing. Just me, my own blood draining into the sea, and an empty kayak smacking against the rocks.

chapter fourteen

When I finish, we're quiet for a while. Peach snuggles close to me, her warm little body steadying my heart. This is the first time I've ever talked out loud about what happened. To anyone. I never even talked about it with Mama. She got the basics from the coast guard and then she told those basics to the grief counselor I went to see for a few weeks before we left California, how when Mum went into the sea, her right leg got trapped underneath those rocks and she drowned, how the same rocks tore across my face and left me scarred for life. But I've never said the words myself. Never had to. Never dared. They just stayed trapped in my chest like prisoners, and now that I've let them out, it feels like they're running wild, finally free, leaving a gaping hole right next to my heart.

Hollowing.

"I've felt guilty like that," Lemon says after a few seconds. "That I couldn't stop what happened to Immy. That somehow, I didn't know something was going on in her brain. Like I should've felt it too. We're twins, right? I should've felt it. It should've happened to me, too. But then I'd be..."

She trails off, but she doesn't have to keep talking. I know. I get it. I feel like I should've been with Mum under that water, trapped by that rock. We should've faced it together, even if it meant...

Even if it meant.

It's not that I wanted to die.

I just didn't want Mum to die alone.

I look out at the dark ocean, all the mysteries underneath, all the danger, all the beauty.

"Do you think Rosemary really is out there?" I ask. "I mean, really?"

Lemon sighs. "Immy thought so. She always dreamed about finding her. That's sort of why me and Kiko and Jules love the myth so much, I guess. For Immy, since she can't love the story anymore, even though we love the story too. But Immy always wondered..."

"What?" I ask before I even realize I'm doing it. I'm even leaning toward Lemon a little, like a kid at story time. I back away and clear my throat. "She wondered what?"

"In seaside towns, you hear a lot of myths about the

ocean," says Lemon. "One myth, a big one, is that those who die at sea stay at sea."

My mouth goes totally dry. "You mean...their bodies?"

"No. Their souls. Who they really are. And Immy always wondered about that. She thought it was so...I don't know. Beautiful. That the sea could claim you like that."

"Beautiful? It sounds terrifying."

Lemon nods. "Yeah. But in a beautiful kind of way, don't you think?"

I just stare at her, my breathing too shallow, too quick.

"Do you...do you ever feel like that with your mum?" she asks. "Like she's still out there somehow?" She waves at the water, but carefully, like she's worried she's saying the wrong thing.

And a week ago, it might've been the wrong thing. But tonight, sitting here with Lemon, it simply feels like a question, a wondering, and nothing I haven't thought before.

"Sometimes," I say. "Just because it was the last place I was with her. The last place we were happy together."

Lemon nods. "Immy liked thinking about stuff like that. How terrible things could be beautiful, how beautiful things could be terrible. She was artsy." Lemon inhales deeply, lets it out slowly. "And she always wondered about that with Rosemary. If her family's souls were still out there in the water and Rosemary knew it. So she went out there to join them and maybe, just maybe, her sadness made it happen. Made it possible."

"Made what possible?" My voice comes out in a whisper.

"Her change. Metamorphosis." Lemon turns to look at me, her eyes narrowed just a little, flicking to my scars, then away. "Sadness can do that, don't you think? Change you that much?"

My mouth opens to answer, but nothing comes out.

"Don't you feel different?" Lemon asks. "Ever since?"

I swallow, but then I nod. "Ever since."

"Ever since," Peach echoes, snuggling even closer to me, and I kiss the top of her head. I wonder if she feels different, if she feels Mum's loss way more than I think she does.

We all sit quietly for a while, listen to the sea. It's almost nice. It's almost . . . comforting.

"I like that it's big, you know?" Lemon says after a few minutes.

"What's big?"

Lemon motions toward the water. "The whole story. Rosemary and the Rose Maid. It's magical. It's bigger than anything I've ever seen or experienced, a girl turning into a mermaid, a mermaid enchanting a whole town, a whole town creating all sorts of art and stories about her. She's just a girl like us, who lost someone, just like us. But she's also way more than that, isn't she?"

I look out at the ocean, take a deep, salty breath. "Yeah. Yeah, I think maybe she is."

"Today at the aquarium, I just wanted a glimpse of her. On our birthday, you know? For Immy."

I nod but don't say anything about the pale flash I saw. Or *think* I saw. I feel Lemon watching me, but thankfully, she doesn't say anything about it either.

"I just wish I could talk to her," she says instead. "Rosemary, I mean. I want to ask her so many things."

Against my chest, Peach whispers something.

"What, Fuzz?" I ask.

She lifts her head and says it louder, bolder. "I wish I was a mermaid."

"Me too," Lemon whispers back, leaning her head against my sister's.

Me too.

The thought pops into my head before I can stop it. I shiver, imagining being under those waves in the dark, all alone and sad. But then I think about the way I used to feel when I would swim in the ocean—free, powerful, surrounded by beauty. Underneath the water, the human world faded away. For that minute and a half that I could hold my breath, I was alone, untouchable, safe, the sun sparkling through the water so everything around me looked like blue diamonds.

Something squeezes my fingers and I look down to see Lemon's hand still wrapped around the top of mine.

I turn my hand up, palm to palm with Lemon Calloway, and I squeeze back.

chapter fifteen

I'm still sitting in the sand, thinking about swimming under the sea and all the things I just shared with Lemon that I never thought I'd share with anyone, when a firework shoots into the sky and explodes in a riot of color over the ocean.

Peach yelps and covers her ears but then, when she sees what it is, turns around in my lap and leans back against my chest. She's quiet, and I feel her sigh a deep, almost happy-sounding breath.

Without thinking, I mimic her, sucking in a lungful of air and letting it out nice and slow. There's something there—a feeling like the wide-open sea. It's not *hollowing*. Not exactly. More like there's *room* inside me. *Space.*

I glance at Lemon, her face upturned toward the glittering sky, an almost-smile on her lips, eyes soft and full of sparklers.

"Happy birthday, Lemon," I say.

She turns to me, the almost-smile flicking into a full smile, just for a second, but before she can respond, we hear a loud crash coming from the dark house behind us, like glass breaking. Lemon and I both startle, whipping to look over our shoulders at the same time and so fast, we bump heads.

"Ow," I say, rubbing my forehead.

"Sorry," Lemon says, rubbing hers.

"What was that?" I ask.

"I don't know." She stands up and turns toward the house, watching it like she's expecting it to sprout legs and take off running. "It came from inside."

"Maybe it was a firework," I say hopefully, but we both turn back to look at the now-dark sky. "Okay, maybe not." I set Peach on her feet and brush the sand off my shorts as I stand up too. "Could it be a raccoon or something, near the trash cans? There are trash cans somewhere, right?"

"I don't know, I haven't been trash can hunting in a while," Lemon says, rolling her eyes.

"Very funny. Well, maybe—"

But I never get to toss out another idea, because right then, a flash of light illuminates one of the house's windows, then goes dark again.

"Okay, that was no raccoon," Lemon says.

"Maybe it's a glow-in-the-dark one," I say, trying to joke, but my heart is pounding.

"A ghost!" Peach says, but with more excitement in her voice than fear. She bounces on her toes and stares with openmouthed wonder at the house.

"I think it's time to go home," I say.

"Go?" Lemon says. "Are you crazy?"

I make a face at her, but that's when I notice her eyes are all lit up like they are whenever she talks about the Rose Maid.

"No," I say. "No way we're going in there."

"But it's the *Lancaster House*," Lemon says, as though that explains everything. "It's supposed to be haunted, and here's proof!" She squats down in the sand and rummages through her tote bag, which I now notice has the words I BELIEVE printed on it with a sketch of a mermaid underneath.

Because of course it does.

She finally pulls out that sky-blue instant camera on its rainbow strap and loops it around her neck. "Let's go," she says, and starts toward the house.

I don't budge. She pauses and looks back at me. "Seriously?"

"Very seriously."

"Hazel, come *on*. For my birthday?"

I scowl at her. "Unfair."

She grins, then clasps her hands to her chest and flutters her eyelashes. "Birthday wish."

"Oh my god."

"Come on, it'll be fun. I've been in there before and it's totally safe."

"Um, yeah, but I doubt you went in there with a poltergeist flashing lights and breaking stuff."

She twists up her mouth. "Okay, fine, we never saw or heard anything spooky in there, but I'm sure it's fine."

"Oh, if you're sure."

"Hazel."

"Lemon." I fold my arms over my chest to hide my shaking hands. "I'm sorry, but there's no way I'm taking my sister into—"

I freeze.

I spin around, my heart immediately in my throat, blood rushing through my veins like white-water rapids.

"Peach," I say, eyes peering through the dark for any glimpse. "Where did she go? Peach!"

Lemon looks around, frowning, then her eyes go wide on mine. She calls out Peach's name too. Our voices echo against the quiet. Way down the beach, the party lights sparkle, but I don't see my sister's tiny form between here and there. There's only silvery sand until it bleeds into firelight.

There's only the ocean.

Panic rushes into my newly spacious heart, filling it all the way back up.

I run toward the water, right to the very edge, but I back up when the surf reaches out for me. "Peach!" But I can't see her. Just a swath of dark. Just a hungry unknown world. I call her name again. Then again and again, because no, this can't be happening, not again, not again, not—

Lemon grabs my arm and spins me around to face her. "Hazel, she's not out there."

I yank my arm back, fear a firework in my chest, but Lemon just grabs on again.

"It's okay," she says, but all I can hear is water rushing in my ears, my hands reaching out for Mum and never finding her. Never, ever finding her.

"Hazel!" She grabs me by both arms now, shakes me. "Hazel, she went to the house."

That pulls my eyes from the water to Lemon's face. My breathing is louder than the waves, a storm in my chest. "What?"

Still keeping hold of me with one hand, she uses her free one to dig her phone out of her pocket. She turns on the flashlight and points it to the sand, then drifts it up toward the house. "See?"

I don't. Not at first, but then, dotting the otherwise smooth, windblown sand leading up to the rocks, I see a set of tiny sneaker prints.

Peach prints.

They end at the wooden path that winds through the rocks and up toward the house's huge porch. Another flash of light fills a window, a different one this time, then goes dark again.

I take off running.

chapter sixteen

S he's got to be outside," Lemon says as we run toward the house. "There's no way she could've gotten in by herself."

I don't say anything, my panic still too close to spilling over to risk a single word. *An old house is better than the ocean,* I tell myself. *An old house is better than the ocean.*

We wind through the rocks to the wooden boardwalk, then take the back steps two at a time. The Lancaster home looms above us, tall and terrifying, its gables and eaves stretching into the starry sky, like a haunted house out of some horror movie. Another flash of light, in an upstairs window this time. My heart triples its pace and I break out in a cold sweat.

"She's going to be right up here, waiting for us," Lemon says. "I just know—"

But her words are cut off as soon as we reach the porch's landing and see the back door cracked open.

"Can she pick a lock?" Lemon asks.

"No way," I say. "Someone must've left it open."

"Who, though? The house tour closes at four every day and—"

"Don't even start talking about some ghost."

Lemon sighs. "I wasn't gonna."

I dig my phone out of my pocket and turn on the flashlight before I rush through the door and into an 1800s kitchen. It's cut off from the rest of the house by a swinging door and has all sorts of ancient appliances—a huge iron stove with copper pots hanging from the brick wall behind it; a large hutch with lots of old-looking plates and cups displayed; a big center island with carefully arranged bowls and spoons on the butcher-block counter, along with a burlap bag of flour next to a wooden measuring cup. There's an apron laid over the edge, as though someone was in the middle of cooking and just left. I know the museum people probably set this up to make it look lived-in or whatever, but a chill still skitters up my arms. If I squint, I swear I see the swinging door...swinging.

I'm breathing too hard, too fast, a horrible sort of harmony to Lemon's own huffing and puffing. I'm frozen, fear cementing my feet to the old hardwood floor. I remind myself that ghosts aren't real, mermaids aren't real, none of this is real.

This isn't my life.

This isn't my story.

My story belongs in a yellow house three thousand miles from here, with two moms and a sister, and with beautiful paintings covering the walls.

I blink the dim kitchen back into view and make myself move toward the swinging door. Lemon grabs a fistful of the back of my T-shirt and I don't swat her away. The weight of her hand feels like the only thing keeping me from floating toward the ceiling. I push the door open and go through.

We walk into a dark, wood-paneled hallway that seems to go on and on until it opens up into a large vestibule. The blue-white light of my phone's flashlight makes everything look freakier, like we're on one of those ghost-hunting shows where all you hear is loud breathing and people whispering *What was that?* and *Did you hear that?* and *Oh my god.* A tall grandfather clock ticktocks beside the front door, a giant Persian rug swallowing our footsteps. On either side of the vestibule, there are two huge rooms—one a formal dining room and one that looks like a parlor, with a bunch of fancy couches and bookshelves.

I can feel Lemon trembling next to me, goose-bumped arm against goose-bumped arm.

Then, a creak, somewhere above us.

A thump, like footsteps.

My eyes fly to the ceiling, as though it's transparent and I expect to see Peach—dear god, let it only be Peach—peering down at me and grinning. I swallow the urge to yell her name, which would be the stupidest thing I could do if there *is* someone else in here, but I have to say something. I have to call to her somehow.

"Peach?" I whisper. "Peach, are you up there?"

I know there's no way she can hear me, but Lemon and I freeze anyway, waiting for Peach's happy giggle, her voice calling back to me, letting me know she's fine and she's just playing a horrible joke on me.

Nothing.

Until...

Thump-thump-thump-thump-thump.

Fast, like running.

"We have to go up there, don't we?" Lemon asks, looking upward too.

"Yep," I say, then grab her hand and squeeze tight, pulling her toward the stairs near the front door. They're dark wood, a thick banister curving all the way to the second floor in a comma shape.

One step.

Creak.

I wince as the old wood's groan echoes through the house, but I keep going.

Step.

Creak.

Step.

Creak.

We keep going like that, slowly. We curve around and are almost at the top—I can see the upstairs landing, see another flash of light from a bedroom down the hall— when a scream splits the shivery air and makes my stomach splash to my feet.

No, not *a* scream.

Screams.

What sounds like several voices screech like banshees and I know, I know, I know one of them is my sister. I drop Lemon's hand and bolt up the rest of the stairs, an idea zooming into my head. I unzip my Safety Pack and fumble inside for my little bottle of hand sanitizer spray. I point it in front of me, phone and spray now poised like weapons.

"What is that?" Lemon says, jogging alongside me and aiming her camera at the darkness with trembling fingers. "What are you going to do, *clean* them to death?"

"It's better than nothing," I say, and continue running as I hit the top landing and fly down the hall toward the screams. Peach careens out of a room at the end of the corridor, arms flailing, mouth and eyes open as wide as they'll go.

I catch her in one arm and hold out the sanitizer with the other hand. I start walking backward, fast, ready to get out of this house of horrors as quickly as possible now that I've got my sister, but I don't realize that Lemon has latched on to the back of my T-shirt again until it's too late. My feet tangle with hers, the back of my head slams into something hard and bony, and she cries out as all three of us go down in a heap on the floor.

"Oh my god, my nose!" Lemon cries out. But it sounds more like *Oh my god, my nothe.* My legs are draped across hers, Peach is literally sitting on my stomach, and I work to get us all untangled.

"We've gotta go," I say.

"It's a real ghost!" Peach wails. "Two of them!"

"My nothe!" Lemon says again, holding her hands to her face.

I finally get Peach on her feet and then dig my right foot out from under Lemon's left, my phone's light swinging in her direction. She pulls her hands back enough for me to see red. Blood. Enough to make my stomach tighten and the scars on my cheek burn from memory. Her eyes go wide when she sees the bright color puddling in her hand. She lifts up her shirt to press it to her face.

"We'll get it fixed," I say, breathing hard. "We'll fix it, okay?"

She nods and I grab her hand and fly for the stairs.

I never get there, though. Another light flashes from down the hall and I swear—*I swear*—I hear someone call Lemon's name.

The three of us freeze.

"Did you—?" I start to say, but get cut off by her name again.

"Lemon?"

The voice is a whisper, raspy and phlegmy, and there is no way I want to know who it belongs to.

I try to pull the three of us toward the stairs again, but Lemon digs her heels in, her eyes wide, half terrified, half curious. Her bloody shirt is still smooshed to her face as she stares down the hallway.

"Lemon, no," I whisper-yell.

Creak.

Creak.

Footsteps across an old wood floor.

Light flashes again, this time spilling from the room Peach ran out of and fixing right on us. It's so bright, I can't see who—or what—is producing it. I hold up the sanitizer, finger fixed on the nozzle.

The light comes closer, grows brighter, bigger.

"Lemon?" Raspy, ghosty whisper. My stomach puddles into my feet, and my mouth waters. I might throw up. I really might puke right here and now.

"Stop!" I yell, aiming my spray at the light. "Stop right there!"

"Lemon, it's—"

"Stop!" I yell again.

"Hazel, don't!" Lemon says.

But it's too late. I press down on the sanitizer nozzle, and a clear stream shoots out into the space in front of me.

It doesn't hit anyone, not directly, but two figures walk right into the spray.

"What is that?" one of them says, followed by some coughing.

I hear a smacking sound, then a different voice. Familiar. "Ugh, it tastes like some kind of cleaner."

"Lemon?" the first voice says again.

"Lemon, what the heck?"

The bright light in front of us drops, revealing two very familiar-looking human faces.

chapter seventeen

Even with their faces scrunched up in between coughs, their tongues sticking out in disgust, I recognize Jules's short swoopy hair and Kiko's glasses. Not to mention their THE ROSE MAID LIVES T-shirts. They're definitely not ghosts.

"What are you doing here?" Lemon asks, her voice thick.

"Us?" Kiko says between a few phlegmy hacks. "What are *you* doing here?"

Jules just shakes their head, then does this sneeze-cough combination that's so loud it rattles the windows. "Ugh, I think some got in my eyes." They rub at their face and sneeze again.

I wince, embarrassment now mixing with my panic.

Kiko's phone is tucked under her armpit, the light angled toward the wall and making all our faces look deathly pale. I tuck the sanitizer back into my Safety Pack and grab my sister's hand.

"Look, let's just get out of here, okay?" I head for the stairs before anyone can argue, yanking once on Lemon's arm as I go. I figure Kiko and Jules will follow if we all flee the antibacterial fumes, but honestly, I can't decide if I'm raging mad that they were the ones lighting up the rooms and scaring us half to death, or relieved that it's them and not someone—or something—worse.

Peach and I make our way down the staircase, Lemon's and Kiko's and Jules's footsteps behind us. I head back through the vestibule, and the kitchen, and spill out onto the moonlit back porch.

When I get there, I pretty much collapse on the wooden floor and pull Peach into my lap. Lemon and Kiko and Jules aren't far behind, spilling out onto the porch and crashing onto the floor as well, all three of them breathing heavy like they'd been running.

My heart is still pounding, fear still pumping adrenaline through my veins. I need a minute. Or fifteen. I squeeze my sister to me and hold her hands. And I smooth over her little nails. And I feel how warm her skin is. How warm and safe and alive.

I press my eyes closed as tight as they'll go. So tight, color explodes behind my lids, fireworks in my brain. Peach is fine, she's with me, and Kiko and Jules aren't dangerous, so all that panic from before is fading away, but another kind is taking its place. The kind that's always with me, part of me, waiting to rear up like a wild animal ever since Mum's and my accident.

Beyond us, the ocean crashes onto the shore. Sand from the porch sticks to my bare legs, works its way under my T-shirt, and finds my back, scratching at my skin. I concentrate on that sand, every little grain.

I'm not on a boat.

I'm not holding my dead mother's hand.

My face isn't rock-cut and bleeding, my eyes aren't crying, my throat isn't screaming so raggedly the paramedics don't know how to treat me without scaring me even more.

Peach curls into my side, and my breathing finally starts to slow.

I'm here. In Maine. My sister is fine. I'm fine.

I sit up, pulling Peach with me, and check her out—her hair's a mess but she seems okay. I'm about to ask her what in the heck she was thinking—running away from Lemon and me like that, going into an empty house by herself, scaring me half to death—when Lemon sits up and my mouth drops open.

Her hair is everywhere. I mean, *everywhere*. It looks like she stuck her finger into an electrical socket just long enough to get a good shock and make her already-wild waves fluff out like a lion's mane. Her face is smeared with blood and snot. There are even some splotches of red up by her forehead, like she brushed her hair from her face with bloody fingers. Her nose, which has stopped bleeding now, is huge, swelling up even as I stare at her, purpling underneath her eyes even more.

"Oh my god," Kiko says, also sitting up now and staring at Lemon.

"What?" Lemon asks. She sniffs and then stares out at us with innocent, totally-unaware-of-how-wild-she-looks baby-deer eyes.

Peach reaches out and pats Lemon on the arm. I pull her hand back in case some blood found its way down there, too.

"Um," Jules says. They're still on their back with their arms and legs splayed to the sides like a starfish, hiccuping every five seconds. Their head is tilted so they can see Lemon. "Yeah, wow."

"What?" Lemon says again when no one says anything. "Do I have something on my face?"

That's when it happens.

A tickling in my stomach, rolling up my esophagus and into my throat. A shifting of all my facial muscles, pulling my lips upward. And then it spills out.

Laughter.

Hard, belly-aching laughter. It echoes around us, but then I realize that Kiko is laughing too, covering her face with her hands like she's trying to stop but can't. Jules curls their legs up and hiccup-laughs at the sky. Then Kiko grabs her phone and taps on the camera, turning it around to selfie mode before holding it up for Lemon to see.

Lemon's eyes go wide, her mouth drops open, and then it happens to her, too.

Even though she looks like she's dressed up for Halloween or something, even though her nose must be sore, she laughs, full-on cackling with her head thrown back, and it all makes me laugh even harder. I hear it, the way my voice sounds when wrapped in a laugh—light and free and relieved—and it's like I'm expelling something dark and heavy with each roll of sheer joy from my stomach, getting rid of little bits of Sadness.

"Oh my god," Lemon says, holding up the phone to her face and inspecting herself more, laughing even while she talks. "I look like I'm in a horror movie."

Her consonants are still a little thick, but she seems okay. Her nose isn't bent weirdly or anything, so I don't think it's broken. Relief filters in between my laughter, and it makes this happy feeling in my chest that much more open and free. I feel like I could breathe in all the air in the world.

Space.

Wide-open space.

Our laughter finally calms down into little hiccups and sighs. I push up to my knees and take a pair of latex gloves from my Safety Pack, slipping them onto my hands. Then I find the travel package of Wet Wipes, remove one clean towelette, and sit back down in front of Lemon. I tip her chin up with a finger and start gently wiping her face.

"See?" I say, cleaning off her cheeks and forehead first. "This Safety Pack is mega-helpful."

"I've always wondered what you keep in that thing," Jules says.

"Gloves?" Kiko asks, a slight edge to her voice.

I shrug. "Blood-borne pathogens."

"I don't have any pathogens!" Lemon says, but then her eyes go soft, settling on mine in a light smile.

I smile back, carefully daubing around her nose now. Some of the blood has grown crusty and my stomach twists just a little, remembering when the paramedics cleaned all the blood off my own face, revealing the gashes underneath that would require stitches, leaving scars that would never fully go away. But I push the feeling down and focus on Lemon.

On right now.

Peach helps out, handing me fresh wipes when one gets dingy with blood. Soon, Lemon's got a clean face, but she's also got two black eyes and a nose that's about twice its normal size.

"Thanks," she says when I'm done. I ball the dirty wipes into my palm and flip them into my gloves as I slip them off, forming a little bag that I tie up and put next to me to throw away.

"No problem," I say. "Figured it was the least I could do, since my head did the damage."

"What?" Kiko asks.

"I slammed into Lemon when we were trying to escape you," I say.

"We thought you were a ghost!" Peach says.

"Or a mass murderer," I say.

"We thought *you* were a ghost or a mass murderer," Jules says, leaning forward and smiling at Peach.

"What are those?" Peach asks. She points to a bunch of bracelets on Jules's arm. They're cloth and wrap over and around each other in four different colors—black, purple, white, and yellow.

Jules's shoulders stiffen a little. They pick at the bracelets, glance at Kiko and then at Lemon. Both girls smile at Jules. "They're nonbinary bracelets," Jules tells Peach.

She scrunches up her little nose. "Oh. What's nonbidary?"

"Nonbinary, Peach," I correct softly, meeting Jules's eyes and smiling.

"Nonbinary," Peach echoes.

"Yeah, um," Jules says, swallowing hard. "It means I don't really feel like a boy or a girl all the time. Sometimes I feel like one or the other, but other times I feel like both or neither. And I like people to use *they* and *them* when they talk about me."

Peach blinks, eyes searching Jules's face as she thinks on this. Finally, she says, "Okay, cool."

We all wait for her to say something else, spout more

questions, but she doesn't. She just sits there with her head against my chest, smiling at all of us.

"Oh, to be young," Jules says, pressing a hand to their chest and gazing adoringly at Peach.

We all laugh, but I can see how pleased Jules is by Peach's peaceful acceptance. Jules's cheeks are a gentle pink and their eyes are bright, relief softening their shoulders.

"What's your name?" Jules asks my sister.

"Penelope Foster Bly," Peach says, "but you can call me Peach."

Jules laughs. "You can call me Jules. And that's Kiko."

"Hey . . . *Peach* and *Lemon*," Kiko says. "Fruit friends!"

"You're all made for each other," I say, rolling my eyes, but then I see how Lemon and Kiko and Jules grin and exchange pleased looks, years of knowledge and experience connecting them like silk ribbons. Something in my chest aches, and then it aches even more when I realize they all lost Immy. They all have a bit of the Sadness, and that connects them too.

"Hey, are you okay?" Jules asks. It takes me a second to realize they're talking to me.

"What?"

"Your head? Where it hit Lemon?"

I wait for Jules to laugh, because compared to Lemon's mess of a face, my head is probably fine, but then I realize they're watching me seriously, waiting for me to answer. They look right into my eyes, gaze never straying to my scars. Jules's hair swoops over their forehead, sticking up in a few places that I don't think they intended, but with our mad adventure in the Lancaster House, I guess that's to be expected. Something about the way they tilt their head at me, smile a little crooked on their mouth, makes a word wing through my head like a hummingbird.

Cute.

"Oh, um." I laugh a little and touch the back of my head, where there is a tiny sore knot. It doesn't hurt too bad, though. "Yeah, I'm okay."

Jules nods. "Cool."

They smile at me and I smile back and then Kiko clears her throat.

"What was that, anyway?" she asks.

"What was what?" I ask.

"Whatever you sprayed at us?" Kiko says.

Lemon and I lock eyes and I feel that same light, carbonated feeling rise up in my throat again. It's not funny. Not really. Hand sanitizer definitely does not belong on people's faces. But the simple fact of it—that Kiko and Jules were traipsing through an empty museum-house by themselves, that we thought they were ghosts, that I almost broke Lemon's nose and then tried to spray Kiko and Jules with a cleaner— feels suddenly so ridiculous and hilarious, two things nothing in my life has been for a long time, that I start laughing again.

"Hand sanitizer," I say through my laughter.

"That's what it is," Jules says, rubbing their face before smelling their fingers. "Purell."

"You sprayed us with Purell?" Kiko says. Her eyebrows are pushed together, but the corners of her mouth tip up just a little.

Lemon is laughing too and points to my Safety Pack. "Hey, she could've thrown a Clorox wipe at you."

"I'm sorry," I say, breathing deeply to try to control my laughter. This is serious. "I know it's not funny, but I really didn't know it was you. I thought we were in danger."

"What else do you keep in that fanny pack?" Jules asks, angling their head to see.

"Safety Pack," Lemon corrects, holding up one finger like some know-it-all, and that does it. We both bust up laughing again and this time it's so intense, tears stream from my eyes. Both Jules's and Kiko's mouths work to stay flat, but finally they give in, laughing and shaking their heads at the same time. Peach giggles right along with us, her hair tickling my chin as she bobs with laughter.

Finally, Lemon takes a deep breath and rubs her forehead. "Why didn't you guys tell me you were coming to the house?"

Jules sighs and picks at a thread on their jeans. "We didn't know if you wanted to go or not. The past couple of years, you don't seem like a big fan of your birthday."

"We're sorry," Kiko adds.

Lemon nods. "No, it's okay. I'm sorry. I know I'm a little...grumpy when my birthday rolls around."

"Understandable," Jules says. "We just wanted to remember Immy. Do something we always did with her again."

"Again?" Lemon asks. "Wait, have you come to the Lancaster House every year?"

Kiko and Jules both nod.

"Didn't seem right not to," Kiko says.

A flash of hurt flares on Lemon's face but fizzles out quickly. "What do you do in there?" she asks.

"Just...what we used to. Walk around, listen for ghosts," Jules says, and smiles at Lemon. "Tell stories about the Rose Maid."

"But who do you tell them to?"

"Us," Kiko says, her voice so quiet I barely hear her. "Immy. I talk to her sometimes, you know? Not just tonight."

"Me too," Jules says. "I talk to her about my drawings. Ask her what she thinks. Is that dumb?"

Lemon shakes her head, wipes at her eyes. "No, it's not dumb. She loved your drawings."

I watch Jules smile—a sad kind of smile, but still a smile. For one mad flash, all I can think about is how I want to see their drawings, tell them about how Mum was an artist too. But then Lemon lets out a long breath and pulls her knees up to her chest. The moment is quiet, that flash thankfully gone.

In fact, everyone goes quiet. I watch Lemon's shoulders rise up and down, up and down in that way I know she's quiet-crying. It's her *birthday*. A big one, too. Thirteen. I won't be thirteen until the fall, but I've thought long and hard about what it'll feel like when the clock hits 7:44 on the evening of October fourteenth, turning me into a teenager. I've wondered if I'll feel different. If I'll *be* different. If I'll even care, since Mum won't be there to celebrate with me.

If I'll keep feeling guilty for getting older and older, just like Lemon does.

Peach snuggles even tighter against my chest and I breathe in her Peach-y smell. The Sadness flows all around us like the wind, all kinds of missing, all kinds of loss. I think about Mum's paintings in Mama's trunk and how much I want to see them. How I know they'll make me sad, sure, but how I know they'll make my heart beat a little steadier, a little calmer, too.

I look through the slats in the porch railing, down onto the silvery sand, the moon-glazed water rushing up to meet the earth, then skittering away again. Over and over. I imagine Rosemary under the waves, in the dark, lonely, filled up with the Sadness too.

Or maybe she's not.

Maybe she found her family, or something at least, out there in the deep, something that turns all the Sadness into nothing but an achy memory. I could use an achy memory. So could Lemon, I bet. So could Kiko and Jules.

"So what else did you guys used to do with Immy?" I ask Lemon.

She lifts her head, eyes puffy and red. For a second, I think I've asked the wrong thing, that achy memories are really just jabs of painful, breath-stealing loss in disguise.

But then she smiles this little mischievous grin that can only mean she's up to absolutely no good. She looks right at Kiko and Jules, who are smiling like Cheshire Cats too. Then the three of them chorus, "Cloudland Bluff!"

I already regret asking. *Bluff* is just a nice, cozy word for *cliff*. I listen as they talk about hiking through the wooded hill to get to the top, how they used to bring binoculars and spyglasses and scan the sea for flukes or flashes of pale hair in the water. Luckily, none of them mentions actually attempting to climb a cliff in the middle of the night.

"There is something we could do tonight that we used to do with Immy," Kiko says. She tucks her legs against her chest and wraps her arms around her knees. "Birthday sleepover at your place, Lem."

She looks at Lemon, whose expression has gone soft. Jules doesn't say anything either. Everyone seems to be waiting for Lemon to make the first move, so I stay quiet too.

"Immy was really great at birthday sleepovers," she finally says, picking at a thread on her shorts.

"She was," Kiko says.

"The best," Jules says.

Lemon nods, then takes a huge breath. "Okay, let's do it."

"Really?" Kiko says, and Lemon nods.

"Yes!" Jules says, shoving a fist into the air.

Kiko claps a bunch of times in a row. "I'll bring all my extra blankets. And fairy lights. We have to have fairy lights."

"Oh, for sure," Jules says. "Lem, do you still have all those jar candles?"

"Yeah, I think so," Lemon says. "And we should have stuff to make butterscotch chocolate chip cookies."

"Yes, oh my god, I need," Jules says, clutching their stomach.

I listen to them all chatter on and on about their plans, a little ache starting to spread through my chest. Finally, they all plan to meet back at Lemon's house in half an hour and they stand up, brushing sand off their shorts and jeans, an excited air connecting them all.

Peach has gone heavy in my lap, not to mention quiet, so I'm almost positive she's asleep. I try to get up, but it's tricky. She's not a baby anymore, that's for sure. Lemon notices me struggling and helps me up.

"Thanks," I say, adjusting Peach so her head flops safely onto my shoulder.

"You're coming too, right?" Lemon asks.

"Oh." I blink at her, at Kiko and Jules. "Um, well, I don't know—"

"No way, little curmudgeon," Jules says. "You're with us."

"Little curmudgeon?" I say.

They wave a hand. "It fits, accept it."

I make a face, but for some reason, a smile tries to worm its way onto my mouth. "I don't know," I say, then nod at Peach. "She's asleep and I need to go check on my mom and—"

"Please," Lemon says.

"Come on, Hazel, it'll be fun," Jules says.

"Yeah," Kiko says, even though the word comes out as a sigh, like she's giving in to something. "We'll torture Jules by talking nonstop in fantasy references."

"Okay, I'm out," Jules says, but they smile.

I smile too. Again. My face almost hurts with how much I've been laughing and smiling tonight. The last time I was this happy, I was—

On the sea.

With Mum. And then I lost it all. I lost *me*. Just like that.

I can't do it again.

I can't be happy like that again, not without Mum.

I can't laugh like this again, feel all this space, only to have it fill right back up in a couple of months, the Sadness fresh and raw with all sorts of new losses.

My thoughts fast-forward to when Mama and Peach and I will leave Rose Harbor, all the goodbyes I'll have to say. For the past two years, waiting until Mama finally takes us home, I've never said goodbye to anyone. I've liked it like that. Mama pulls us into these towns, these memory-less places I can walk into without knowing a soul and walk right out of three months later the same person. No goodbyes. No memories. No inside jokes or fluttery feelings when you lock eyes with someone you think is cute. Goodbyes mean losing someone who meant something to you. Goodbyes mean gone and missing and remembering faces that made you smile, inside jokes that only feel like a hole in your heart once that person has left you.

Goodbyes mean Sadness.

A sleepover tonight is nothing but a goodbye tomorrow.

"I've...I've got to get Peach to bed," I say, backing up in earnest now. "I'll...I'll see you. Happy birthday, Lemon."

And then I turn and start walking, fast, holding my sister tight against me, leaving them all behind before they have a chance to do the same to me.

chapter eighteen

By the time I get back to Sea Rose Cottage, I'm ready to put Peach to bed and crash. I'm exhausted from carrying my sister the half mile back to the cottage, all the time worrying Lemon was going to chase me down and badger me into coming to her sleepover.

She didn't.

When I open the door, Peach still nestled in my arms, I look behind me, squinting through the dark for Lemon's phone light or a glint of the moon off Kiko's glasses.

Nothing.

I swallow hard, push down some feeling I can't figure out that keeps trying to rise up in my throat. I walk into the living room and lay Peach on the couch, shake out my aching arms. A single lamp on the side table lights the room, but the house is quiet.

"Mama?"

I tug my phone out of my pocket and check the time. Nine thirty.

I check for missed calls, texts, voice mails.

Nothing there, either.

I tap Mama's name and press my phone to my ear. It rings for what feels like a thousand years before there's a click, followed by a surge of noise—crowd noise, laughter, loud and wordless—and finally, Mama's voice.

"Hazel?"

"Mama?"

"Hey, sweetie, how are you?"

"Fine. Um, where—"

"Hang on a sec, Haze."

Then her voice fades, just a little, as though she's holding the phone away from her mouth.

"Okay, yes, one more glass," I hear her say. Then she laughs, clearly not talking to me. "No, this *has* to be the last one." More laughing and then she comes back at full volume. "Hazel, honey, you there?"

"Yeah," I say through clenched teeth. "Where are you?"

"We're still at the Solstice Fire. It goes all night, apparently. It certainly is a party out here!"

We.

"You're with Claire?" I ask.

"Yep—oh my god, Claire, no, do *not* order more fries. I'm stuffed!"

More laughter. More talking to someone who's not me, who's not Mum, and who definitely isn't part of our family.

"You found Lemon, right, sweetie?" Mama asks. "She texted Claire a few minutes ago and said you did, that she was okay."

"Um, yeah."

"Good. You did a good thing, baby girl, I'm proud of you. Are you home?"

I nod, even though she can't see me. Suddenly, all I want is her here. I want to talk to her about how I laughed tonight, about goodbyes, about this feeling I can't get rid of, about the way my stomach felt funny when I noticed the way Jules chews on the side of their lip when they're listening to their friends. I want to talk to her about Mum, about Claire, about how I'm scared that Mama is forgetting Mum.

That she'll forget me.

That we'll all just disappear one day, the Sadness swallowing us whole.

"When are you coming home?" I ask. I barely get it out. My throat is closing up, tears rising like a flash flood in a narrow canyon.

Mama doesn't notice, though.

"Oh, honey, in a little while," she says. "Claire needs

this, you know? Just some time. I do too, if I'm being honest."

"Time for what?"

"Just...time. To have a little fun."

Tears spill over now. *Time away from you. To have fun without you.* I know she didn't say those words, but I feel them anyway. It's always there since Mum died, the distance between Mama and me, distance when I need her close, close, close.

"Get Peach to bed, okay?" Mama says. "Love you!"

I hear Claire's voice say something in the background, pulling another laugh from Mama, before the line goes dead. I sink down onto the couch next to Peach, whose mouth is open a little, hair spiraling out on the throw pillow.

I know I should get Peach into bed and just go to sleep, but I can't seem to make myself move toward our room. The walls stare back at me, all of them white and blank except for a few generic paintings of the beach, the kind I've seen in dozens of motels and rental houses between here and California.

I could be anywhere.

I could be anyone.

I stand up, opening the front door and letting in the cool, salty air. Under the moonlight, the ocean is all silvery waves, peaceful. I go out onto the porch, close my hands around the rough wooden railing. Footprints litter the beach below, probably made just minutes ago by Lemon and Kiko and Jules. Down the way, Lemon's house is lit up. Warm. Probably full of laughter and noise.

I pull my gaze back to my little stretch of sand, our cottage quiet and nearly dark. I think of Rosemary Lee a hundred and forty years ago, maybe standing just like this on the Lancaster porch, lost even before she went into the sea, no one left to say goodbye to.

Then she vanished.

Like she never even existed in the first place.

A different kind of panic surges into my heart, moving my arms and legs and pushing me back into the cottage. Inside, I quickly stuff my backpack with toothbrushes, some pajamas, nothing else. Then I scoop Peach into my arms again and head out into the night.

chapter nineteen

I can hear it before I even knock on the door. Music, loud and vibrant. Something from a musical if I had to guess, all well-trained voices and lots of instrumentation, a girl singing about defying gravity. Every single window is lit with a golden glow, full of an energy and warmth that make me take a deep breath.

I shift Peach onto my hip so I can ring the doorbell, my arms and back sore from carrying her across the beach on the uneven sand. The bell sounds through the house, but underneath the music, the chime is like flies buzzing around a tornado. I ring it again, and then a third time, my sister growing heavier by the second. She lifts her head and mumbles something about dinosaurs before flopping her cheek back onto my shoulder.

Nothing.

My brain says go back to Sea Rose Cottage—put Peach to bed and go to sleep, forget this whole ridiculous idea—but my hand does something different. It reaches out and twists Lemon's doorknob, and then my eyes nearly cry in relief when the door swings open to reveal a small entryway that opens into a living room, a fire roaring in the gas fireplace even though it's the end of June. The music blares from the back hallway, voices laugh and shout, but I feel frozen to the spot, taking in the kind of house I haven't seen in two years.

A *home*, cozy and bright and calming all at the same time.

There's the huge cream-colored sectional couch, bright pillows in kelly green and navy spilling everywhere, a fleece blanket piled up in one corner with a book still open and facedown. Driftwood end tables flank the couch, softly glowing lamps and a mug with cats all over it still half full of cold tea or coffee on top. Even more books spread across a big tufted ottoman in the middle of everything.

And the smell—it's not stale, like every rental I've ever walked into. It's warm, like candle wax and laundry, a whiff of cinnamon left over from some meal made recently. The big island in the kitchen, which opens up into the living room just like our kitchen in Berkeley used to, is filled with the kind of stuff that says *life* and *family* and *We live here*—papers and mail, books and hair elastics and half-filled water glasses, a phone charger curling up on itself like a snake.

The walls are covered in art, not like Mum's, but not generic landscapes, either. No, all these pieces mean something. I even see a framed piece between two windows that looks like a self-portrait, clearly done by Lemon in a school art class, different scraps of paper making up her red hair and freckles.

And then there's the driftwood mantel over the sea-glass-tiled fireplace.

Framed photographs cover the entire surface, smiles beaming out at everyone who walks through the front door. I walk closer, Lemon's face growing clearer with every step.

And not just Lemon.

Lemon and Immy. Clementine and Imogene.

Over and over, there they are, red pigtails that grew into wild waves, matching blouses and jeans and backpacks on what looks like a first-day-of-school picture. Third grade, maybe. There's a couple of the twins with Claire and a dark-haired guy I assume is their dad, and then one photo of Lemon and Claire alone, at the very edge of the mantel. They're on the beach, and it's clearly a selfie, Lemon's head resting on Claire's shoulder, a sad smile on both their faces. A smile I feel right in my gut.

But Immy is here. She's *remembered* here. Here, in this home, she's still alive.

I want to sink onto the couch, right in the little corner where one section meets the other. I want to curl under that fleece blanket, read whatever book is lying there, pull Peach close to me while surrounded by all the stuff that makes a place *ours*, all the little things that make it home.

Except it's not ours and it's not home.

We haven't had a home in two years.

We've had houses. Cottages. Apartments. Duplexes. The road. But we don't have a home. Not anymore. I close my eyes and picture our house in California, the big, squashy couch and art on the walls and the kitchen where Mum and Mama cooked our meals, talked and danced and loved and even argued every now and then.

The sting in my chest is almost unbearable. But instead of wanting to run to Mama, demand that she take us back to Berkeley, back home, I just want to be here. Lemon's home. At least for tonight. A place where someone she lost still feels close, still feels treasured.

Another laugh bursts from the back hallway, jolting me out of my thoughts. I blink away some rogue tears, then hoist Peach up higher in my arms. I walk toward the voices, the music, stopping in front of a door covered in stickers of mermaids and other sea creatures—which means it absolutely has to be Lemon's room—and lift my hand to knock.

I freeze.

My nerves crawl up my throat, making it hard to swallow.

What if I'm not welcome? Lemon invited me over, sure, and then I ran away, a huge nonverbal *Take your invitation and shove it* if there ever was one. I'm thinking of what I'm going to say or do, when Peach twitches in her sleep. Her foot lashes out, kicking the door with a hard *thump*.

The music turns down and the door flies open, revealing Lemon, a question wrinkling her eyebrows, which...

I squint at her.

...are covered in bright teal glitter.

As are her eyelids, her cheeks, and her lips. Even her bruised nose has a dot of teal on the end.

Behind her is the most elaborate blanket fort I've ever seen, spanning her entire room from wall to wall, warm fairy lights strung everywhere and wrapped around anything that will hold them. Kiko and Jules are inside the fort on the floor, where there's a whole still-steaming pizza in its delivery box, at least five lit jar candles in a wide circle around them, and a huge basket of makeup. Their faces are similarly coated in glitter, their eyebrows pushed together with the same question.

"Um...hi," I say.

A beat passes.

Then Lemon's glittery face breaks out into a huge grin and she throws her arms around me, Peach still fast asleep and smooshed between us.

chapter twenty

Turns out, the sparkly makeup all over Lemon's and Kiko's and Jules's faces is mermaid makeup, because of course it is.

After I put Peach down in the bedroom right next to Lemon's—which still has a mint-green comforter on the bed and mermaid posters on the walls, so I know it must be Immy's room—I sit down under the blanket fort, marveling at the construction.

"Wow," I say, gently touching a spot where one blanket drapes down to form half of a doorway, which they've tied open with a piece of twine. There's a wooden pole in the middle, causing the whole structure to actually arch up like a tent. Binder clips hold white fairy lights in place, and when I look up, I see glittery stars on strings hanging from more clips.

"I know, right?" Jules says.

I nod. "It looks . . . magical."

Except when I say it, my voice echoes with Kiko's and I realize she said the same word at the same time. She lifts her eyebrows at me. She's not smiling. In fact, she looks downright skeptical. My stomach twists and I look away from her.

"See?" Jules says. "Magic in the real world."

"You guys built this all tonight?" I ask. "Like, since we left the Lancaster House?"

Lemon shrugs and flops down onto a pillow, tucking her arms behind her head. "We've had a lot of practice."

"The first one we made was—what?" Kiko says. "When you and Immy turned eight?"

"Yep," Jules said. "Except that one collapsed on us in the middle of the night and Immy woke up screaming her head off, thinking she was being suffocated."

"No, that was you," Lemon says, nudging Jules's knee with hers.

"Oh, yeah," Jules says, winking at me. I feel my cheeks warm. That wink does something to Jules's whole face that just makes them so . . . I don't know.

The word *cute* pops into my head again and I realize I'm staring at Jules while they stare right back at me.

"Um," I say.

Jules laughs softly and scrapes a hand through their hair, making it stick up in every direction.

So cute.

I shake my head, then utter another brilliant "Um."

"Oh," Kiko says, looking between Jules and me.

"Oh indeed," Lemon says, now nudging Kiko with her other knee. She's grinning, while Kiko looks annoyed, and I have no idea what's going on.

"Oh indeed-shmeed," Jules says, slapping both girls' knees. Then Jules clears their throat. "Now, since we are in a magical tent, you need the proper garb."

"Huh?" I say, while Lemon and Kiko shout agreements, clapping their hands and watching Jules like they're about to sprout fairy wings.

What they end up doing is way worse.

They come at me with a tiny brush, a bunch of glittery teal powder dotting the end.

"Whoa, wait, what?" I say, ducking out of their reach.

They pause and Lemon and Kiko bust up laughing.

"Come on, just a little blush," Jules says.

"That is not blush," I say, pointing at the brush.

"It's *mermaid* blush," Lemon says.

"Mermaid...," I start, but then I notice that Lemon's hair is plaited into one of those fishtail braids and they each have on a navy sweatshirt with sparkly iridescent flukes embroidered on it, teal definitely one of the colors shining from the scales.

I look down at my Wonder Woman shirt, suddenly very aware that I'm the odd kid out. The only one here who doesn't have a history with any of them. The only one who never knew Immy. The only one without a closetful of mermaid tops. But somehow, right now, it doesn't feel like I'm the *only one*.

It feels different. Like space.

It feels like *part of*.

I sigh, roll my eyes but smile, then lean forward and let Jules turn me into a mermaid.

We don't go to sleep until after two o'clock in the morning. There's cookie-making and movie-watching and reading Kiko's favorite comic book series—about a Muslim girl who's this amazing superhero—in the blanket fort. We even sing a very quiet "Happy Birthday" to Lemon and eat a bit of the cake her mom made her. It's beautiful, a real work of art if you ask me, three layers with all the blues fading into each other just like the ocean zones, a freckled, redheaded mermaid swimming through the twilight zone.

Claire comes home right around eleven, which means Mama must be home too. We're all sprawled on the sectional in the living room with a bowl of popcorn between us—I can't remember the last time I ate so much junk—watching a Pixar movie. Claire leans over the back of the couch and wraps her arms around Lemon, her face right next to her daughter's. Lemon reaches her own arms up, tangling them around her mom's neck. They stay like that for a long time while Kiko and Jules and I glue our eyes to the screen. I hear some murmuring, see Lemon nodding out of the corner of my eye, then hear Claire whisper "Happy birthday, baby" to her before they let go of each other. Then Claire stands there, watching us watch a movie, a sad-happy smile on her face.

She catches my eye and her smile grows a little wider.

I look away, pretending I didn't see her. Instead, I take out my phone, waiting for Mama to call or text me, asking me where I am, where Peach is, but my phone stays dark and quiet.

"Your mom knows you're here, sweetheart," Claire says.

I look up at her. "She does?"

"I texted my mom while you were putting Peach to bed," Lemon says, stuffing some more popcorn into her mouth. "So she knew how many people were over here."

I nod but keep my phone in my hands, still waiting for Mama to text. When she still doesn't after an hour, I turn my phone off.

Later, we all lie down in the fort, smooshed together like sardines in a can, extra blankets piled on top of us, at least five pillows underneath us. I'm right in the middle, next to Lemon, Jules and Kiko on either end. The two of them fall asleep almost immediately. Jules's mouth hangs open a little, their arms tossed over their head, while Kiko curls up into the tiniest ball I've ever seen. She's like a little squirrel hibernating. Lemon's still awake, though. I feel her stir next to me, light and restless. Even though my body feels exhausted, I can't seem to fall asleep either.

This is my first night away from Mama since Mum died, my first night away from any parent ever. I never did sleepovers, even before Mum died. I had friends at school and on my swim team, but I've always been a mama's girl, preferring home and family to all the uncertainties that come along with best friends. It's weird and I feel a little outside of my skin, but when I take a breath, the air flows nice and smooth.

"Can you believe how late my mom got home?" Lemon whispers.

I frown at the stars hanging above us, remembering how much fun Mama seemed to be having when I talked to her earlier. My throat goes thick as I think about it. I try to swallow it down, feel happy that Mama was happy, but I can't do it.

"Hmm," I eventually say.

"Do you think they like each other?" Lemon asks. "Like, *like* like?"

I breathe in. Out. Dread trying to rush into all the new space inside me. I shrug in a way that seems to satisfy Lemon's question. She sighs and then leans her head on my shoulder. I stiffen for a second, then relax, tiredness finally starting to settle over my body like a weighted blanket.

"Thanks for this," Lemon whispers, her eyes on the stars.

"For what?" I ask.

"For coming over. I mean, I have fun with Kiko and Jules. Of course I do. They're my best friends, but it's hard sometimes. Like Immy's always there with us, but she's not, and it's just...I don't know. But with you, especially tonight, it felt sort of new, you know? New and familiar at the same time, which is the best way it can be, don't you think?"

I nod, but I don't think I really know. Everything's always new, all the time. That first Christmas Mum was gone, we were living in Santa Fe and Mama bought a tree, but she strung it with white lights instead of the colored strands we always used to use. She bought a bunch of cheap, generic ornaments at a drugstore instead of using the Popsicle-stick ornaments that I made in first grade and the Baby's First Christmas ornaments with Peach's and my baby pictures stuffed into them. On our birthdays, we have cupcakes now, never a cake. On Thanksgiving, Mama still makes a big dinner, but it's quiet, not filled with Mum's and Mama's friends like it used to be.

Everything is new now. Everything is different, almost every day.

I hear myself release a long sigh. I'm not sure if Lemon hears it, but when she grabs my hand and squeezes it, I squeeze back.

I wake up before everyone else. I almost forget where I am, but then I feel this weight on me, much heavier than Peach. Lemon's wrapped around me like a vine, her arm slung over my waist, her leg twisted around my ankle. I lie there for a while, the room going from dark to a soft lavender as the sun comes up.

Peach will be up soon.

Mama will want to see us.

My chest tightens, thinking of Mama. I work my way out from under Lemon, peeling back the blankets until I'm free. Lemon groans and flips over, cuddling in close to Jules on her other side. I look at them for a second, Lemon and Jules and Kiko, and my cheeks twitch, a smile trying to fit itself onto my mouth.

The smile goes into hiding when I find my phone in my bag and turn it on, the screen still blank once it powers up.

No text.

No call.

I shove it into my backpack, teeth clenched as I change out of my pajama shorts and back into my cutoffs, as I throw my bag over my shoulder and sneak out of the room. I'm about to slip into Immy's old room, wake up Peach, and head home to find out what in the world Mama is doing, when I hear clanging around in the kitchen, like mugs clinking against each other.

My fingers tighten on my bag, and before I know what I'm doing or why, I'm standing in the kitchen doorway, watching Claire pour soy milk into a mug of coffee and then sit on a high stool tucked under the island. She opens a mustard-colored book, which is when I notice she's got a Mason jar full of pens and markers next to her. She takes out a black pen and scribbles something down, then goes over it with a lavender-colored highlighter.

It feels sort of like spying, but I watch her for a second without saying anything, staying as quiet as I can. She's oblivious, wearing dark-framed glasses with her short hair a complete mess on top of her head, like a fire swirling up to the sky. In the couple of weeks she's been in our lives, I haven't really looked at her. Not like this. I study her, suddenly wishing I could dig under her skin, figure her out, see all the reasons Mama seems to like her so much.

Do you think they like each other? Like, like *like?*

Lemon's question from last night pings around in my brain as I watch Claire take a sip of her coffee, write something else in the book. After a swipe of a light green highlighter, she sighs and rubs an eye under her glasses. Then she just sits there like that, quiet and staring out in front of her with a glazed-over gaze, and it hits me.

She lost her daughter.

Immy was hers, just like Lemon is hers, and yesterday must've been just as hard for her as it was for Lemon. Maybe harder. Maybe—

I shake my head to get rid of the thought, swallow hard against my thickening throat. Except as I do, my bag slips off my shoulder, making a soft sound as it slides down to my elbow. Claire's head snaps up, swinging in my direction, eyes wide.

She relaxes when she sees it's me.

"Oh. Hi, Hazel."

I swallow and try to say something, but my voice isn't working yet, so I nod. She smiles at me.

"Did you sleep well?"

I shrug, determined not to talk to her and to just turn around, but somehow my feet edge themselves into the room, step by step.

"I'm amazed any of you could fall asleep with all the sugar you ate last night." She grins and gestures to the giant Tupperware container only half filled with butterscotch chocolate chip cookies, Lemon's beautiful birthday cake now missing a few pieces on its cake stand.

"We managed," I say.

She smiles, flips her black pen over her knuckles. I've always wanted to do that, but every time I try, the pen ends up flying across the room or onto the floor.

"I'm so glad you came over last night, Hazel," she says. "It means a lot to Lemon."

"It's no big deal," I say.

She glances at me as she slips a turquoise highlighter out of the jar, uncaps it. "I don't think that's true. Sometimes, very small things are very big deals."

I don't know what to say to that, but I've reached the island now, my traitorous feet carrying me all the way to just a couple of steps from Claire. I glance down at the pages in her book, which are covered with neat black writing—the ink thick and almost markerlike—and blocks of delicate color. It's pretty, so neat and organized. I can't help but admire it even as I tell myself to stop.

"What is that?" I ask.

She glances down at her book and runs her hands over the paper. "My planner."

"Your planner?"

She nods.

Now that she's said it, I notice section headings lining the top of both pages, *Monday, Tuesday, Wednesday*, and so on. Still, the spread looks like art—organized art, but still art. I even see a space at the bottom that she's filled with a doodle of a little cat, some books on a tiny bookshelf, a mug of something warm complete with delicate steam lines rising from the top. "But aren't planners just, like, a place to write down stuff you have to do? Like appointments and to-do lists and stuff?"

"Sure. All that's in here. But I like to make it look pretty, too."

"Oh."

I tilt my head and she angles the book so I can see more. Every bit of writing is also highlighted, but not with bright colors. Instead, the page is full of dusky pink and sky blue, twilight purple and buttery yellow, green like spearmint tea.

"Everything is color-coded," she says. "I have a color for the restaurant, for appointments, for anything having to do with Lemon, for exercise, for errands. Everything."

I nod, taking in the spread. She's even written a word in a little box at the top of each day of the week, words like *peace* and *balance* and *confidence*. She's got a busy life, writing everywhere, but somehow, the way she's put it into this planner, so neat and organized and, yes, pretty, it makes my pulse slow down just looking at it.

"It keeps me organized," she says, "but it also just keeps me..." She trails off and I glance up at her.

"What?" I ask. "What does it keep you?"

She sighs. "Calm."

I blink at her, but yeah. That's the exact word I was thinking about, the exact word that describes her book.

"Why... why do you need to stay calm?" I ask.

She laughs. "Well, everyone does sometimes. But, well, this planner helps me because I can get a little anxious."

"Anxious?"

She nods and looks down at the pages. I wait, unsure what to say. That word—*anxious*—the grief counselor used it back in Berkeley. She used it a lot, even in just the couple of sessions we had. I never knew what to do with it. Neither did Mama, and then we just left and I've barely heard that word since.

"I used to worry a lot," Claire goes on. "After Immy...
I worried all the time. About Lemon, about me, about Lemon's dad. I couldn't sleep and I would have these...these
times when my chest would get all tight and I couldn't
breathe. Lemon would have to help me calm down, poor
girl."

I suck in a breath—quietly, but I know Claire hears it,
because she tilts her head at me—as I think of my panic
attack on the beach, how Lemon knew exactly what to do.

"My therapist recommended a planner," Claire says
after a moment. "It doesn't fix everything, but it helps me
feel more prepared. If I write everything down, order my
day as much as I can, I know a little bit better what to
expect. Of course you can't plan everything, but routine,
seeing what I need to do all laid out before me...it helps.
And spending time on making it something I like looking
at, well, that's a stress reliever too."

We fall silent after that, as we both look over everything she's planned for this week. On yesterday's space,
there's not a lot written. Instead of a big to-do list, she's
drawn a mermaid. Red-haired and freckled, just like the
one on Lemon's cake. Then, near the bottom of the day's
rectangle, I see another word.

Evie.

I take a deep breath as she closes the book and hops off
the stool.

"Are you hungry?" she asks.

I frown, *I need to get home* right on the tip of my tongue. But for some reason, I can't get the words out. She shifts into action, pulling eggs and butter out of the refrigerator, bread and cinnamon and sugar from the pantry. I watch her start what is very obviously French toast and sink onto the stool she just vacated. I place my hand on top of her planner, the engraved design of flowers and vines soft and textured under my fingertips. We stay like that, quiet, calm, as she whisks up the eggs, soaks slices of thick bread in the mixture, then places them on a sizzling pan. Finally, she slides two pieces onto two plates, drizzles everything in butter and syrup and cinnamon and sugar, and sits down next to me on the other stool.

We eat quietly and I'm glad. I don't want to talk to her, but I can't seem to get myself to storm out of her house, either.

"How is it?" she finally asks, motioning with her fork toward my plate.

I shrug as I shove another bite into my mouth. No way I'm telling her this is the best French toast I've ever had in my life.

chapter twenty-one

O n a Friday in mid-July, after Ocean Club is over, Lemon tells Kiko and Jules to meet us back at her house in an hour. Ever since her birthday a few weeks ago, we've been hanging out there at least once a weekend. Usually, Peach comes with me during the day, but if we hang out at night when she's already in bed, Jules loves to bring out these freaky books called *Scary Stories to Tell in the Dark*. The pictures alone are enough to give anyone night-mares. Still, I don't say no when they dig the books out of their bag. There's something amazing about reading scary stories with other people in a fairy-lit blanket fort.

Something magical, even.

"I have a surprise," Lemon says, literally rubbing her

hands together like some villain as we jog down the steps to exit the library.

"Oh, god," Jules says, covering their face.

Kiko shakes her head. "No way. No surprises."

"You guys have such little faith in me," Lemon says.

"The last time you said you had a surprise," Kiko says, "we ended up eating fish eggs."

"It was caviar," Lemon says. "As in fancy, rich-people food?"

"Fish. Eggs," Kiko says.

"Okay, okay, can we stop talking about fish eggs?" Jules says, holding their stomach. "And I've got a surprise for tonight too. Well, actually, it's for Hazel, but you guys are part of it."

"Wait, what?" I ask.

Jules shrugs innocently.

"I know what it is, I know what it is!" Lemon says, clapping her hands at least ten times really fast and grinning at me like a total fool.

Kiko rolls her eyes, then pulls Jules in the direction of their houses, while Lemon and I head toward ours.

"So what's the surprise?" I ask Lemon as we walk. The sky is crystal clear, so blue it almost feels as though the sea got tipped upside down and is floating above us. The air is dry and warm and it finally feels like summer. If I was a different kind of girl, a two-years-ago kind of girl, I'd be itching to go swimming. A pool, a lake, the sea—it didn't matter, as long as I was covered in water.

"If I told you, it wouldn't be a surprise," she says.

A flicker of anxiety sparks in my belly. "I'm not great with surprises."

"Mine is good," she says. "It's . . . romantic."

"Romantic?" I ask. "A rom-com movie binge?"

She laughs but shakes her head. "Better."

I blow out a breath. I would've liked a rom-com movie binge. Not because I like rom-coms necessarily, but movies are safe. Easy. Get some popcorn, a few blankets, some pillows, all of us squashed into Lemon's huge couch. I can do that. I *have* done that, three whole times since her birthday.

"I'm more interested in Jules's surprise, though," she says.

"You're not gonna tell me that one, either?"

She shakes her head, then skips ahead of me and turns around, walking backward so she can see me. "It's good too. Trust me."

"That's dangerous," I say, pointing to her feet.

She ignores me and keeps on heading down the sidewalk backward. "They're so sweet, don't you think?"

"Jules?"

"Of course Jules."

"Um. Yeah, I guess," I say.

"You guess?"

"Okay, yeah, they're sweet."

"And cute?"

I frown at her, a squirmy feeling starting in my stomach. "Sure."

"Sure? That's it?"

I shrug.

"They think you're cute."

I stop walking. Right there in the middle of the street. I touch my scars, the bumps on my cheeks that will never, ever go away. "What?"

Lemon stops too, her eyes flicking to my fingers at my scars and then back to my eyes. "They told me so."

"Really?"

"Yeah."

The words jumble in my head—*romantic* and *cute* and *Jules and me*. I don't understand why Lemon is even talking about this. Have I done something to make her put all those words together, think about Jules and me as...I don't know, *Jules and Hazel*? And why, *why*, does the slight possibility of a *Jules and Hazel* make me feel like a million lightbulbs have replaced all my blood?

I can't decide if it's a nice feeling or not. I'm suddenly sweaty, nervous, thoughts cartwheeling out of control. I think back over the past few weeks and all the time I've spent with Jules.

It's a lot.

More than I've ever spent with anyone other than my swim team and schoolmates, Mama and Peach and Mum.

But Kiko and Lemon are always there too. Half the time, so is my little sister. Nothing we do screams romance. We go to Ocean Club. We sit on the beach, far from the water, and eat lunch every weekday. Sometimes, after Ocean Club, Lemon and Kiko and Jules will hang out, so I'll go home and pick up Peach and then we'll meet up with them for frozen yogurt at the Pink Mermaid, this shop downtown that has wild flavors like Rose Maid Mint and Seashell Sherbet. I go, mostly because the first time Lemon invited me, I said no, and she followed me the whole way home, babbling on and on about the wonders of the Pink Mermaid's toppings—all of them, from the cinnamon drops to the peanut butter cups, shaped like tiny mermaids—until I finally gave in just to shut her up.

Also, Mama is writing nonstop lately and the *tap-tap-tap* of her laptop makes me think of home, of California and Mum. My mind starts somersaulting, wondering what she's writing about, if it's romantic, who she'll get to read her first draft because, *before*, it was always Mum.

So, yeah, I've been with Jules a lot. We've gone to the movies to see the new Pixar film. We've eaten truffle fries from the Rose Maid Café. About a week after the sleepover, we all went to the Lancaster House when it was actually open and looked at all the stuff that used to belong to Rosemary Lee. The rooms felt completely different in the daylight. In the parlor, the walls were packed with framed photos, maps, even blueprints of the *Skylark*,

Captain Lee's ill-fated ship. Several cases gleamed in the afternoon light, trinkets waiting under the glass.

I walked up to the closest one and peered down at an old-fashioned hairbrush, a silver-plated mirror, and a smaller brush with warped bristles that I was horrified to realize was a toothbrush.

"Creepy, right?" Jules said, frowning down at the nineteenth-century toiletry items. Their shoulder touched mine.

I laughed, relieved they didn't think this thing Rosemary Lee supposedly stuck in her mouth once upon a time was magical. "Um, yes."

"There's better stuff, I promise," Jules said, then pointed to a corner where at least seven other people hovered. "Anne Lancaster's journal is over there. It's under glass, so you can't touch it, but the curator here puts on these special gloves every morning and turns the page."

"How generous," I said. "All you'd have to do is come here every day for an entire year and you'd get to read the whole thing."

Jules's smile dipped. "Yeah, silly, right?"

I tilted my head at them. "You've read the whole thing, haven't you?"

Jules opened and closed their mouth a few times before saying, "I mean, probably not the *whole* thing."

I laughed and got that swoopy feeling in my stomach that I'd been getting more and more around Jules. I didn't know what it meant. It sort of felt like nerves, sort of like excitement. I tried to ignore it, but it's hard to ignore your gut.

"It's actually really beautiful," Jules said. "Anne's writing. And sad. Really sad."

"Yeah, I remember a few lines from *Coastal Lore*. 'She has the sea in her soul now—' "

" 'I fear one day it will claim her completely.' " Jules nodded. "Yeah."

I pressed my fingers to the cold glass case. "Do you think it did?"

"What?"

"Claim her completely?"

Jules sighed. "I think...she was sad. And I think sadness can change you, you know? That kind of loss? It makes you different. It's made *me* different, losing Immy. And she wasn't even my family. Who knows what it can really do to some people. Maybe it did take her over completely, and she just...she just..."

I couldn't look at them, but I felt my mouth open, heard my voice speak. "Lost herself."

"Yeah," they said softly. "Something like that."

I nodded, gazing on that gross toothbrush, but a flash flood of tears welled in my eyes.

"Hey," Jules said softly, touching my shoulder gently. Quickly, fingers there and then gone. "You okay?"

"Yeah." I sniffed, blinked the tears away. I hadn't told Jules, or Kiko, for that matter, about Mum. And I didn't want to tell Jules now. Getting it all out to Lemon once was hard enough, and I had no interest in reliving that moment in the middle of a museum. "Yeah, I'm fine."

Jules nudged my arm with theirs, smiling that crooked smile, and we went on meandering around the room. Lemon was right, what she said about the Lancaster House that night on the beach—there is a *feeling* here, a presence, a heaviness that weighs on each room like an invisible mist.

Upstairs, you could walk around and see the bedrooms, including the one that Rosemary used to sleep in. The five of us went up there together, and once we were alone, Lemon lifted five sea roses out of her backpack. We each placed a flower on the tiny twin bed—even me, because Lemon pretty much stuffed the thorny plant into my hand and I had to take it or risk a skin laceration—right on top of the rosette quilt yellowing with age.

It was a serious moment, but something about it felt light, too, all of us being there together again but in a totally different way than our midnight adventure.

On our way back toward the stairs, Jules paused on the hallway landing and sighed heavily.

"You okay?" Kiko asked.

Jules nodded and ran their hands along the banister. "I was just remembering."

"Remembering what?" Lemon asked.

"Right here," Jules said, looking around wistfully, sighing again. "Right in this very spot…"

"Yeah?" Kiko said. "What?"

Jules's eyes settled on mine, a smile just barely twitching at the side of their mouth. "...is where Hazel nearly poisoned us all with her mighty hand sanitizer."

"Hey!" I said, but it was too late. Everyone roared with laughter, even Peach.

"Ah, memories," Kiko said, fake coughing and rubbing her eyes.

"I didn't mean to," I said, but a laugh worked its way up my belly too, falling out of my mouth even as I tried to defend myself. The heaviness I'd felt just moments before lifted like I'd shaken off a coat in the heat of summer.

We all laughed the whole way down the stairs, earning us several annoyed glances from somber tourists who clearly just wanted to get lost in a sad story.

I remember thinking about the whole day later that night in bed, what Jules and I talked about, change and sadness, how sometimes you can't *not* change. Changing is survival. Changing is how you keep the Sadness from claiming you completely. Or, like Jules said, maybe the changing *is* the claiming. I thought about the me I was before Mum died. I barely knew that girl anymore. Even my reflection was different.

But then, in the next second, while Peach rolled over in the bunk underneath mine, shaking the whole bed frame, I

thought about how Jules made me laugh. Made me feel...
I don't know. *Part* of something.

As I walk back to the cottage with Lemon now, my
stomach flutters, remembering.

I've never liked anyone before. Not *like* liked. But it's
not something I was ever interested in. I remember making
faces at a movie or TV show whenever the actors would
kiss on-screen. I remember Mum laughing when I did it,
one arm around Mama on the couch and tousling my hair
with the other hand.

Just you wait, kiddo, she said. *Just you wait.*

I never really knew what I was supposed to be waiting
for, but maybe... it's this? I *do* think Jules is cute. And funny.
And smart. And my stomach feels weird when I'm around
them, but does that mean *like*? A stomachache—that's it?

The questions spin on and on as we walk. By the time
we get to Sea Rose Cottage, I've nearly forgotten about
Lemon's and Jules's surprises, my mind completely crowded
and confused.

"I'll see you in an hour or so?" Lemon says as she keeps
heading off down the beach. I nod. Wave. Walk up the
porch steps to the door. I stop before going in, trying to
process what I think Lemon was telling me.

Jules.

Me.

Cute.

Like?

A smile starts to form. I wonder what Mum would say—

I freeze.

My smile drops.

Because there's no way I can know what Mum would say. I can guess, but I can't know. In a blink, she disappeared from my life and I couldn't do anything to stop it. I was *right there* and I couldn't stop it. That's how fast your life can flip totally upside down, crushing you, knocking you sideways until you can't breathe, until you're sure, you're *sure*, you'll never get another deep breath ever again.

In a snap.

Everything gone.

That's how fast Kiko and Lemon and Jules could disappear too. All it'll take is Mama and Peach and me leaving, or all of them deciding I'm not worth it, I'm too *changed*, too lost, too much, too little. All these smiles, these memories of the past few weeks, these . . . these . . .

Friends.

The word hits me like a punch in the gut.

Friends.

Gone in a blink. A moment.

Other words spill into my mind, water filling a hollow cup. *Goodbye* and *loss. Change. Heartbreak. The sea, cold, dark, deep blue. Rocks* and *sirens. Paramedics*, pressing on Mum's chest, *scars* on my face in the mirror, under my fingers, always there.

I shake my head, press the heels of my hands to my eyes. Breathe.

It takes me another minute, but I get my lungs back to normal enough to put my hand on the doorknob. I push open the door and start to call for Mama—I just want to see her, talk to her, talk to her about *friends* and what to do, how to handle all this. Or talk to her about home. It's been over a month. Maybe she'll agree. Maybe she'll see it's time to go back to our old life, back to where we were happy, where we were a family with Mum.

But when I walk in, I stop short. I never even get to call out for her.

Mama and Claire are sitting at the kitchen table, a pot of tea between them, their heads bent close together. They startle, pulling back from each other. Claire's pale face goes super red and then Mama puts her fingers to her mouth like she and Claire just... like maybe they...

"Hi, sweetheart," Mama says, clearing her throat. "How was Ocean Club today?"

I just blink at her.

Claire wraps both hands around her mug and smiles at me, her cheeks still pink. "Hi, Hazel. Did Lemon head on home?"

Blink.

"Hazey!" Peach yells, flying out of her room with her purple tutu around her waist and Nicholas in her arms. She launches herself at me and I catch her, swinging her up onto my hip. "Are we going over to Lemon's?"

"Um..." Suddenly, going to Lemon's feels impossible. Seeing Jules. Feeling all these new feelings I can't talk to Mum about, can't talk to Mama about because she's... she's...with Claire. She's not worried about goodbyes. She's happy. She's probably told Claire everything about Mum, talked to her like I wish she'd talk to me. She's... replaced Mum. Replaced me.

I can't stay here. I can't go into my room and close the door and pretend Mama and Claire weren't just...that they aren't...

"Yeah," I manage to say.

Peach beams, squeezes me tight as I turn back toward the sea.

"Hazel, honey—" Mama starts, but I don't let her get anything else out. I open the door and slam it on my way out without another word.

chapter twenty-two

I walk fast.

So fast, Peach complains, but I can't slow down. I need to get away, away from the cottage and the kitchen table and Mama and Claire and whatever was going on before I walked in.

Kissing.

They were *kissing*.

Or they were about to. Or they just had. Or maybe they've already kissed a hundred times and I've just never seen it, never noticed. Maybe they've held hands, walked slowly down the beach, snuggled on a couch while they watched a movie.

A memory flashes through my mind. Mama and Mum, the Christmas before Mum died. We'd just finished opening presents, and Mama's breakfast casserole was baking in the oven. Peach was asleep on the living room floor, amid all the wrapping paper, her new stuffed baby penguin snuggled in her tiny toddler arms. I was curled in Mama's big armchair reading *Ultimate Oceanpedia*, which I'd just gotten from Mum. It was filled with the most recent ocean facts, along with gorgeous photographs taken by the best underwater photographers in the world. My favorite photographer was this woman named Marisol Rivera. She was amazing, capturing the darkness and light and life of the sea like no one I'd ever seen, and this new book was full of her stuff.

I was absorbing new facts on the status of the world's coral reefs, listening to Mama and Mum talk in the kitchen, when their voices suddenly went quiet. "Have Yourself a Merry Little Christmas," sung by Judy Garland, which was Mama's favorite holiday song, clicked on. Our kitchen and living room were one big open space, so when I looked up, I could see them standing by the center island.

They were dancing.

Slow-dancing.

Mama was wearing the typewriter apron I'd just given her, and Mum had a dusting of flour on her nose from the snickerdoodle cookies she'd made for us to decorate later, but none of that mattered. Mum had one arm around Mama's waist, the other holding Mama's hand against her heart. They swayed, Mama's chin resting on Mum's shoulder, because she was just a little shorter. Mum spotted me watching, a soft smile on her face as she winked at me. Then she said something to Mama I couldn't hear and Mama laughed, pressed a kiss to Mum's neck.

Perfect.

That's what I thought right then. I remember it, clear as day, the word filling up all the space in my head. Mama and Mum, they were perfect. They were meant to be. They were one true loves and fairy tales and all that gooey, happy romantic stuff Mama wrote about all the time.

Now it's like Mama's forgotten all about that, all about Mum, all about her heart shattering into a million tiny pieces when Mum died. All about the week after the accident, when Mama barely talked, barely ate, barely slept, and I had to take care of Peach all on my own with a bandage covering my cheek.

She's forgotten how much it hurts to love someone and then lose them.

But I haven't.

I hug Peach tighter, tears welling in my eyes and blurring my vision. Before I know it, I'm at the stairs leading up to Lemon's back deck, which is set high off the ground on stilts. I don't want to be here, but I don't know where else to go. Luckily, she must be inside, so I sit down on the bottom step, curling Peach into my arms while I try to think what to do.

"What's wrong, Hazey?" my sister asks, little brow furrowed when she sees my face.

I shake my head. "Nothing."

"Something," she says, putting her hand on my scarred cheek. It just makes me cry more. Soon, I'm sobbing, don't know how to stop, don't know why I'm even so upset. Peach leans her head on my arm, pats my leg. Even puts Nicholas in my lap, which only makes me cry more. I take him, that pilly little purple narwhal, and kiss the top of his head.

Peach beams, but her eyes still flash with worry. I want to tell her I'm okay, but I think I'd be lying. I don't think I've been okay in a long, long time.

Above us, on Lemon's deck, I hear the glass door in her kitchen slide open, her voice drifting out. "...wait for her on the beach," she says.

Peach leaps off my lap. "Lemon! We're here!"

"Peach," I whisper. "Don't."

She makes a face at me. "But you need your friends."

"I don't have...they're not..." But I can't get it out. Instead more tears well and spill over, my skin itchy and tight now from the salt.

"Cherry, is that you?" Lemon calls.

"Yup!" Peach says. Even now, weeks later, she's a sucker for these ridiculous fruit names Lemon throws out.

"Excellent!" Lemon says.

Footsteps shuffle over the porch floor, more than one set. I lift the hem of my T-shirt and rub the cotton over my face, hopefully soaking up most of the tears and snot. Then I breathe.

Or try to.

Breathe.

In.

Out.

By the time Lemon, Jules,˙and Kiko tromp down the steps, my eyes and face are dry.

My hands are shaking, though. Like I just gulped down a bowl of sugar.

"Hey!" Lemon says. "You're—" She stops, frowns at me. "What's wrong?"

I shake my head. "Nothing. I'm fine."

Jules tilts their head at me, and Kiko crosses her arms. I feel another sob—or a scream—rising up in my chest, but I swallow it down. Act normal, make some excuse to leave. A headache. Exhaustion. Sudden diarrhea, I don't care. Any excuse is better than faking wanting to be here.

"Um, okay," Lemon says. She walks over to Peach and picks her up, the bulging tote bag on her shoulder swinging. "Hey, Blueberry, do you think you could go collect some shells for me?" She grabs a pink plastic bucket off the patio table under the porch and hands it to Peach. "The prettiest ones you can find."

"Wait, what?" I ask, but Peach is already wiggling out of Lemon's arms and taking off for the sand. "Lemon, what the heck?"

I watch Peach skip along the dry sand, the water at low tide and far away, bending here and there to plop a shell into her bucket. Off in the distance, the narrow wooden dock behind Lemon's house juts out into the water. A little boat bobs in the waves near the end, tied to a wooden post.

"She'll be fine," Lemon says.

"Shells won't bite her," Kiko says.

I glare at them both before turning my gaze back to Peach. Another shell. Then another.

"Besides," Lemon says, "this is grown-up stuff."

"Grown-up stuff?" I ask. "What are you talking about?"

"My surprise. Are you ready?"

"Fish eggs, right?" says Kiko. She and Jules crack up.

Suddenly, I feel like rolling my eyes. Didn't we just do this in front of the library? Lemon made them eat fish eggs, yeah, gross, move on.

"Actually, I think—" I start to make some excuse to leave, but Lemon plops down at the little patio table and tips her tote bag upside down.

Books tumble onto the table, five paperbacks, all of them with familiar-looking colorful covers featuring illustrated grown-ups in various states of adorable romantic bliss.

Evelyn Bly is printed across the top of each and every one.

"Why do you have my mom's books?" I ask.

"Your mom's an author?" Jules asks. They sit down across from Lemon and pick up a book, setting their own tote bag on the ground, black with a rainbow arching from corner to corner. "Like a real published one?"

I nod but don't say anything else. I'm not allowed to read Mama's books yet. And if what I remember about that first day we met her and Claire on the beach is correct, neither is Lemon.

"Whoa, really?" Kiko says, following Jules.

"Lemon," I say.

"Hazel," she says back, but in a drawling sort of way that clearly means *Get over yourself and have a little fun, why don't you?* "Haven't you ever looked at these?"

"No," I say. I've looked at the covers, sure, read the back descriptions. But Mama's most recent book came out a whole year before Mum died, which means I was nine years old and couldn't have cared less about the kissy stuff she writes about. And *after*, Mama's creative spark sputtered out and I've been too focused on taking care of my sister and trying to get back to California to give Mama's books much thought. Still, she's been writing so much lately, I have wondered what her new book is about, what romantic stuff she can possibly be writing now that Mum's gone.

Not that I'd ever admit any of this to Lemon.

"They're amazing," Lemon says, waving me over.

I don't move.

Lemon eyes my frozen position for a second before she picks up a book with a bright blue cover.

Three Days in June, Mama's first book.

"This one," Lemon says, brandishing it like a work of art. "Oh my god, this one is so good."

"Wait, you read it?" I ask.

She nods. "Last night. I found all your mom's books piled up on the kitchen table yesterday morning."

She eyes me meaningfully and I just shake my head at her. "And?"

"And," she says, "*my* mom got them all out and wants to reread them." She eyes me again.

"And?" I say again.

"Ugh, oh my god, Hazel, help me out a little."

"I think she means," Kiko says, "that her mom likes your mom."

"Oh, she totally does," Jules says.

I don't say anything. My fingers curl into fists, nails biting into my palms.

"Thank you, Kiko," Lemon says. "I swear, the past few weeks? My mom has been in the best mood. I mean, the best. Happier than I've seen her since..."

She trails off, her eyes going soft for a second before she snaps back into excited mode.

"Anyway, she had to go into the restaurant last night and when she did, I pounced. I read this whole thing in, like, two hours."

"What's it about?" Jules asks, taking the book and looking at the back.

"It's about these two lonely women, Calla and Mac, which is short for Mackenzie, isn't that the cutest? They meet on a secluded beach where they're both renting houses by themselves and they fall in love. But then they have to go back to their regular lives and don't talk for a year, but then they see each other again when they both take separate trips to India at the same time. They keep finding each other, over and over again, like they're totally meant to be."

"Wow," Kiko says. "Sounds...romantic?"

"So romantic," Lemon says.

"And it's about two girls?" Jules says.

"Totally," Lemon says. "A lot of her books are about two girls."

"Cool," Jules says softly, opening the book up to the first page.

"Can we not do this?" I say. I don't like where this is going. I don't want to hear what Lemon thinks about romance, especially not where Mama is concerned.

"No, we cannot *not*," Lemon says, laughing and picking up a purple-covered *Harriet and Henry Are Not in Love* and snuggling with it. Literally, she *snuggles* it against her chest.

"Is there a lot of, you know...," Jules starts, but twists up their mouth in thought.

"Is there a lot of what?" Lemon asks.

Jules slides their eyes to me, then away, but I swear their cheeks go pink. "Kissing," they finally whisper.

Now I swear my own cheeks go pink. No, not pink. Red. Volcanic lava red.

Lemon grins really slow and the dread in my belly increases. "I thought you'd never ask, my curious friend." She snatches *Three Days in June* back from Jules and flips through the pages until she settles on one. "Listen to *this*."

Oh, god. "Lemon, no, don't—"

" 'Calla felt as though she had four hearts instead of one, all of them beating wildly as Mac stared at her from across the room. She couldn't understand it. She'd only known the woman for a single day, but she felt as though Mac had always been there, hovering at the edge of her life and waiting to crash through.' "

"Lemon, please just—" I say, but she's not having it. She dives back in as though I didn't even speak.

" 'Suddenly, Mac was right in front of her, with her long blond hair and freckled skin, and all Calla wanted to do was kiss her. It felt like the most important thing in the world, kissing Mac right here, right now. Like kissing her might change everything, the moon, the tides, all the little aches inside Calla's heart. At that very moment, Calla would give anything to kiss Mac Christenson. Just once.' "

"Oh. My. God," Kiko says, pressing her hands to her heart. "That is so ... It's just ..."

"Right?" Lemon says.

"It's pretty good," Jules says, nodding.

"Do you think this is how your mom feels about Hazel's?" Kiko asks.

"Oh my god, I hope so," Lemon says, laughing. "She's writing a new book, isn't she, Hazel? I bet it's super romantic. I mean, it has to be, right?"

"Your mom is really pretty," Kiko says to Lemon. "So is Ms. Bly."

"Isn't she?" Lemon says. "She's so—"

"Mrs."

Lemon looks at me. Blinks. "What?"

"It's *Mrs.* Bly."

"Wait, what?" Jules says. "Your . . . your mom's *married*?"

"No, she's not," Lemon says. "My mom wouldn't do that. Hazel, tell them."

"Tell them what, Lemon?" I say. Lemon flinches at my voice. It's cold and sharp. I can hear it, meanness edging each syllable, but I can't seem to smooth it out. My heartbeat is everywhere, fingertips and toes, throat and stomach and temples. "That my one mum is dead and my other mom's free for the taking?"

Jules inhales sharply. "What? Your mum? Who—"

"That's not what I meant," Lemon says softly. Too softly. I hate all this softness—wide eyes and gentle words. I'm tired of her excitement and her smiles, how it's like she's sad about Immy one minute and the next, the world is all romance and glitter and rainbows. How does she *do* that? How does she live like that? How does the hollowness not swallow her up?

"Hazel, I'm sorry," Lemon says. "I just—"

"Sorry for what?" I say, and then suddenly, I need to *say* everything. The words start spilling out, like I'm running down a hill and can't stop. "Sorry that I was there when she died and my whole family fell apart?" My voice rises, the wind in a circling storm. "That Mama hasn't spoken of her since and, half the time, I feel *crazy*, because it's like it didn't even happen? Like I'm worried and scared and lost and freaked out all the time for nothing, because that's just who I am? That all I want is to go home? Or are you sorry that, yeah, Mama's acted really happy since your mom came along? So happy, like Claire is everything, when I've been *right here* for two years and she's all but ignored me? How about that? Are you sorry about that?"

Only when my voice echoes against the wooden pillars holding up the porch do I realize I'm yelling. Lemon's lips tremble, tears already shining in her eyes. Jules stares at me openmouthed. Kiko glares, all her suspicions about me, I'm sure, confirmed right there.

I'm mean, hard, cold, no good as a friend, no good as a person.

"Hazel," Lemon says. "I'm sorry, I thought—"

"No, you didn't. You didn't think at all," I say. "You never do. You just barrel right along, full blast, never *thinking* one bit about—"

"Hey!" Kiko yells. Loud.

We all jump. I shut my mouth.

"Kiko," Jules says, but they look pained, anger and hurt creasing their forehead a little.

Lemon reaches for Kiko's hand. "Kik, it's fine."

"No, it's not *fine*, Lemon," Kiko goes on, grabbing on to Lemon's hand and then glaring at me. "From day one, you've acted like this, like we're dirt under your shoe or something. You're constantly rolling your eyes about the Rose Maid myth, even when you know that's something that's really important to us. That we *like* it. You hang out with us, but you're never really *with* us and I'm sick of it." She motions to Lemon and Jules. "You may have fooled these two, but I see you. You and that stupid fanny pack."

"Kiko," Lemon says, but it's soft and she's crying.

"You don't care about anyone but yourself," Kiko continues, ignoring Lemon. "And you can't talk to my best friend like that. I'm done."

Then she tosses Mama's book to the table and looks away, toward the sea, like I'm not even there anymore.

"Yeah," I say, turning my back on them and taking off toward my sister. "I'm done too."

chapter twenty-three

The weekend passes quietly.

Mama spends it writing. When Peach and I get back from Lemon's, Claire is gone and Mama is in her chair, typing away. All afternoon and evening, I wait for her to bring it up, what I saw, what she and Claire were doing at that kitchen table when I walked in, but she doesn't say anything. She just writes. Picks up her phone, smiles at it and types out a text, then writes some more.

My mind rolls over and over, trying to figure out a way to talk to her about it—not about Claire, but about going home. I don't want to know about Claire. Claire is just...a distraction. An old friend, and Mama's just lost in remembering or forgetting or I don't know what. But she promised me. She *promised* we'd go home someday.

My phone is quiet. In the past few weeks, Lemon has usually spent the weekend either blowing it up with texts and pictures or knocking on our door and asking if we want to walk on the beach or go into town. I haven't always said yes, but she's always been there, and now I jump at every little creak and groan out on the porch, thinking it's her.

I don't want it to be her. I never did. She probably hates me now, just like Kiko hates me, and Jules...

No, I don't want it to be any of them, but I keep looking for them all anyway. It gets so bad on Saturday I finally take my book and close myself in my room just to stop myself from constantly looking up at every little noise outside.

Peach is quiet too, sitting on the living room floor making beaded bracelets. When I ask her who they're for, she just shrugs and keeps stringing them together, one with purple and yellow and white and black, then one with pink and red and orange, then another with sparkly silver beads alongside navy and aquamarine.

I sit out on the porch a lot, staring at the ocean. It's the only time I don't feel like I'm coming out of my skin. I keep thinking about what Kiko said, how I don't care about the Rose Maid myth, but I think she might be wrong about that.

I think I care about it a little too much.

Rosemary Lee feels like a...well, not a friend necessarily, but like someone I know. When I think about her, she seems so familiar to me, so…present. Like she's right here with me, watching the sea too.

She has the sea in her soul now.

That's what it feels like when I watch the water—like some tiny piece of my soul is out there, out in those deep waters, all alone.

Is that what Rosemary felt like?

Like her soul belonged under those waves, like she was so different now that she couldn't even live on land, couldn't find a way to belong anywhere else? That's what I feel like all the time—like I can't figure out how to be this girl, this person who watched her mum die, this sister, daughter.

Friend.

I shiver in my bed on Sunday morning, thoughts of mermaids and Mum, changing and belonging flitting through my mind. I haven't slept great since Friday, since my fight with Lemon. I dream all night long, endless blue water surrounding me, pale hands reaching up from the depths to mine, even paler hair swirling through the sea like silk ribbons in slow motion.

After breakfast, I take a mug of mint tea with lots of honey and go sit out on the porch. The ocean is there, as always. Today it's gray in the shallows, dark blue in the deep. Clouds layer the sky, and I wonder what the world looks like in California today. What the Pacific is doing. Downtown Berkeley is probably still sleeping, but in a few hours, it'll be full of people out for Sunday brunch, shopping in the vintage stores, browsing in Mrs. Dalloway's, Mum's favorite bookstore on College Avenue.

I think about our yellow house on Camelia Street, the way it always smelled like coffee and paint and the wild roses that bloomed in our backyard. Peach learned to walk in that backyard. I did too, though I don't remember it, but there are a thousand other memories I do have.

I stand up from the Adirondack chair and head back inside, determined to ask Mama about going home soon. She's sitting in the armchair, as usual, typing furiously on her laptop, that crease between her eyes that means she's concentrating. I know better than to interrupt her, but I don't care anymore. I don't.

"Mama?"

She keeps typing.

"Mama."

She startles and looks up. "Oh, Hazel, honey, would you go get my hand cream out of my bathroom?" She shakes out her hands, inspects a dry patch on her knuckles, then goes back to typing.

I just stand there, breathing in and out, pulling the words out of my heart one by one. When I've got them all collected, I finally set them free.

"When are we going home?"

Peach looks up from where she's coloring in her coloring book on the floor.

Mama sighs. "Hazel."

"You promised me. You promised me we'd go."

She swallows and nods. "I know that."

"So?"

She bites her lip and moves her gaze to the window, to the sea. "Sweetie, it's still summer. We'll talk about it when the cottage's lease is up, okay?"

I just want her to say it, say that we're going back to Berkeley, no new towns, no bland rentals that don't feel like home and never will, say that we'll be in *our* house by the end of August. Say we'll get our life back, that she'll talk to me like she used to, that we'll hang up all Mum's art and remember how we used to be.

But she doesn't. She just looks at me with this sad glint in her eyes that feels familiar—the Sadness, peeking out from behind her own heart—and smiles a smile that barely moves her mouth. She used to smile at me with all her teeth showing, crinkles around her eyes. Now she has the Sadness smile. Ever since Mum died, that's all I get.

She only smiles big and wide for Claire now.

I turn away to go get her hand cream, because I can't bear to see her smile like that anymore.

Her bathroom is small, white, plain. A single generic painting of a seashell over the toilet. White shower curtain, cream-colored ceramic counters and sink. Nothing like Mum and Mama's old bathroom, with Mum's art everywhere in deep greens and blues and a big glass shower.

I pull at the rectangular mirror on the wall that doubles as a medicine cabinet. It swings open, revealing Mama's hair creams and gels, face cleansers and moisturizers. I spot the little jar of hand cream, this stuff she's been using for years that she has to special order from a local shop in Berkeley. I open it up, smell the familiar meadowy smell, like clean air and grass. The smell is like a punch in the stomach, memories of home hitting hard and fast.

I cap the jar and am about to close the cabinet when I see it.

A key.

Right next to Mama's tube of toothpaste. A little tarnished brass key.

Before I can talk myself out of it, I scoop it up and put it in my pocket. I walk out into the bedroom and crawl under the bed, pulling out the big navy trunk. Hands shaking, I manage to fit the key into the padlock on the second try. The lock clicks open. I stare at it for a few seconds, my heart ballooning in my throat. Down the hall, I hear Mama's keystrokes flying.

I jump up, then walk back to Mama as calmly as I can and place the jar of hand cream on the side table.

"Thanks, sweets," she says, never moving her eyes from her laptop.

I watch her for a second. She's definitely in *The Zone*. Peach is working hard on a page in her coloring book, Moana soaring over the sea in her boat, a determined look in her eyes. I get my sister a snack, Goldfish in a little plastic bowl and a cup of water, and kiss her on the top of her head.

Then I go back to Mama's room, click the door shut as quietly as I can, and open up Mum's trunk.

chapter twenty-four

The first thing I notice is the smell.

Like paint and wood, wild roses and coffee and this perfume Mum used to always wear called Isle—dewy and fresh and calm.

Home.

The scents knock me back like a punch. My own trunk, my clothes and books, don't smell like this anymore. They smell like the road, like eight different rentals, eight different towns with no memories.

I take a deep breath, tears already gathering in the corners of my eyes, and look back into the trunk.

Paintings.

They take up most of the space, barely fitting. Peach's is on top—all crimson and russet, golds and pinks and plums.

That tiny green river. Tears spill over. I haven't seen this painting in two years. I haven't seen *Mum* in two years and that's what this feels like. Seeing Mum. Not just remembering her, but seeing her. Her mind, her beauty, her humor and talent, her love.

I move Peach's painting to the side and take out mine. I sit back on my heels, balancing the canvas on my legs.

The sea.

Me.

It's all right there, everything Mum saw in me. Calm and wild, dark and light, mysteries and wonders. I run my fingers over the thick paint, the glossy blues, the way the waves seem to undulate just like in the real sea. I hug the painting to my chest and let myself cry, sure I'll never be able to put it back.

Holding on to my painting, I peer into the depths of the trunk. My favorite book, *Ultimate Oceanpedia*, is in here. I remember giving it to Mama a few days after Mum's memorial. Or rather, throwing it at her. Not angry with her, but angry with the ocean, at my love for it, telling Mama I never wanted to see the book or the sea again. I ripped all my posters off the walls too, left them in a shredded mess in a corner of my room until Mama took them away. She must've put my book in the trunk, figured I meant what I said, that I wanted to forget it all. I lift it up, heavy with glossy pages full of beauty and mystery. I don't open it, though. I can't. Instead, I just set it aside, carefully, like it might break, and look deeper into the trunk.

There are a few other smaller paintings that Mum did. One that hung in Mum and Mama's room, all creams and browns and blush colors, two women curling around each other.

Mum and Mama.

Mama and Mum.

True loves.

There are some old art magazines that featured Mum's work, a half-full bottle of Mum's perfume, a lavender-scented candle that used to sit on Mum's nightstand, a coffee cup with a picture of Mum's face asleep on a pillow, her pale hair wild and her cheek creased from the sheets. Mama took the picture as a joke, but then I remember Mum had the photo put onto a mug and gave it to Mama the Valentine's Day before she died. They always gave each other funny presents for that holiday, something to make each other laugh.

"What's more romantic than my snooze face?" Mum said, and Mama roared with laughter, then drank out of that mug every day for the next month.

It's our old life, opening up in front of me like a flower in spring.

At the very bottom, there's a dark green photo album that I know holds all sorts of pictures of our family. I stare at it for a few seconds, my painting still in my arms, trying to ready my heart to see us, see how we used to be. Mama doesn't keep any pictures around of Mum, not like Claire keeps ones of Immy all over their house. I've always assumed it was because we moved around too much. Framed pictures aren't easy to travel with, glass and frames that could snap or break, but now, seeing the album hidden away like a secret, that's exactly what it feels like.

Hiding.

Forgetting.

My fingers are touching the album, ready to pick it up, when I spot a tiny royal-blue velvet box next to it.

A ring box.

My stomach cramps, my throat suddenly dry, like my body knows what it is before my mind does. I pick it up, frowning at it for a split second before opening it, my mind catching up right before I see what's inside.

There's Mum's wedding ring. Platinum with the hand-engraved pattern of flowers circling the whole thing, a tiny blue diamond inlaid in the middle.

And right behind it, nestled into the same slot, is Mama's.

Mama's wedding ring, pale green diamond sparkling at me.

Mama's wedding ring, which as of our first night in Rose Harbor was still on her finger.

When did she take it off? And *why*? Because of Claire? Because…because she doesn't…because Mum's not…

I can't finish my thoughts, tears blurring my brain as much as my eyes. These tears feel different, though. They feel hotter, flow faster, a kind of anger burning right in the center of my chest like a tiny flame. I take out my phone to text Lemon, to see what she thinks, but then I remember our fight, I remember how Kiko hates me and Lemon is rooting for our moms to get together, like some romance novel.

I remember the romance novels.

Mama's new romance novel.

I bet it's super romantic. I mean, it has to be, right?

That's what Lemon said about it, right after Kiko asked her if her mom liked Mama.

No. No. No.

I try to breathe. Inhale. Exhale. Try, try, try.

"Hazel!" Mama calls from the living room.

The ring box falls out of my shaking hands, plonking onto the wooden floor. I carefully collect everything—the paintings, the mug, the candle—and place it back in the trunk. Snatching up the ring box, I stare at those rings—my parents' wedding rings, the start of our whole family, both of them abandoned, forgotten—and then pull them from their tiny slot and slip them onto my forefinger.

I finally get a good breath.

The rings fit perfectly.

"Hazel, sweetie, what do you want for lunch?" Mama calls again. "Peach, go check on her for me."

I place the empty ring box in one corner, close the trunk quietly, and lock it back up. I put the key in Mama's bedside drawer, right under the deck of cards, and slip the rings off my finger and into my pocket.

Then I head off in search of Mama's laptop.

chapter twenty-five

It takes the rest of the day for Mama to separate herself from her laptop. Between writing and constantly checking her phone and grinning—not smiling, but *grinning*—as she reads whatever the screen says and types a reply, she's barely looked up at the actual people in her family since we ate turkey sandwiches for lunch.

And even then, she kept checking her phone.

"Who do you keep talking to?" I finally asked her as Peach and I got our shoes on to go for a walk. Even though it had turned overcast and gray outside, I needed to get Peach some exercise. Mama sat in her chair, computer on her lap, thumbs flying over her phone.

She paused at my question, just for a second, and met my eyes. I could almost hear what she was thinking, those mom gears turning as she tried to figure out what to say. It was the sigh that did it—a big inhale and exhale that confirmed everything Lemon hoped was going on, everything I saw between Mama and Claire a few days ago at the kitchen table. Still, I didn't want her to say it. I wished I could tuck my question back into my mouth, take Peach on a walk all the way to California.

Mama sighed again. I looked down at my shoelaces, tied them in triple knots.

"I'm talking to Claire," she said. "We're going out to dinner tonight. You and Peach are going to hang out with Lemon over at her house."

"Yay!" Peach chirped from the floor next to me, where she was concentrating on making bunny ears with her laces.

"Where are you going?" I asked.

"Hmm?" Mama said, her eyes back on her phone.

"You and Claire. Where are you going?"

Mama glanced at me. "Just out to eat. A place in town called Rilla's. We won't be late. Not like the night of the Solstice Fire, I promise."

The question *Is it a date?* was right there behind my teeth, but I swallowed it back down. I didn't want to hear it from Mama's own mouth. That would make it too real. Instead, while Peach hunted for sea glass washed up on the shore—I made her stick to dry sand, far away from the ocean's edge and far, far away from Lemon's side of the beach—I typed *Rilla's* into my phone's browser.

It was a restaurant in downtown Rose Harbor, just like Mama said. What she failed to mention was that it was a *fancy* restaurant right on the water. The online photos showed candlelit tables with white tablecloths, couples in nice clothes and pearls smiling at each other over glasses of red wine, diamond rings sparkling on their fingers.

Romantic.

That's what Rilla's was. Dim and golden-lit and romantic.

Now, hours later, I can't get the restaurant's romantic scene out of my head while Mama gets ready in her bedroom and I stare at her laptop. It's right there, just sitting on her chair. I've got Peach busy with her beads and bracelets in our room and the shower has just turned off in Mama's bathroom, so I know I've got a few minutes.

I ignore the alarm bells going off in my head and pick up the laptop. I flip it open...and am immediately stopped by a screen asking for a password. I try everything. Peach's and my birthdays, our first and middle names, Mama's, even Mum's. Nothing works. I hear Mama in her room, opening her closet door, rummaging through bathroom drawers. I'm running out of time and I have to know. I have to know what she's really thinking. Mama's writing is her whole life and when Mum died, that part of her died too.

I have to know what's come back to life.

A thought pops into my head. It's a hopeful thought, dangerously so, but it's all I can think of. I type it in.

39CameliaStreet

I tap Enter and Mama's computer springs to life. I breathe out, feel a relieved smile pull at my mouth. Maybe all of this with Claire isn't what I think it is after all. How could it be, if Mama's still typing our old address, the last place where the four of us were a family, Mum's *home*, into her computer every day?

Hope blooms in my chest like a wildflower. I almost close Mama's computer right then, scared the feeling will wilt, but then I see the file on her desktop.

SYLVIE BANKS BEGINS AGAIN

I click on the little icon, and Mama's fancy writing program boots up. It opens to where she left off, fifteen chapters in. I scan the page she's on, but nothing makes sense. There's a character named Sylvie who's working in her garden, and she keeps thinking about some woman named Gemma, who must be the love interest. At least I think she is, but there's another woman's name on the page—Bryn—so I'm not sure who's who or what's going on. Sylvie just keeps wrestling with some stubborn snapdragons and worrying about what Bryn must think of her.

I scan the program's sidebar, which is just a bunch of

chapter numbers, but then, near the bottom, there's an icon titled *Synopsis*.

I click on it and read.

Sylvie Banks is heartbroken. She's also a complete hermit. Ever since the love of her life, Bryn, died two years ago in a tragic accident, she's barely left her house, and she definitely hasn't thought about meeting someone new. She spends her evenings alone with her cat, reading and working on her design business from the comfort of her living room. Real pants are a thing of the past, and she's more than happy to stay in her sweat pants sipping hot tea for the foreseeable future, thank you very much.

Then she meets Gemma.

Or rather, she meets Gemma again. Gemma Brownlee and Sylvie Banks were childhood best friends until Gemma's family moved away when the girls were twelve, but not before the girls shared a goodbye kiss, a kiss that neither woman has ever forgotten.

Suddenly, Sylvie finds herself feeling things again. Friendly things, Sylvie tells herself, but it's not long before her friendly feelings for Gemma blossom into something decidedly more romantic. Gemma, for her part, makes no secret of her interest in Sylvie, but she's haunted by her own share of ghosts.

Can both women put aside past loves and losses to make room for a new one true love?

"Hazey?"

My head shoots up to see Peach standing in the doorway of the living room.

"Why are you crying?" she asks.

I touch my scarred cheek, and my fingers come away wet.

"I'm not," I say, wiping my face. "I'm fine." But my voice trembles, my throat aches with the effort to hold it all in.

Peach points. "That's Mama's computer."

"I was just...looking something up. Did you make a new bracelet?"

She frowns but holds up one she's been working on for a few days, colors blurring in my vision. I give her a thumbs-up, but she keeps her frown. I need to close Mama's computer. Put it away. Forget this story she's writing.

This story where Peach and I don't even exist.

Where Claire is her new one true love and Mum is...

Mum is *past*.

Mum is gone.

Mama *begins again*. Fresh. Like nothing before even existed.

But my fingers won't move. They won't close the laptop.

"Go get your jacket, okay?" I say to my sister.

She nods again, turns, and does what I ask, but I know I can't have this thing in my hands when she comes back. In Mama's bedroom, I hear her diffuser whirring, drying her curls, which means her makeup is done and she's dressed. Drying her hair is always the last thing she does when she's getting ready to go somewhere.

I look back at Mama's story. I click on the title right above the chapter headings at the very top of the sidebar. When I do, the whole book unfurls on the screen, chapter after horrible chapter.

Thirty-three thousand, two hundred forty-one words.

I press Command-A, highlighting every single letter.

Then I hit Delete.

chapter twenty-six

After Mama leaves to meet Claire, wearing a beautiful one-shoulder coral dress with a tulle skirt that I've never seen before tonight, I sit on the porch for a long time. Then I get up and start to pace. Then I go to the railing and look down at the beach, the sea, the water rolling and churning, Rosemary somewhere underneath.

"Aren't we going to Lemon's?" Peach asks more than once.

I keep putting off giving her a flat-out no. I tell her we need to eat dinner, then that Lemon's not home yet, then that I've got a headache and I'm waiting until it goes away. I don't think she buys it. Ever since my fight with Lemon, Peach has been quieter, more observant, watching me closely with a little pucker between her eyebrows.

Or maybe she was always like that and I'm finally noticing that she sees and feels so much more than I ever thought. Part of me wants to tell her about Mama and Claire, tell her about Mama's book, what I did, just to tell *someone*. Over the past few weeks, I've gotten used to being with Lemon, with Kiko and Jules. I never divulged my deepest secrets or fears—well, except to Lemon on her birthday—but they were still *there*. I spoke words, laughed, locked eyes and smiled, shared my thoughts on the last movie we saw.

All this stuff about Mama and Claire, the wedding rings I slipped onto my finger the second Mama walked out the door, it all churns in my stomach, a sour brew that doesn't belong there, that wants out. I can't tell Peach, though. I can't tell Lemon or Kiko or Jules. I tell myself I don't *want* to tell them, that I can handle this just like I've handled everything else since Mum died. But I have to do something. I have to…

I look down at the rings on my finger, glinting in the pale evening light like the moon.

I have to tell Mama.

All this time, two years, day after day, that's who I need. That's who I've kept quiet for, because I was there when Mum died and I didn't save her and I don't want to remind Mama, I don't want to make her sad, I don't want her to tell me again and again that we're not going home. So I've been quiet. But I need her. I need her to tell me, too. To tell me this is all happening, that it's okay that I barely recognize myself anymore, that I'm still me, I'm still *hers*, that Mum is gone but we're going to be okay.

We're going to be us again.

Mama is who I need.

My mother.

"Peach, let's go," I tell her, turning away from the sea to where she's sitting on the porch floor, doing nothing but hugging Nicholas to her chest and looking through the wooden slats of the porch railing at the ocean.

"Are we going to Lemon's now?" she asks, getting up.

"No, we're...we're going into town. To get some dinner."

Her face falls, but she nods. I make sure my Safety Pack is fully stocked and that Peach goes to the bathroom before I lock the door and head toward the porch stairs.

And run right into Lemon Calloway.

I suck in a breath. Something flares in my chest under all the panic and worry. Something...happy. That's what it is. It's happiness. Relief. To see Lemon. I push it away, though. Remember that she wants Mama and Claire together. Remember that we're leaving, we're going home to California. Remember that I don't need her.

"What are you doing here?" I ask.

She looks up at me from the bottom stair, a tote bag on her shoulder. She doesn't smile. Not even a little. That relief shifts, turning into more worry, more fear, more Sadness. But I'm used to those feelings. I know what to do with those feelings.

"I thought you were supposed to come over," she says, voice soft.

"We are!" Peach says, then jogs down the steps to meet Lemon, wrapping her little arms around Lemon's waist.

"Hey, Raspberry," Lemon says, ruffling her hair.

"Her name is *Peach*."

I say it sharply. I don't know why. Peach loves her fruit names. Peach loves Lemon. But all that worry, fear, and Sadness is swirling like a hurricane gathering strength, outer bands lashing out.

Lemon frowns, swallows again. "I just came to..." She takes a deep breath. "I don't know. Look, I'm sorry for what Kiko said. It's not how I feel."

"It is," I say. "At least a little, or you would've called or texted me. You would've come over before now, banging on the door like you always do."

The words flow out before I can stop them. My throat goes thick as I say them, some emotion I don't want or need flying right into the hurricane.

"I just...," Lemon starts, but trails off, shaking her head. Then she takes the tote bag off her shoulder and sets it down on the step. I recognize it. It's the one Jules had the other day at Lemon's. Black with a rainbow through the center.

"This is for you," she says, motioning toward it. "From Jules. I mean, from me and Kiko too, but it was Jules's idea."

I eye the bag, a twist in my stomach. "Their surprise?"

She nods.

I take a step closer. Then another. The tote bag is open, dark fabric peeking out. Then I remember what Kiko said, how she's done, how I'm stupid and was never really *with* them.

Maybe she's right.

I'm not.

I don't belong here.

"Look, it doesn't matter," I say, then walk past the bag, past Lemon, taking my sister's hand as I go. "Peach and I are heading into town, okay?"

"Can I . . . can I come with you?"

I turn around to face her. *Yes* almost flies out of my mouth, but I stop it in time. "No," I say, and Lemon goes pale.

"Hazey!" Peach says, pulling on my hand. "I want her to come!"

"We're going to find my mom, okay?" I say. "I need to talk to her."

Lemon frowns. "But your mom is with—"

"Yeah, I know that."

Lemon rubs her eyes. "Hazel, look, I know this is hard for you. I'm sorry I got so excited. It's just that I want my mom to be happy, and your mom is—"

"My mom belongs in California," I say. "And so do we."
Then I walk away, pulling my sister along even though
she keeps looking back.

Peach complains for a few minutes, whining that she wants
Lemon, but I just ignore her. Eventually, she goes quiet
and presses closer to me. I know she's angry with me, but
she still tries to comfort me. She must notice I'm a rattling
sack of bones, my whole body shaking and trembling as
we walk to town. I squeeze her to my side, my arm tight
around her shoulders, which makes it harder to walk, but I
don't care. I need her close. Need her closer than ever.

Rilla's is by the pier, the non-fisherman part of town
that most people call the Village. The Pink Mermaid is
down here too, along with all sorts of novelty shops and
cafés, the one-theater cinema. I walk fast, trying to avoid
looking too hard at the places I've been with Lemon and
Kiko and Jules. Finally we get to Rilla's. It's on the water,
with soft lighting and huge windows facing the sea.

It's been about two hours since Mama and Claire left
for dinner, so I'm not sure if they'll still be in there or will
be out somewhere else. I lead Peach toward the restaurant,
stopping at the front door. There's absolutely no way we
can go in there. We're dressed in jean shorts and T-shirts.
Plus, before I talk to Mama, I want to see Mama and Claire
together without them knowing I'm there. I keep hoping

this all isn't really happening the way I fear it is, that they're just friends, best friends even, but that's all. I want to see what's really there, what Mama really feels, how far Mum is gone from her heart.

If she's even still there at all.

"What are we doing, Hazey?" Peach says. "I'm hungry."

"Yeah, we'll get food soon. We're just...walking around for a second. It's a nice night, right?"

She frowns at me, knows I'm up to something. Still, she lets me take us up the path that leads to the water. There are bushes of sea roses everywhere, little dots of fuchsia growing darker as the sun sinks completely behind us. It's dusk now. Lampposts line the sidewalks and pier, casting amber spheres onto the ground.

There are a lot of people milling around the pedestrian courtyard near where the pier stretches out into the Atlantic. It seems like it's date night for everyone, tons of couples holding hands and laughing or just being quiet and watching the water. Some families are out too, kids swinging on the little playground, picking sea roses and handing them to their mothers.

"Mama!" Peach says, just loud enough that I'm terrified Mama heard her.

"Shh," I say as quietly as I can.

"Why?"

"Just...where? Where's Mama?" I look around, frantic, needing to see her and also terrified she's already seen us.

Peach points to a bench in one of the green spaces in front of the pier. Two women sit there, Mama in her coral dress and Claire in a dark green jumpsuit and gold heels. They sit close, shoulders pressed together. Their backs are to us and they don't seem to have heard Peach's exclamation.

I walk as quietly as I can toward the bench. There's a large rosebush behind them and to the side, and when I reach it, I squat down, pulling my sister down with me. She scowls at me but obeys. The greenery blocks Mama from our view, but I can hear their voices.

"...never been so full," Mama is saying, laughing as she talks. "I'm not sure I'll ever be able to eat lobster again."

"You say that now, but by tomorrow afternoon, you'll be dreaming of that lobster bisque again, trust me," Claire says. "It's a problem. I'm constantly trying to get Rilla to tell me what she puts in there to make it so amazing. I can't figure it out."

"It tasted like magic in a cup."

"So true. I'm woman enough to admit she's a better chef than I am."

"Not possible," Mama says.

They laugh. Sweat breaks out on my forehead, my upper lip, tingling under my arms and back.

They're just talking about food, I tell myself. *Food is fine. Food is normal. Food isn't love.*

"It really is beautiful here," Mama says after a few seconds of silence.

"More beautiful than California?" Claire asks.

I freeze. My heart slams against my ribs so loud I'm sure everyone in town can hear it.

Mama sighs. "Just different."

"Different can be good."

"Well, we've had plenty of that. It's what we needed after Nadine."

After.

"I understand that," Claire says. "How many places have you lived?"

Mama doesn't say anything at first. Then, "Eight, I think."

Claire inhales sharply. "In two years?"

"I know. It sounds...god, am I a terrible mother?"

"What?" Claire says. "No. Evie, no. You do what you have to. I understand that."

"Hazel hates it. She just wants to go home. To...I don't know. Right after Nadine died, she didn't want to talk about any of it. *Couldn't* talk about it. Neither could I. I thought I was doing the right thing, what we both needed. But now I'm not so sure."

"Hazel seems...," Claire says, then sighs. "I don't know, Evie. She's been through a lot, and grief is hard. God knows there were times I felt like I was losing Lemon, too."

What? Mama feels like she's losing me? That's not right. I'm the one who's losing *her.* I glance at Peach. She's got her head down, picking at the grass, but I can tell she's frowning, her little forehead creased.

"How'd you get her back?" Mama asks.

Claire sighs. "I gave her space. Let her talk about Immy, about her dad, whenever she wanted. I actually suggested moving, you know. Somewhere new. But she didn't want to leave Rose Harbor."

Something that feels like hope wells up in my chest.

"We still haven't talked about Nadine," Mama says. "Not once."

"Why not?" Claire asks.

"I...god, it's so hard, Claire. Hazel. She looks...she looks just like her, you know?"

I hear Claire sigh, but she doesn't say anything. I feel like my breath is caught in my lungs. Stuck forever. I do look like Mum. Exactly like her. Is that why...do I... *remind* Mama of Mum too much?

"I feel responsible," Mama says. I shake my head, confusion building. "Hazel lost her *mother*. I love her so much, and I'm just trying to protect her from more pain. Talking about Nadine hurts, and Hazel was *there*, Claire. She's got these scars for the rest of her life and I just thought...she needed a fresh start. She needs to feel like a normal kid, you know?"

"I do."

"But lately, I feel her slipping away more and more.

267

Changing. Like maybe I've handled all of this wrong and she needs something I can't give her."

"You can, though."

"Maybe. I never know what to say to her. Because how can I make this better? *How?*"

"Again, all understandable," Claire says.

"Was it hard?" Mama asks. "Staying here after Imogene?"

Claire doesn't answer at first.

"I'm sorry," Mama says after a few seconds. "We don't have to talk about it. I can't imagine what it must—"

"No, it's okay," Claire says, her voice soft, thick as though she's got tears stuck in her throat. "I want to talk about it with you. I want you to know this part of me."

"I want you to know this part of me, too," Mama says softly.

My nose starts to sting, tears building. *I* don't even know this part of Mama. I feel like a stranger is sitting with Claire on that bench, some woman who lost her wife, a woman I don't know.

"It was hard," Claire says. "It still is. Like I said, I wanted to leave too for a while. But in the end, for Lemon and me, this is where Immy was born. This is where she lived and where we loved her."

Mama doesn't say anything. The bush blocks them from our view, so I can't see what they're doing, but it doesn't matter.

Relief swells in my chest.

Yes, yes, yes, beats my heart.

Because Claire said it. The perfect words. What I've been trying to get Mama to see for two years. Home. California. Berkeley. That's where Mum lived and where we loved her. That's where we need to be. Surely if *Claire* says it, Mama will finally get it. She'll finally take us home.

"Evie," Claire says. "I'm sorry, I didn't mean—"

"I'm okay, I'm okay," Mama says. A laugh edges her words, but her voice is thick and I realize she's crying.

"It's okay to start fresh, too," Claire says. "There's no right way to handle grief, Evie. If there's anything I've learned, it's that it's deeply personal. Loss is almost like... like... the closest relationship you have. The most intimate. It knows all your secrets, all your weaknesses."

"God, that makes so much sense," Mama says. She sniffs and I want to run out and hug her, tell her it's time, it's time, it's time to go home.

"And it's a little different when you lose a child," Claire says, and I can definitely tell she's crying now. Softly, but still. "I just want to preserve all I can. Keep it safe for Lemon. For her memories of Immy."

"I can't imagine," Mama says. "Claire, I'm so sorry."

"I'm sorry too."

A beat passes, sniffs and rustling, like maybe they're hugging. I don't dare look.

Finally, Mama says, "I've thought about going home

so many times. Part of me wants to. Hazel wants to. I think she believes life will be just like it was. She doesn't understand..."

"I know," Claire says. "It'll be different, no matter what."

"It's not just that," Mama says, her voice growing thicker and thicker, more tears. "I haven't told her..."

"Told her what?" Another beat. "Told her what, Evie?"

Mama takes a deep, shaking breath. "When we left California, I promised her we'd go back at some point. That we just needed some time to get used to things. But she doesn't know... she doesn't know I sold the house."

It's quiet for a second. A lifetime. An eternity.

Mama's words sink in like a leaf in quicksand. Slowly, then all at once.

"Oh, Evie. She thinks you're going back to the house?" Claire says.

Breathe. I need to breathe.

"I think so. She loves that house. So do I, but I couldn't... I can't do it without Nadine. It was Nadine's and my first place together. We got *married* in the backyard, and it just... it's filled with..."

"Ghosts."

"Yes. I couldn't breathe there. Couldn't be a mother... maybe I made the wrong choice. I don't know."

"You need to tell her."

"I know. I know, I will."

My house—39 Camelia Street. Gone? No. Someone else's? No. It's not possible. It's mine. It's Mum's. It's *ours*.

Peach's little hand grabs on to mine. She looks at me, her eyes wide. She can see I'm losing it. She squeezes my fingers, likes she's trying to keep me on the ground, keep me from floating away, but I feel like I'm already gone. Lost. Under the ocean and out of control.

But Mama doesn't know. She's right there, feet away, and she doesn't know. Her date keeps going, Claire keeps talking. There's a rustling sound, like clothes shifting, like they're moving closer. Or maybe farther away. I pull my hand from Peach's and press my palms to the grass and start crawling.

"Hazey," Peach whispers, but I ignore her, peering around the rosebush until I can see Mama.

They've definitely moved closer. They're both sitting on the bench so that they're facing each other. Claire has Mama's hand in hers. As I watch, Mama tips her head closer...closer...until her forehead touches Claire's.

"I'm glad you're here, though," Claire says. "Is that bad to say?"

Mama shakes her head. I see a tear slip down her cheek. "No. It's not bad. I'm glad I'm here too."

My throat goes tight. How can she be glad and crying at the same time? How can she say she's glad to be here, when the whole reason we're here is because Mum is gone? A scream starts to unfurl in my chest, like a ball of yarn coming unraveled.

"I don't want you to leave at the end of the summer," Claire says. "Is *that* bad to say?"

Mama laughs, forehead still against Claire's. "No. I . . . I don't think I want to leave either."

What? No.

"Then don't," Claire says, lifting her head from Mama's. They stare at each other. "Evie, don't leave. Stay here."

Mama opens her mouth to say something, but nothing comes out.

"Stay with me," Claire says. "I know you need to put your kids first and you have a lot to work through. So do I. We can go as slow as you want. But let's see what this is. Because it *is* something, right? I'm not imagining it?"

My heart thumps so loudly I'm sure it's about to crash through my ribs, through all my blood vessels and skin at any moment, spilling onto the grass in a bloody mess. I wait . . . wait . . . wait . . . for Mama to tell Claire she *is* imagining it. That Mama can never stay with Claire. That she promised me we'd go home. She promised Mum to love her forever and ever.

It crashes through my heart again, anew—Mum's gone. Our *home* is gone.

So of course Mama doesn't say any of that. She doesn't

say anything at all. Instead she leans forward and kisses Claire.

She *kisses* her.

Right here, right now, right in front of me, my mom kisses Claire Calloway. She kisses a woman not my mum. She kisses her and Claire kisses her back and then they pull away and smile at each other and sort of laugh and Claire says "Is that a yes?" and then Mama just kisses her again, not saying anything, just kissing and kissing and kissing like she's in one of her romance novels. Except this isn't a novel, it's not a fairy tale, and I feel Mama floating away from me, leaving me alone, going away with Claire to some happy place I can never follow because the Sadness, the Sadness is too heavy, it's too thick and it's got my heart in its claws, squeezing it and squeezing it until it's not my heart anymore, until it's not even *me* anymore.

It's Sadness itself.

"Stop," I say, but my voice is quiet. No one hears me. Mama touches Claire's face, keeps on kissing her.

"Hazey?" Peach says behind me.

"Stop," I say, louder this time. The waves crash in front of us, bashing against the rocks and swallowing my voice.

"Hazey!" Peach says. I feel her tug on the back of my shirt.

"Stop," I say, louder. I'm on my feet now. I'm moving. "Stop, stop, stop!"

I yell it.

Mama hears me this time. She pulls away from Claire and blinks up at me, her mouth hanging open.

"Hazel, what in the world—"

"Stop!" I say. "Just stop. Stop doing this. Stop kissing her and stop talking about staying here." My fingers curl into fists, so tight I feel my nails bite into my palms. Peach runs out from behind the bush and latches on to Mama, crawling into her lap.

"Sweetheart," Mama says. "Let's just calm—"

"Tell me it's not true," I say. "Tell me you didn't sell our house. Our *home*."

She sucks in a breath. "Hazel, let's—"

"No, no, I'm not calming down. We're going home. You promised me and you promised Mum and I'm . . . you can't . . . you can't leave me . . . you can't—"

"Hazel," Mama says. She's standing now, Peach holding on to her skirt. Mama's hands are on my arms. She's close, her brown eyes right in front of my blue ones. "Stop. Take a breath. We need to talk about this calmly—"

I shake my head. See Claire stand up and cover her mouth with her hands. Everyone's staring at me, frowns curling their mouths downward and shoving their eyebrows together, but I don't care. If I can get Mama to see, to promise, that's all that matters.

"Let's go home," I say. "Now, please. We can get our house back, right? We don't have to wait until the summer's over, we can go now, go back where we belong, where Mum lived and where we loved her."

I hear Claire inhale sharply, but I don't look at her. She doesn't matter, nothing matters except Mama and me and Peach and Mum.

"We don't need them," I say. "We don't need a new family. I don't need another mom and you don't need another wife and I don't need another sister. We don't need them! Please." I pound the space over my heart as I talk. "See *me*. Love *me*. Tell *me* you miss Mum and you're worried about me and you feel like you're losing me."

My throat feels raw and I realize I'm yelling. My chest goes tight, something that feels cold and heavy settling in my stomach.

"Hazel," Mama says softly. She touches my scarred cheek. "Stop it."

I shake my head, but Mama takes my face between both her hands.

"Say her name," I say.

"What?"

"Mum. Say it. *Mum*. To me, not to Claire. Talk to *me*!"

My throat is raw. I'm screaming, people we don't even know are looking.

"Hazel, it's okay to move on," Mama says. "I know it's scary, but it's all right. It's what Mum would've wanted, honey."

There. She said it. Mum. But she didn't say it the way

I wanted her to. She's still telling me to forget. She's still telling me I'm like this for no reason, that I should be over it, I should be fine. Moving on means forgetting. Moving on means she's really gone and I really am all alone.

"We're still here, sweetheart," Mama says. "*You* are still here."

I blink at her. At Peach and Claire. They all look at me like I'm a stranger, like I've changed into some terrifying marvel they don't understand. Suddenly, they all feel a million miles away. And Mama's right, I'm still here. I keep trying to pull them back with me, back to Berkeley, back into safety so they'll never leave me, back into the life we had with Mum, but they don't want it. They don't want me.

They've already moved on.

I pull away from Mama. Her hands float out in front of her. I think she says my name. I think she screams it when I move even farther away, when I start to run, but I don't stop. I keep going, my feet pounding the pavement, running and running and running...

chapter twenty-seven

I don't stop until I get there. I hadn't even realized I was headed this way, but when I see the little dock stretching out into the water, the boat bobbing in the sea, I know this is where I was going all along.

I stop on the beach, staring over at Lemon's house. She's nowhere to be seen, the blinds on the back windows shut tight.

Behind me, the ocean roars, the waves churned up by a windy night. I wait as long as I can, but it's pulling me, calling me.

Home.

Finally, I turn to face it. I walk down the dock, right to the very edge. The boat is there, like it's been waiting for me. I stare at it for a long time. The Sadness is here, holding my hand just like always, but something else is there too.

Longing.

You were meant for this.

The sea is in her soul now.

The water curls and rolls, creating a space for me. This is where I was last happy. Where I last felt like me. Maybe I am like Rosemary, the Sadness has changed me so much that I don't belong anywhere else now. The sea is my soul, my soul is the sea. My home.

I brace my hands on the boat's edges and hop inside. The ocean tosses the little skiff like it's a plastic toy. I tip sideways, my shoulder slamming into the side, but I barely feel it. Instead, it just feels right. I'm where I belong, the only place that makes sense.

The wild, senseless sea.

I untie the boat, then grab the oars. The waves seem to help me along, carrying me farther and farther from the dock. And the farther and farther I get, the easier I breathe. Out here, completely alone, nothing but dark blue underneath me and dark sky above. How did I avoid this for so long? Rosemary knew the answer. She knew she belonged to the sea, after losing her whole family to the wind and waves. She knew this was the only place she'd ever feel like herself.

One day it will claim her completely.

I'm far enough out now that the waves have calmed. I

stop rowing and look around, dark blue everywhere, not another soul in sight. I can't even see the shore anymore. I can't see Lemon's house anymore. Can't spot Sea Rose Cottage. There's nothing, nothing, nothing, but me and the deep blue sea.

The tears start without my permission, but I don't fight them. They pour like rain, bumping over my scarred cheek. Here, I'm not holding anyone back. Here, I'm not spouting mean words to my friends. Here, I'm not confused, I'm not worried, I'm not nervous.

But I'm alone. Really, truly alone.

Out here, I'll always be alone.

The thought settles inside me. It opens up, but not like *space*. Not like *freedom*.

Like *hollowness*.

Rosemary's out here all alone. No friends, no crushes, no one to tell secrets to, no one to paint sparkly teal makeup over her eyelids and cheeks. No one to eat frozen yogurt with. No one to laugh with. No one to cry with, to feel the Sadness with.

My mind reaches out for something to fill the *hollowness*, something, anything, and it latches on to the Solstice Fire, Lemon and me on the beach, her hand in mine, our Sadness tangled together and me feeling...me feeling...

Right.

Safe.

Understood.

Home.

I shake my head, because no. Mum is home. California is home. Thirty-nine Camelia Street is home. And if it's gone, then...then...

Maybe I am too.

I lean over the edge of the boat, stretching an arm out toward the water. My parents' rings glint on my finger. My moonlit reflection appears, my face. I know it's me, the girl below moving as I move, frowning as I frown, wiping tears away as I do the same.

I reach farther, dipping my fingers into the sea.

I wish I was a mermaid.

I stretch even farther, the frigid water gulping at my arm up to my elbow now. My face gets closer and closer to the sea, waves bobbing me closer still. Just a little more and I'll find her. The water reaches my shoulder...neck...

And then the ocean swallows me whole.

chapter twenty-eight

C old.

That's all I feel at first.

Heart-freezing, brain-blurring cold.

Shock fills my whole body. It takes all my concentration not to open my mouth and gasp water into my lungs. I press my lips together, squeeze my eyes shut as I drift down...down...down...

Finally, the cold settles around my heart like a blanket, and my body wakes back up, moves around a little to get used to its new surroundings.

I open my eyes.

Deep blue all around.

Quiet.

Calm.

Alone.

For a second, all I feel is relief. I'm here. I'm in the sea, right where I belong, and I don't feel any fear. I don't feel any worry. I just feel right. Like coming home after a long time away. I wave my arms through the water, spin my body like a ballerina. I look down, waiting for my legs to meld together, beautiful iridescent flukes unfurling where my feet used to be, waiting to change so when I go back up to the surface, I'll fit. I'll know what to do, how to be.

None of that happens, though, and for a split second, I'm surprised. Something like disappointment settles into my chest. I swish my legs around, as though I could coax them into some magical metamorphosis. I've already changed. I'm already barely *me*. So why not this? Even while my brain knows it's impossible, I still want it to happen. I want my body to match my heart, to change and shift and mold into something untouchable, something that could never lose everything again.

But nothing happens. My heart beats in my chest, alone and altered while the rest of me stays the same. I go to take a deep breath, to think of what to do next, how to get rid of this cold, immovable heart, but I can't. I've still got lungs. Legs. I don't fit here, either.

I squeeze my eyes shut, twist my body again, trying to make it work in its new home.

Home, I think as hard as I can. *Home, home, home.*

But then something happens.

Pictures bloom in my head. Not of the sea or 39 Camelia Street, but Lemon's tear-streaked face on her birthday, her hand in mine as we gazed out at the sea and talked about mermaids.

Faces—new faces I didn't even know three months ago, Kiko and Lemon and Jules—breaking into smiles and then laughter on a museum's back porch, chasing ghosts who ended up being friends.

Peach running toward the sea, kicking her feet in the waves and shrieking from the wonder of it, the hugeness of the ocean, loving with her whole heart all the time no matter what.

Mama.

My mama.

Smiling at her phone. Typing up a new story. Slow-dancing with Mum. Resting her forehead against Claire's. Crying on the couch back in California after Mum's funeral when she thought I was asleep, hiding all her memories in a trunk, sipping her morning tea on the porch wrapped in the Sister Quilt, watching the Atlantic roll over the earth.

Jules smiling at me, talking about sadness and change while staring at a creepy toothbrush.

Sparkly eyeshadow swept over my eyelids.

Blanket forts filled with stars.

Lemon's huge, squashy couch.

Mermaid cakes and mermaid T-shirts and mermaids who look just like me.

Mum's paintings. Mama's books. Peach's little bracelets. *Home.*

My eyes fly open, deep blue everywhere. Just the ocean. Power and mystery. Beauty and fear and serenity and violence, but the sea nonetheless. Not love, not a person or a family or a friend.

I twist around, looking up and down for light, but it's all dark blue. Nothing but dark blue melting into darker and deeper blue above and below. I can't find the surface, the waves, have no idea which way I'm facing. My lungs feel like they're shrinking. I flail, swimming one way, then another, but I have no idea which way to go.

It's too late.

I'm lost.

I'm alone.

Panic begins filling me up, darkening my vision. I need to scream, to cry, tell Mama I'm sorry. I open my mouth, to tell the ocean instead, but then I see a flicker of color.

A flash, that's all it is, but it's bright in all this navy. It's enough to shock me into calm, into watching and waiting. The color grows and grows, swirls of silver white in the dark. It gets closer, swimming toward me, and I realize that all that silver white is hair.

A girl's hair.

No. Not a girl.

Something else.

She swims toward me, her face like mine, slender body covered in a tattered blue dress. Lace at her throat. Her tail flicks out behind her, two beautiful flukes pushing at the sea to get to me.

And then she's there. Right in front of me. We stare at each other, blue eyes for blue eyes, pale hair for pale hair.

I'm not like you.

She reaches out a hand and places it on my scarred cheek, shakes her head as though she heard me even though I know the words were only in my mind. She frames my face with both of her hands. Her palms are cold as she touches our foreheads together.

If you find her, beware.
If you find her, be keen.
She'll sing you into madness
or grant you one dream.

Terror fills my heart and I shake my head. I just want air. I want Mama, Lemon, Peach. I thrash, trying to escape her, but she braces her hands around my arms, holding on tight, shaking her head and frowning. Something slips from my finger—Mama's and Mum's wedding rings, escaping into the deep.

No!

I scream it, reach for the rings, but the ocean swallows my voice, the cold freezes my body.

She squeezes my arms and then...she leans forward and kisses my scarred cheek. When she pulls back, I see the faintest trace of a smile on her mouth, but then the ocean is moving. Soaring and swirling around me, dark blue shifting into lighter. Her hands grip my arms, pulling and pushing, and I realize it's not the sea that's moving.

It's me.

Light flashes above me. Red and blue circling around a dark shape. My body breaks the surface. I feel arms around me. Stronger than Rosemary's. Deep voices shout words I can't make out. A boat bobs in the water. Not mine, but a ship, huge and haunting. I'm hauled out of the sea, blankets piled around me as a clear mask is strapped to my face. Air flows, clear and clean and real.

A woman in a beautiful dress and dark, curly hair breaks through all the unfamiliar faces. Mama. My mama. I try to call out to her, try to tell her I'm back. I'm here.

I'm here.

I'm here.

I'm here.

But my voice is gone, swallowed up by lungs desperate for more, more, more air.

"Hazel," she says. Just that. My name. The one she and Mum gave me, only me. For the first time in two years, she pulls me into her arms. For the first time in two years, she buries her face in my hair, hugs me tight with all her strength. For the first time in two years, I wrap my whole self around her, cry into her neck like a little girl, like a daughter who needs her mom. For the first time in two years, right here in the middle of the sea, I'm finally home again.

chapter twenty-nine

The paramedics on the coast guard ship say that I have mild hypothermia, so they take us to the hospital in Portland, where we have to stay overnight. As we ride in the ambulance, the plastic mask still over my face, I wait for my breathing to shorten, to go hot and then cold, for my whole body to feel like one giant heartbeat.

The panic does come—I remember the ambulance after Mum's accident, the sadness on everyone's faces as they treated me, the constant reassurances that I was okay when I knew I wasn't, I knew nothing would ever be okay again.

But it's all different this time. Mama's with me. She's right next to me and she's telling me I'm going to be okay and I think I believe her. She keeps looking me right in the eye, keeps holding my hand. She keeps and keeps and keeps.

Once we're in my hospital room, the smells are familiar, the scratchy sheets and blankets they pile on top of me, the nurses' uniforms. Again, it's all the same, except for Mama. When Mum died and I was hurt, Mama was at the hospital with me, but she kept having to leave to deal with stuff about Mum and even when she was in the room, she was a zombie, barely there, blank stare or silent crying. I remember wanting to talk to her, tell her I was sorry, ask if it was all real, or just have her hold me in my hospital bed.

She never did.

But now, it's not like that.

She's clear-eyed and calm. She helps me change into a gown, keeps hold of my hand while a nurse in green scrubs with tiny dancing wedges of cheese all over them takes my vitals. Mama keeps talking to me, telling me Peach is with Claire and she knows I'm okay, telling me she'll stay with me all night, telling me it's all going to be okay now.

She keeps.

And keeps.

And keeps.

And my heart is a little fast. My lungs are a little strained. But I keep too. I keep calm, keep breathing, one breath after another, and soon, they actually feel like deep breaths.

"How did you find me?" I ask once the nurses finally leave us alone. Mama crawls into the narrow bed with me, wraps her arm over the four fleece blankets they've piled on top of me to keep me warm.

"Lemon," Mama says. "After you ran away, you were so upset, I knew you needed some space, but then Lemon called her mom, told her she'd seen you on their dock getting into the boat. She saw you rowing out to sea."

"Did she...?"

...*say anything else about me?* I want to ask, but I swallow the words. Surely Lemon hates me good and proper by now.

"She was worried about you," Mama says, squeezing me tighter. "Claire will tell her you're okay."

I nod, but I'm not sure Lemon will care at this point.

"I was worried about you too," Mama says, touching my scars. "Oh, baby, I'm so sorry."

I turn to look at her. Her eyes are dark, wide, shiny with tears. My throat goes tight as I think about everything I heard her and Claire talk about, everything I saw.

"Did you really sell our house?" I ask quietly.

She winces but then nods.

I suck in a breath, the news hitting me again, the Sadness settling over me. "Why?"

"I just..." She sighs, hugs me tighter. "It's hard to explain. But...your mum and I bought that house before you were born. We bought it to live in together, raise our family together. And after she..."

She swallows, takes a breath. We've never talked about this before. Never. And even though the Sadness is right there, snuggling with us like a third family member, I don't want her to stop talking. I don't want Mama to change the subject or even make me laugh or ignore the Sadness like she's been doing for two years.

I want this.

Sharing the Sadness. Mum's name, her *life*, right here with us.

"After she died," Mama goes on, "all that togetherness left with her. I still had you and Peach, yes, but I didn't know how to be in that house without her. I didn't know how to do the life we had without her. Not then. Maybe if we'd stayed, if I hadn't made that choice so quickly, it would've gotten better. But back then, leaving was what I needed to do to keep going, to keep *us* going, and I knew your mum would understand that."

I frown, letting those words sink in. For the past two years, I kept waiting for Mama to deal with losing Mum just like I was—trying to keep everything the way it was as much as I could, wanting everything familiar, wanting everything safe and planned, even boring.

But Mama needed change. She needed different.

Maybe she even needed forgetting.

Still, I can't believe she really wants to forget. She can't. Mum's... *Mum*. Mama's true love. Peach's and my mom. She's... everything. But then I remember how happy Mama's been lately, remember her kissing Claire, remember her saying she wanted to stay in Rose Harbor.

It feels like forgetting, hollow and lonely, and tears creep into my eyes.

Mama frowns at me. "Baby?"

"Do... do you love Claire more... than you love... Mum?"

I'm full-on crying now, words choppy as the idea of Mama and Claire taking the place of Mama and Mum reaches right into my lungs and squeezes.

"What?" Mama says, her voice breathy. "No. Honey, *no*."

The machine monitoring my heart beeps a little faster, my pulse speeding up as the words spill out. "But... you kissed her and you... took off your wedding ring and I... I know you're writing about her. Your book is about starting over, it's about *love* and I deleted it and I'm—"

"Hazel." Mama takes my face in her hands. "Hazel, honey. Shh. It's okay. Breathe."

And I do. Mama leans her forehead against mine, warm skin on cold.

"Shh," she says again, until I quiet down.

Then she just lies there for a second in silence, smoothing my hair behind my ear. I wait, not sure if I even want her answer anymore. But eventually, she gives it to me anyway. She backs up so she can look me right in the eye.

"Hazel, listen very carefully, okay? I need you to hear me."

I manage to nod.

She takes a deep breath. "No one—and I mean *no one*—will ever replace your mum. Not in my heart, not in yours, not in our lives, or our memories."

More tears spill over. "But...but you never talk about her. You never even say her name. And Claire makes you so happy. It was like you just..."

"Forgot Mum?"

"Yeah."

"Oh, honey." More tears spill over her cheeks. She doesn't wipe them away, and I'm relieved. Her tears loosen up my tongue, my icy heart, all the thoughts and feelings I've balled up into a tight little knot and tucked away in the corners of my mind for the past two years.

"And then it was like she never even existed," I say. "And all this"—I get a hand free and point to my face, pat my heart—"everything about me and what happened and all these things I feel now were just...my fault. I couldn't stop worrying all the time, being scared all the time, and that was just...who I was."

Mama frowns. "Tell me more about that. Worrying and being scared."

So I do. I tell her all about why my Safety Pack feels

like it's keeping me from floating away sometimes, how I can't handle Peach being in danger, how I'm always waiting for something bad to happen, worrying that I won't be able to keep everyone safe.

"Just like I couldn't keep Mum safe."

Mama sucks in a breath. "Sweetie. No. Do you... Hazel, what happened to Mum was *not* your fault."

"But I was there," I say through my tears. "I was there, just me, and I couldn't—"

"No. Baby, *no*." She sighs. "My god, Hazel, I had no idea you felt like this." She takes my face in her hands. "Baby girl, sometimes, things just happen. It's not fate and it's not fault, it just is. What happened to Mum was horrible and tragic and goodness knows I've thought a million times what I could've done to prevent it."

"You... you have?"

"Of course. I've thought if I'd just insisted you two stay home, or suggested a different day, or if I'd been sick that day, or Peach or you, and asked Mum to stay home to take care of us, or if it'd been raining or freezing cold. A million little things I wish had fallen into place to prevent it."

I breathe out, breathe easier.

"But they didn't, baby," Mama says. "And you couldn't have done anything to stop what happened."

I nod, not sure if I believe her yet, but right now, in this moment, just hearing her say it all feels... different. Feels better.

Mama takes my hand and presses it to her heart. "Hazel, honey, none of the things you've been feeling are your fault. This is *my* fault. I thought I was doing the right thing by tucking all of it away. I thought that was what you needed. What I needed. And maybe, also, I just didn't know what to do with you after Mum died."

Hurt laces through me, thin and sharp. Mama must see something change on my face, because she hurries to keep talking.

"No, not like you were too much to handle," she says. "Not like that. But you'd been through so much, so much trauma, being there when it all happened. I didn't know the right way to handle it, and locking it all up seemed best. That's what I *thought* I was doing, at least. But maybe... oh, honey, it hurt to talk about her. Especially at first, and then it became a habit and even when I wanted to talk about her—because I did, Hazel, I did want to talk about her with you, remember her with you and Peach—I didn't want to upset you or bring up memories of the accident. So I stayed quiet. And now I see it was the wrong thing. I let you think things I would never want you to believe, and I'm sorry."

I cling to her, my mother, cry on her shoulder. She lets me and it feels so good. It feels right. It feels hard and achy, too, the Sadness hovering right around us, but maybe that's how it should be right now.

"Tell me about Lemon," Mama says after a while.

"What about her?" I sniff, wipe my eyes.

"Well, I know you two had a fight the other day. Is everything okay?"

I don't say anything for a while. I don't know how to explain it, how much Lemon scares me—Kiko and Jules, too. But how much I think I want them all in my life and what that means about Mum. How can I make friends, be a friend, when Mum can't do anything? How can I lose them all again when we leave Rose Harbor? So I tell Mama the truth. "I don't know."

Mama sighs and leans her head against mine. "You know what I think? What I *know*?"

"What?"

"I *know* Mum would want you to be happy. She would want you to laugh and make friends and not be so scared all the time. You survived a terrible accident, honey. You *lived* and Mum would want you to *live*. And living, letting love in, letting yourself be happy, also means hurting sometimes. That's the risk we all take."

I let out a long breath and lean my head on Mama's shoulder. My head feels full. My heart, too. For the first time in two years, it feels really and truly *full*, no hollowness anywhere inside me. And some of the stuff I'm filled with is hard, it hurts. But a lot of it is good, too. A lot of it is love and relief and comfort. Maybe nothing is all one thing or the other—safety or danger, love or hate, friend or friendless, happy or sad. Maybe we're all a mix of everything. Maybe we're all a mess, a glorious, scared, happy, safe, loved, sad, worried mess.

And maybe...that's okay.

Maybe it's better than okay.

Maybe it's beautiful.

"Hazel?" she asks when we've been lying there for a while, the lights dim, our breathing nice and even and slow.

"Yeah?"

"Did you say you deleted my book?"

I freeze up. "I...um..."

She squeezes me tighter. "It's okay. Just tell me the truth. No secrets between us anymore, okay?"

"Okay. Um, yeah, I figured out your password and I read the synopsis and I just...it made me..."

"Sad. Scared?"

I nod.

She leans her head against mine. "It made me sad and scared too. But I think maybe that's why I started writing it, writing about loss and grief and sadness. About finding life and happiness even while you feel all those other things. I needed to write that story to believe I could be and feel all those feelings too. Does that make sense?"

I nod, shame pulling tight at my chest. "I'm so sorry, Mama."

Mama wipes tears away. She's hurt. I can tell. I hurt her, taking all her hard work, all her...I don't know...her *heart*, and just throwing it away.

"I bet it was really good," I say. "Lemon probably would've loved it."

A laugh bursts through Mama's tears. "Lemon?"

"Oh, she's a fan. Major."

Mama smiles, then kisses the top of my head. "Well, lucky for Lemon I've got a copy saved in the cloud."

Relief loosens my shoulders. "You...you do?"

She nods, but then her face grows serious. "Hazel, please don't violate my privacy again, okay? We have to trust each other."

She says it kindly, with her forehead pressed against mine, but tears still spring to my eyes. But then again, I guess they should. I deleted her book. Or at least, I tried to. Her work. It's not okay. But after I nod and Mama wraps me up in her arms, she doesn't bring up my horrible act again. She keeps loving me anyway. Maybe that's what real love is. Real family. Real friendship.

Loving anyway.

chapter thirty

The next day, after they release me from the hospital and we go back to Sea Rose Cottage, Lemon and Peach are waiting for us on the porch steps.

I freeze when I see Lemon. I'm dressed in gray hospital-issued sweat pants and a black T-shirt, my sea-salted clothes from the day before in a plastic bag in my arms. Her wild red hair blows in the wind and she's wearing the same T-shirt she was wearing on the day we first met—THE ROSE MAID LIVES.

Something desperate rises up in me.

I just want to tell her.

I want to tell her everything.

I want to tell her that I saw Rosemary, even if I really didn't and it was just my brain trying to survive the cold

Atlantic. I want to believe it, for Lemon, for me, for that need we both have for something *big* in our lives. Something that means there's more than just us, more than the Sadness.

I want to tell her I'm sorry.

I want to tell her—to *ask* her—to be my friend.

"Hazey!" Peach says, and launches herself into my arms. I pick her up, holding her close, breathing in her Penelope Bly smell, clean clothes and that blueberry hair gel Mama uses to tame her curls, that unidentifiable scent that's one hundred percent my sister. My strong, brave little sister.

"Hey, Fuzz," I say, squeezing her tight. She burrows into me, like she never wants to let me go. Mama wraps her arms around both of us and the three of us stay like that, hugging, a family of three, for the first time...

...maybe ever.

We've *never* held each other like this, all of us wrapped up together without Mum. I feel tears tighten my throat, the Sadness that she's gone forever rising up. But there's something else there too.

Space.

Space for something new. A new way to be a family. A way to *live* together. Like Mama said, I survived a terrible accident, but I haven't been living like it. I've been living like I'm trapped under the sea, no home, no family. With Mama and Peach with me, I know none of that's true.

They are my home.

"Hey, Lemon," Mama says, her voice thick as she pulls back from us but keeps her arm around me.

"Hi," Lemon says, taking a step closer from where she's gone over to the railing, giving our little family of three some space. "Um, my mom's inside, cleaning. Hope it's okay we're here. Peach wanted to be here when you got home."

"Of course," Mama says, then tilts her head. "She's cleaning?"

Lemon shrugs. "There are also three casseroles in the fridge and I think she might have hand-washed all your sweaters."

Mama laughs, shakes her head, but then her smile dips, replaced by a crease between her eyes. "Lord, she didn't need to do all that. I'll just go check on her, then."

I feel a momentary wave of panic. I haven't been away from Mama since I came out of the sea—literally not an inch away except for when one of us needed the bathroom and when Mama called Claire this morning to check on Peach and stepped outside the room for about fifteen minutes.

But then she kisses me on the top of my head and says, "It's okay, honey," really quietly. "We're gonna be okay." Then the wave recedes, slow and steady. It's not gone. I'm not sure if it will ever be totally gone.

This morning, Mama and I talked for a long time over my rubbery hospital eggs about going to see someone again about my anxiety. A therapist. Even though I saw someone by myself for a couple of sessions right after Mum died, before we left California, it wasn't enough. Because then we left and we've been on the road ever since, moving from place to place, pretending that the quiet between Mama and me meant *okay*. So this time, Mama said, we'd see someone as a whole family as well as Mama and me each seeing someone alone.

"I think we just need a little help navigating our feelings and everything you've been through," Mama said. "What we've all been through."

"I think we need a little help too," I said, and I meant it. I did need help with all my worrying and fear. I needed help with *living*. And when Mama said it was okay for us to need help, for us to not know how to do it all on our own, I believed her.

"Hi," Lemon says to me after Mama disappears inside. She's got that tote bag with her again. Jules's tote bag. "How . . . how are you feeling?"

Suddenly, I'm nervous. Flutters erupt in my stomach, like a thousand birds taking flight. Peach slides to the ground but keeps hold of my hand. "I'm okay."

Lemon nods. "Good. That's good."

I take a step closer, that desperate feeling growing stronger, cutting right through all the wings in my gut. "Lemon, I'm sor—"

But I don't even get to finish my apology, because

Lemon gulps me into her arms. She holds me so tight I feel my bones crack, my lungs squeezing out all their air. At first I lock up—I'm not exactly used to all this hugging, especially with someone who's not a tiny curly-haired five-year-old—but then I melt. That's what it feels like. Melting. Thawing. All my meanness, fear, impatience, contempt. All the stuff that kept me so far away from accepting Lemon, from accepting *me*, from accepting friendship. It just...melts.

Because Lemon Calloway, she sees me. The real me, the way I am right now, Hazel Foster Bly.

And she loves me anyway.

"I was so scared," she says when we finally let go of each other. "When I saw you row out into the ocean." She slaps my arm.

"Ow."

"What were you thinking?"

"I don't know. I was...thinking about Rosemary."

She narrows her eyes at me, and then that Cheshire Cat smile—the one that means Lemon is up to absolutely no good—spreads slowly across her face.

"Oh no," I say. "You're not gonna make me eat fish eggs, are you?"

She laughs. "Maybe someday."

Someday. The word jolts through me, surprising and

strange. In eight towns, there's never been a *someday*. Mama and I didn't talk about what's going to happen in August, after our lease runs out. There's no home to go to anymore in California. But there's our town, my old school, our old neighborhood. Mrs. Dalloway's bookshop and hiking to Point Reyes.

There's a lot of Mum there.

But . . . Mum's *here*, too. She's wherever I am. Wherever Mama is, wherever Peach is. For the first time in two years, *someday* fits somewhere else besides Berkeley.

"But first," Lemon says, "mermaids."

"Mermaids?" I ask.

"Mermaids!" Peach says, jumping up and down.

Lemon pats the tote bag swinging from her shoulder. "Mermaids."

Once our feet hit the sand at the bottom of the steps, Lemon takes off toward her house, red hair flapping like a flag. Peach leaps alongside her while I struggle to keep up. Running in dry sand is a lot harder than you'd think.

"Come on!" Lemon yells behind her.

"Why are we running?" I yell back.

She spins and runs backward. "Because we can—now move it!"

I roll my eyes at her, but I keep on running.

Because she's right.

I can.

The sea wind zings through my hair, leaving salt on my cheeks and lips. The ocean rushes by on my right, huge and blue gray and beautiful. I slow down just enough to watch the waves roll in and roll back out. I still feel a blip of fear looking at all that power, but it's the good kind. The awestruck kind. I feel my mouth smile and keep smiling, taking in this vast world that I used to love so much.

That I *do* love so much.

When we reach Lemon's house, she and Peach both run up her porch steps, fly inside, and disappear into the back hallway before I even get through the door.

"Hey, wait up!" I call, but they don't. I slide the door closed, take in Lemon's now-familiar living room. The photos, the couch, the art on the walls, the messy kitchen counter. I feel a pang of sadness.

My house is gone.

But maybe Mama's right. Maybe it was gone already, without Mum. I close my eyes, try to imagine a different house as our home, filled with Mum's paintings, photographs of Mum and Mama and of Peach and me growing up, our mess, our lives. The ocean just outside our windows. Fuchsia sea roses blooming among bright green leaves by the dunes.

My eyes flip open.

Home.

But before I can process what I just pictured—what I

think I *want*—I hear Lemon's loud whisper from her bedroom. "She's here, she's here! Quick. No, not that color, the teal!"

"Lemon?" I call.

"Back here!" she calls, then there's lot of laughter, hushing, whispered *Hurry up*s. Familiar voices I never thought I'd hear again.

I walk to Lemon's bedroom, heart fluttering like a tiny baby bird trying to take its first flight. I lift my hand to knock, but before my fist touches the wood, the door flies open and there are Jules, Kiko, Lemon, and Peach, all covered in mermaid makeup—Lemon's and Peach's clearly rushed and smeared—all of them laughing and grinning and hanging on to each other.

"What in the world?" I ask.

"Mermaids! Mermaids!" Peach says, jumping up and down.

"I hereby call the first official meeting of the new and improved MerSquad to order," Lemon says, her hands on her hips. She and Kiko and Jules are wearing the same navy THE ROSE MAID LIVES tee.

"MerSquad, huh?" I ask.

Jules grins. "Well, that's what everyone calls us anyway."

"That's what they call *you*," I say, folding my arms over my chest, but I'm smiling. Jules smiles back, this small, slow spread of their mouth that's sort of crooked and one hundred percent cute. I feel myself redden and their cheeks go red too and I can't stop from smiling even bigger.

"Oh my god, make out already," Kiko says.

"What?" both Jules and I splutter, but then our eyes meet and we turn red all over again.

"Oh, someday, they totally will," Lemon says.

"Lemon!" Jules says, smacking her arm.

"What's a make-out?" Peach asks, and the four of us bust up laughing.

"Never mind, Fuzz," I say, still smiling and blushing, half mortified and half excited. It's not a terrible feeling.

"Okay, first things first," Lemon says, pulling me into the room. Her curtains are closed, the only light coming from one lamp by her bed and the fairy lights swirling around the blanket fort. Everything feels warm and soft and I let Lemon lead me into the fort, where we all sit cross-legged, facing each other. Peach crawls into Kiko's lap and Kiko snuggles her close, which is when I notice that everyone has new beaded bracelets around their wrists. Bracelets I've seen before but never seen on them.

Kiko has one with sparkly silver, navy, and aquamarine beads—her favorite mermaid colors.

Lemon's wearing perfect-for-her gold and red and orange and pink.

And Jules.

Jules's bracelet is purple, white, yellow, and black. The same colors they had explained to Peach were nonbinary colors. Colors that made them feel strong and sure and like themselves.

Peach remembered. My sweet sister made our friends bracelets that fit exactly who they all are.

I reach out and squeeze her foot, winking at her while Jules digs through the makeup basket and starts dipping a brush into teal glitter.

"May I?" they ask, holding the brush out to me.

I don't even have to think about it. I nod, lean forward, and let Jules paint me into a mermaid. After they're done, I hold up a mirror and I look...

"Beautiful," Jules says.

"Really?" I ask, touching my scars.

"Yeah, really," they say.

"Ugh," Kiko says. "Don't make us say it again."

I laugh, blush, then go quiet as I put the mirror down. "Kiko...I'm..."

I wait for her to help me out, but she just lifts an eyebrow. She's not going to give an inch, and I guess I don't blame her. I take a deep breath, roll my shoulders back. After all, everything she said to me the other day was right. I was a jerk, but she's still here. She's with me, in this little blanket fort.

"I'm sorry, Kiko," I finally say. "I'm sorry to you, too, Jules. Lemon. Everyone. I just..." I look down, fiddle with the mirror's handle. Then I just say it. I want to get used to saying it more, because it's true. Because it's my life.

Because it changed me and it's going to take a while to figure out this new me.

And I'm going to need friends to do it.

"My mum died," I say. "Two years ago, in a kayaking accident. Lemon knows about it, but I wanted you to know too. I was there when it happened, and I couldn't—"

—*save her* is what I almost say. I'm so used to thinking it, feeling it. But those words, they're not the truth. Guilt still edges around my heart. Maybe it will for a long time, that I survived and she didn't. For today, though, I manage to stop the words, swallow them, and simply motion to my scars. "That's what these are from," I say. "And I guess I'm still working through a lot of it."

Kiko's eyes go soft. She nods. Jules reaches out and takes my hand, squeezes my fingers. I squeeze back and that's that. Lemon smacks a kiss to my cheek, then tickles Peach's belly so she's laughing, and then we just...

Move on.

And it feels good.

"Okay, okay," Lemon says. "We're almost all properly outfitted for our meeting. But before we can discuss costume ideas for the Rose Maid Festival and what sighting party we want to go on..." She reaches behind her and grabs that black-and-rainbow tote bag.

"What is in that thing, anyway?" I say.

"Well, I'm glad you asked, my friend," she says, then

hands the bag to Jules. "You do the honors. It was your idea."

They nod, then dip into the tote bag and take out a pile of navy-blue cloth. They shake it out and a T-shirt takes shape. Two of them, in fact. One bigger and one smaller.

"No MerSquad member should be without one," Jules says as they lay one out in front of me and the other in front of Peach.

I smile, reaching out to touch the soft navy cotton, the seafoam-green script.

THE ROSE MAID LIVES.

Peach squeals and Kiko helps her pull it on. I slip my own on over my plain black tee.

It fits perfectly.

chapter thirty-one

Later, we all go out to the beach, run up to the wind-whipped waves, and kick our bare feet in the cool water. Well, everyone else but me does. I hang back at first, chest tightening as Peach barrels toward the sea in her mermaid shirt with her arms spread wide. My feet are inches from the surf but still on dry sand. At least I took my shoes off. I look down, wiggle my toes, squishing them between and around centuries of crushed-up shells and organic matter, something I haven't done in two years. A smile tugs at my mouth.

Still, stepping closer to the sea feels like walking off a cliff right now. I look up, look out, look at all that endless blue, mysteries underneath, whole worlds, and my stomach flutters, nervousness and excitement crashing like a tsunami inside me. I remind myself I've been *under* those waves. I went under, went deep, and I survived.

Twice.

I'm still here.

But my heart won't seem to catch up to my brain. Or maybe it's the other way around. I don't know, but it's strange, to want something so much and be so terrified of it at the same time.

I watch my friends—that's who they are, my *friends*—splash in the waves with my sister, Lemon twirling Peach around in the surf just like I would do if I could.

I feel the moment Jules notices me just standing there, because they stop trying to skid across the sand just a few steps away from me and lock eyes with me, tilt their head in a question.

"That's a great activity if you want to break your ankle," I say, but I'm smiling.

They smile back, then jog over to me, shoulder lightly grazing mine as we look out at the ocean together.

"So," they say.

"So," I say.

And then we just stand there, silent, except it doesn't feel silent. My body is a riot of noise inside—heart drumming, blood zinging, palms so sweaty I'm sure they must be making a sound like a river burbling over rocks.

"So," I say again.

"So," they say back, a little laugh just underneath the tiny word.

And then...our hands meet. I don't know if I reached for them or they reached for me. Maybe it happened at the exact same time, which feels like magic, but it also feels so real, because our palms press together and then each one of their fingers slips in between each one of mine so we're all tangled up, and I couldn't stop the grin from curling onto my mouth if I tried, but I don't try because I'm holding hands with Jules and they're holding hands with me and they're grinning too.

"So," Jules says.

"So," I say.

"Walk with me?" they say, then tug me toward the water a little.

I freeze. I don't let go, but I pull on their hand enough that they freeze too.

Jules frowns, eyes soft.

I look out at the water again. My heart feels like the south end of a magnet, the sea the north, the pull so strong I feel tears starting to form in my eyes.

Jules keeps hold of my hand, but they turn toward Lemon and Kiko and Peach, and Jules must give them some sort of MerSquad signal, because soon all of them are running up to me, salt water splashing behind them.

Lemon takes my other hand. Kiko takes hers. Peach latches on to Jules's other hand and bounces up and down.

Lemon squeezes my palm. I look at her and my eyes must be full of fear, because her expression goes soft and she leans her forehead against mine.

What's more, I let her.

"We're right here with you," she says.

I nod against her, take a deep breath.

I want to walk with Jules in the surf.

I want to be able to look out at the ocean and not think about everything I lost, everything I fear I'll lose again, but feel...

...love.

Happiness.

Freedom and belonging and awe and curiosity.

Space.

I roll my shoulders back and nod again, nod so they can all see me.

"Yay, Hazey!" Peach calls from the end of our line, and I love her for it. She knows exactly why they're all standing in a line, holding hands with me in the middle. She knows me through and through, her little five-year-old heart loving me no matter what.

"Love you, Fuzzy," I say, winking at her.

"You can do it," she says, giving me a thumbs-up with her free hand. "You're a mermaid!"

I blink at her. "I'm a..."

I glance down at my THE ROSE MAID LIVES shirt.

"Okay," I say. "But before we, you know"—I swing

Jules's and my joined hands toward the water—"I need to tell you guys something."

"You actually are a mermaid?" Kiko asks from the end.

Everyone busts out laughing.

"No," I say, laughing too, but then my smile drops. I gaze out at the water again, mysteries rolling over and over each other with every wave. "I...when I was in the water, I was out pretty far."

"Yeah, no kidding," Lemon says. "I ran down to the dock and couldn't even see you."

I nod, take a breath. "Yeah. And then, when I went in, I went down pretty deep and I..."

"Wait, don't tell us—you saw the Rose Maid," Kiko says, but she says it in a teasing tone, sarcasm pulling at her vowels. Everyone laughs again.

Everyone except me.

It only takes a second for them all to notice, and their laughter drops flat and fast into the sand. The three of them start talking at once.

Lemon: "Wait, what?"

Jules: "Hang on, hang on, hang on."

Kiko: "Say what now?"

Peach just stares at me.

"I didn't see her," I say. "I mean, I didn't *actually* see her."

"But you saw...something?" Jules says.

I shake my head, then nod, then shrug. "I don't know. I was...I mean, technically, I guess you could say I was drowning—I couldn't find the surface or the bottom, everything was the same dark blue and I didn't know which way to swim. I was starting to panic and—"

I slip my hand free of Lemon's for a second, look at my fingers. They're bare. "I lost my moms' wedding rings."

"You what?" Lemon asks.

Tears pile up, just like that, there's no stopping them. I hadn't noticed before right now. How had I not noticed? "My mum, Mama, their wedding rings. I found them in Mama's trunk a few days ago and I was upset and I just wanted to wear them, but then, when I saw Rosemary, I freaked out and they slipped off my finger—"

"When you saw *Rosemary*?" Kiko shrieks. "What?"

"Shh," Lemon tells her.

Tears river down my cheeks, a steady stream as I think about those rings floating in the sea. Mama will be heartbroken. She may have taken off her ring, but I know she'll be upset that I lost them. Even though I was wrong to delete her book, her words are replaceable. These rings aren't. They're custom-made, one of a kind, symbols of the promises Mama never got a chance to keep.

Lemon takes my hand again and curls it against her chest. On my other side, Jules squeezes my fingers. My friends give me a second. I breathe. Still, I can feel a million questions shooting down their arms and into my fingers.

"I didn't see her," I say again, sniffing, letting the sea air dry the salt on my cheeks. "I think I just...wanted to?

So maybe my brain thought her up. Lack of oxygen or something."

"Or maybe you *saw* her," Kiko says, voice dreamy now.

I shake my head. Magic isn't real. But as I look at my friends, my sister watching me with wide-eyed wonder, all of them *here* and holding my hands, wanting to listen to me and help me and just... *be* with me, I realize that's not true.

Magic is absolutely real.

"What did you see exactly?" Jules asks softly.

So I tell them about the pale-haired girl who looked like me, lace collar at her throat, iridescent tail curling out into the dark water. How she held my shoulders and kissed my cheek and how it felt like she pulled me to the surface.

How it felt like she saved me.

When I'm done with my tale, they're silent.

For what feels like forever.

"Hello?" I say.

"I mean," Lemon finally says, clearing her throat. "You look like her, so I guess it would make sense that you saw... yourself? Saving yourself?"

Her nose and eyebrows wrinkle up as she poses her theory. Then, at the exact same time, she and Kiko and Jules all say "Nah!" and start screaming. I mean, literally screaming. Kiko curves around so she joins up with Peach and soon they're all jumping up and down in a circle, yanking me along and squealing. They start chanting "The Rose Maid lives, the Rose Maid lives!" over and over and I can't help but laugh and join in, even though I know we're all just playing make-believe, hoping for something huge and fantastical in our little lives.

As I watch their faces, smiles and tears from laughter, eyes shining, I'm not sure if the Rose Maid lives or not, but I do know this.

Hazel Bly lives.

"Ready?" Jules asks me.

I swallow.

"She's so ready," Lemon says.

We're still on the beach, the Rose Maid celebrated and forgotten again. For now, at least. The sun is starting to sink behind us, late-afternoon light soft and hazy. Jules holds my hand again, fingers intertwined, Lemon holds my other, palm pressed to palm. Kiko is at the end, Peach latched on to Jules.

I close my eyes.

Breathe.

"I'm ready."

Then we run, all five of us connected, straight into the sea. The water hits my feet, my bare legs, my head and my heart, cool and familiar and beautiful, like coming home.

chapter thirty-two

Lemon walks Peach and me back to Sea Rose Cottage. Sand sticks to my feet, my legs, salt water dotting the hem of my shorts, and my sister is just as dirty. When we reach the porch, Peach dashes inside, calling for Mama, yelling about how we're all mermaids and I went into the sea.

"Peach, don't!" I call after her, but Mama appears in the doorway anyway, concern wrinkling her brow.

"You okay?" she asks.

I wave a hand. "I didn't go *in* in. Just…you know, splashed around."

Mama's face softens, eyebrows popping into her curls. "You did?"

I nod. "It's not a big deal."

But we both know that's not true.

"Well," she says, doing nothing to hide her huge smile, even though her voice is calm. "That's good. Come in soon, okay? I've got dinner going."

"Okay."

"Lemon, your mom went home a while ago." Something sad flashes across Mama's face, there and then gone. "She told me to tell you."

"Thanks, I'm heading there now."

Mama opens her mouth like she wants to say something else but seems to change her mind. She waves goodbye to Lemon and then disappears inside. I don't know how I'm going to tell her about the rings. My own fingers feel naked, empty, and I only wore the rings for a day. I can't imagine how hers feel, after years and years of marriage.

"I hope they can still be friends," Lemon says after the door closes. She walks over to the railing and looks out at the sea.

"Who?" I ask after I join her.

"Our moms."

"Oh. Wait, what?"

Lemon frowns at me. "Your mom called this morning to check on Peach and...well, okay, I eavesdropped and I'm pretty sure your mom called things off."

I blink at her. "Called things off?"

"I mean, they weren't actually together, I know that, but from what I could tell, your mom said it wasn't, like, the right time or something. My mom said okay, but she's sad. She's been sad all day, I could tell."

I wait for relief to hit, happiness. I wait and I wait and I wait.

"It won't affect us, right?" Lemon asks.

"What?"

"Just...before. When I talked about our moms together, I know it upset you, and I'm sorry. I wasn't thinking. My dad left. He and my mom didn't feel that way about each other anymore—they chose to be apart—so I know it's way different than what happened with your moms."

I don't know what to say. It is way different. And for weeks, I've felt like I've been carrying around this tiny flame of hatred for Claire. Now that I know Mama's broken it off, I should feel relieved. I should be ecstatic. Mama's heart is safe, we can move on, just the three of us. Maybe go back to California. Even though our house is gone, everything else about our old life is still there.

Except that's just what it is...it's all old, part of a life, a Hazel, I don't even know anymore. We could go back... but we can't ever go *back*.

And maybe that's how it should be. When you lose someone, *the* someone, shouldn't you be changed forever? Doesn't that mean they mattered, that your life with them mattered?

My mind swirls, a million thoughts I can't figure out.

One feeling keeps popping up, though, waving its hand to make sure I see it. And it's not relief.

It's sadness.

Sadness for Mama, for Claire.

I shake my head, unsure what to say to Lemon about it all. Finally, I say, "I'm sorry," because it's true. I am sorry.

She shrugs. "It's not your fault. I get it. It won't affect us, right?"

"No way," I say, but I swallow a sudden knot in my throat. Because it feels like this all might be, even in the smallest way, my fault. I don't know what else to say about it, though, so I change the subject. "Thanks for today."

She frowns at me. "For..."

I shrug. "For just... being there." I pluck at my shirt. "For this."

"That, my friend, was all Jules."

I blush, a smile creeping onto my mouth.

"Uh-huh," Lemon says. "So I thought."

"Shut up," I say, nudging her shoulder. She nudges back, laughing.

"Immy would've loved today," she says. "Your story about the Rose Maid." She looks at me, eyes shiny. "She would've loved *you*."

"Me?" I shake my head. "I'm an acquired taste. I'm not—"

"She would've loved you."

I stare at her for a moment, then smile. "I think I would've loved her, too."

Lemon nods once, a silent *Exactly* or maybe a *Thank you*, then turns back to the sea. "Do you think she's really out there?"

I go to stand next to her. The ocean is dark, the sun nearly asleep now. "Do you really want me to answer that question?"

She laughs. "No. I guess not. I like believing."

I nudge her shoulder and she nudges back before turning around and walking backward toward the porch steps. "I'll see you tomorrow?"

"Yeah, sure, um, please turn around before you fall down the stairs."

"What, you mean, like this?" She teeters her heels off the top step, windmills her arms like she's actually going to fall.

"Lemon!"

"Help me, help me!"

"Lemon Calloway."

She rights herself and smiles. "Okay, okay. I'll text you tomor—"

Her smile shifts into a frown, eyebrows shoved together as she looks at something over my shoulder.

"What's wrong?" I ask, turning to look, but all that's there are the two Adirondack chairs and a weather-worn wooden patio table.

She doesn't answer but brushes past me. I follow her, spotting the pile of wet sand in the very center of the table right before she scoops it into her palm. She opens her hands, sifting through the sand with a finger. The porch light glints off something small.

Two small somethings.

Rings.

Both platinum, engraved with vines and flowers, one inlaid with a blue diamond, the other with a green.

"Are these...?" she starts.

"Yeah," I finish. "They are."

I stare down at them, almost afraid to touch them, relief and wonder swirling in my gut.

"Are you sure?" she asks.

"Positive."

"But you lost them in the ocean."

"I did."

I *know* those rings were on my finger when I went into the sea. I *know* I saw them float into all that deep blue. But my eyes aren't lying. Because Lemon sees them too. Here they are, as real as I am, sitting on Lemon's hand in a pile of wet, salty sand.

We look up at each other, eyes as big as dinner plates.

"She granted you one dream," Lemon says.

"What?"

"Like the poem. *She'll sing you into madness or grant you one dream.*"

I don't say anything else. I just reach out, taking the rings from Lemon as gently as I can, as though they might crumble into ash at any moment. I turn on the little water spigot next to the door meant for washing off sandy feet and rinse them clean. Then I slip them back onto my finger.

When I go inside, Mama calls me to dinner, but I head straight to my bedroom, eager to change out of my sandy clothes.

"I'll be right there!" I call back.

I slip on a pair of pajama pants and a fresh, salt-free T-shirt. I hold my new mermaid shirt in my hands, my moms' rings glinting on my finger. I hug the shirt to my chest—yes, *hug*—breathing in the briny ocean scent before heading to my hamper to toss it in to be washed. As I do, something on my desk catches my eye.

A book I've never seen before.

Or rather, a book I've seen one other time, on a cool summer morning, its pages filled with neat handwriting and color.

I pick up the goldenrod-colored planner and flip through the pages. They're all beautifully blank, waiting to be filled with...

...with me.

My life.

My world.

On the desk, next to where the planner was, there's a bundle of two black pens and the same kind of highlighters Claire used—lavender and aqua and soft orange, cloudy-sky gray and spring green—tied together with a piece of twine, along with a purple sticky note filled with black writing.

For Hazel, it says in pretty cursive. *For calm, for beauty, for peace.*

My eyes sting, just a little, and I hold the book to my chest for a second before I set it back down on the desk and open up the cover. There's a space to put my name, my address if the book gets lost. I slip one of the pens from the bundle and uncap it, then write in my best handwriting:

Hazel Foster Bly

On the line where my address should go, I pause. But then my pen touches the paper again, letters spilling out to form a few little words.

A few words that never felt so right.

Late that night, long after Peach has gone to sleep and Mama has turned off her light, I slip into Mama's room. She's awake, because she turns over as soon as I open the door, and she says my name.

"Yeah, it's me," I say.

"You okay?" she asks.

I nod but step closer to her bed. She turns the covers down, pats the mattress. For the first time in two years, I slide into bed next to my mom and she wraps me up in her arms.

"Couldn't sleep either, huh?" she asks, her voice thick, like she's been crying. She's been quiet all evening. Not like the old kind of quiet, like we were both avoiding each other because we thought that was what the other needed. After dinner, the three of us snuggled into the Sister Quilt on the couch and watched a movie. Mama kept smoothing my hair back, kissing the top of my head, like she was constantly checking that I was there. It was nearly suffocating, but I loved it. I didn't realize how much I'd missed her these past two years, missed the simple touch of her hand, the warm feeling of her body wrapping around mine.

This was home.

Not a house. Not a state. But a heart. Lots of hearts, all connected to mine.

"Not really," I say now.

"Any particular reason?"

I don't say anything for a few seconds but finally let my question spill out. "Did you break up with Claire?"

She stiffens, just for a beat, then squeezes me tighter in her arms. "What?"

"Lemon said you did. Called it off or whatever."

Mama sighs. "I did. I just...I think I need to focus on

you right now. On us. You and me and Peach. But you don't need to worry about any of that."

I go quiet again, letting all that settle. She pretty much just made all my dreams come true. Me and Mama and Peach, the three of us together. Mama connected to me and me to her. But something doesn't feel right. Something keeps niggling at my heart, like a soft knocking on it that won't give up.

I think about today, about Lemon and Jules and Kiko, how they forgave me. How it was *hard*, facing them again, and how it's still a little scary, thinking about being with them, part of their group. What if I mess it up or hurt them again? What if they hurt me? What if Mama and Peach and I leave Rose Harbor? What if I really do like Jules so much that sometimes I feel like I can't breathe, and they break my heart?

What if, what if, what if.

But then I think about Mum.

It hurts so much to be without her because I love her. It breaks my heart, because she mattered. And everything that's happened with my friends—my hurting them—hurts too, because they matter. It all matters, just like Mum mattered. I wouldn't go back and *not* have Mum, even if I knew I was going to lose her. I'd still want her. I'd still want the ten years we had together.

"Mama?"

"Hmm?"

I lift myself up on my elbow so I can look at her. And then I tell her what I should've told her months ago.

"Mum would want you to be happy."

Even in the silvery darkness, I can see her frown. "What?"

"She'd want you to be happy. To make friends and laugh and not be so scared all the time."

Mama's mouth drops open as I echo exactly what she told me in the hospital. "Honey, I'm not—"

"You like Claire. I know you do."

She sighs. "I do. But—"

"And no one can replace Mum. Right?"

"No. Never."

I nod. It hurts to say all this. To let go of the family I always thought I'd have. But this is where we are. And Claire isn't Mum. She never will be. She's Claire, whoever that is to my mama. Just like I'm Hazel and Peach is Peach. Every person, a different heart connecting to others. It's not *replacing*. It's not *forgetting*. It's *expanding*. It's *space*.

"So be happy, then," I say.

"My brave girl." Mama tucks my hair behind my ear. "But, sweetheart, our lease runs out soon and I...well, I promised you we'd go home."

I smile at her. "Yeah. About that."

Mama watches me as I disappear under her bed. I pull out the trunk, Mum's trunk, and then pluck the key out of the nightstand drawer.

"What—"

"I'm sorry." I sit back on my heels, squeeze the key in my palm. "I know I should've asked, but I...I was scared Mum was disappearing and I needed her. I needed her stuff, things that reminded me of her. Paintings, her smell, photos. And I knew it was all in here."

Mama pushes the covers back and clicks on the lamp before sinking down onto the floor next to me. She takes the key and opens the lock, lifts the lid. All the familiar smells hit us both. She sucks in a breath, presses her hand to her chest.

"I know," I say, tears already clogging up my throat.

She nods, rubs my back, and then we spend the next thirty minutes with Mum. Just me and Mama and Mum. Remembering. Laughing. Looking through the whole photo album and talking and sharing stories. The Christmas when I got Rollerblades and Mum spent the whole day gripping my hand on the sidewalk so I wouldn't break my tailbone. Swim meets where Mum would bring cowbells and kazoos to cheer me on, aggravating the opposing team's parents so often, she racked up multiple complaints. Mum and Mama's first date, which featured a fancy gallery opening in San Francisco and ended with milk shakes at McDonald's.

"Mum hated all that fancy art-world food," Mama says. "You know her, she needed her cheeseburgers."

"The greasier, the better."

Mama shakes her head. "God, the times I told her to feed you a vegetable. And she'd say——"

"French fries are vegetables."

We laugh and then we cry and it feels good. It feels perfect. It feels like what we both need. I find my *Ultimate Oceanpedia* and finally open it up, colors and marine life and wonder coming to life right in front of me. Mama wraps her arm around my shoulders as I flip through it, sadness mingling with missing mingling with relief. I've missed this—the facts, the knowledge, the love I had for the sea. The love I still have.

"Thank you for saving it," I say.

Mama nods. "I knew you'd want it back. Or at least, I hoped you would. It's one reason why I chose Rose Harbor. I wanted...I hoped...you'd be near the sea and remember. That maybe the ocean could help you in a way I didn't know how to."

I nod. She was right, in a way. I did need the sea. I needed Mama more, but I needed that ocean, too. I needed to remember who I *was* so I could love who I am.

I'm just closing the book when Mama picks up the ring box and flips it open. She gasps, eyes frantic for a split second, but then I slip the rings off my finger and press them into her hand.

"It's okay, Mama. They're here."

She opens her palm and takes a breath.

"I'm sorry," I say. "I just wanted...you took yours off and it scared me."

She nods. "It's okay, honey. I did take it off. I thought... I don't know. Maybe if I took it off, I would feel...less guilty."

"For...?"

She shrugs, wipes her eyes. "Everything. The accident. How I've handled everything since. Selling our house and needing to leave California." She takes a breath. "Liking Claire."

I nod, then fish in the trunk, searching for something I remember seeing before. I find it in a corner, curled up like a little snake. A silver chain, thin and delicate. I take the rings from Mama and slip them onto the chain. Then I get up on my knees and fasten it around Mama's neck. The rings settle right over her heart, clinking together softly.

"There," I say. "Perfect."

"Perfect," she says, cupping her hand over the rings.

"Mama?"

"Yeah, baby?"

"About California."

She sighs but doesn't say anything. Just waits for me to go on.

"I don't think we should go back."

Her eyes pop wide. "What?"

"I mean...I do want to go. But maybe just to visit. I think...well..." I don't know how to say it. Or maybe I do and I'm scared, because it's huge. This thing in my heart. This desire. This feeling, one I haven't felt in two years, not since the four of us were a family. So instead, I go back to my room and find my new planner. When I get back to Mama, I hand it to her and she frowns down at it.

"What's this?"

"Claire gave it to me."

"She...she did?"

I nod. "To help me with my anxiety. To...feel calmer, organized."

Mama runs her hand over the cover and smiles.

"Open it," I tell her.

She tilts her head at me but does what I ask, opening the cover to the first page, where my name and address are written in thick black ink.

Sea Rose Cottage
Rose Harbor, Maine

Mama sucks in a breath, her eyes snapping up to meet mine.

"Hazel. Are you sure?"

I don't answer. Instead, I stand up and pull on the trunk's handle, dragging it out of Mama's room.

"Hazel, what in the world?" Mama says, setting my

planner on the bed and following me. I don't stop until I've got the trunk situated in the middle of the living room. I click on a lamp, and the bland room comes to light, all bare walls and generic prints.

I take out one of Mum's paintings. Mine. All the blues and greens and grays of the ocean, calm and adventure at the same time, the deepest, most beautiful, most mysterious sea. I carry it over to the fireplace and set it on the mantel. Next I slip a few photos from the album—me and Mum, Mama and Peach right after she was born, me holding Peach as a baby, all four of us smiling on the beach, Mama and me on our old couch, making kissy faces at the camera. I set them up on the mantel. They need frames, but this'll do for now.

I place Mum's candle on an end table. I put Mama's silly mug right next to it. I take down a seascape and hang Peach's painting on its hook on the wall next to the window.

When I'm done, I step back and take it in. Mama comes up next to me and puts her arm around my shoulders, pulls me in close. Even with just these few additions, the room looks completely different. Looking at all the stuff that used to be in our house in California, it hurts. Right where my heart keeps on beating, it's achy and raw, but it feels right, too.

It feels like home.

chapter thirty-three

Two weeks later, I'm standing in front of a large white boat called the *Lonely Rose*.

My hair has grown longer over the summer, past my shoulders now. Last night, Lemon insisted I sleep with it in braids, so that when I woke up this morning, my locks were what she calls beachy waves, perfect for what's going on this evening.

The Rose Maid Festival.

In addition to my waves, I've got on an old-fashioned blouse that Kiko and I found at a vintage clothing shop in town. It's ice blue, with lace at the throat, tucked into a skirt that Kiko actually made. It's the prettiest thing I've ever owned—long and flowy, all these different blues and greens and grays swirling together so it almost looks like a mermaid's tail.

But mostly, I simply look like a girl from a long time ago. A girl who really lived.

The day after Mama and I spent all night making Sea Rose Cottage look more like our home, Peach and I went with her over to Lemon's house so she could talk to Claire. They took a long walk on the beach. I watched them head off, a tiny pang in my heart, but that pang was all mixed up with happiness, too.

Because I knew walking with Claire right then was what Mama wanted.

And I knew Mum would want whatever made Mama smile like that.

While they were gone, I distracted myself by crawling into the blanket fort with Lemon and Peach and brainstorming ideas for costumes.

I knew exactly what I wanted to do.

Who I wanted to be.

It was a small thing, dressing like Rosemary, but for me, it was my way of remembering her, thanking her. Saying that she—the girl, not the myth—mattered.

Lemon and Kiko and Jules and I spent the next two weeks planning and shopping, sewing and gathering props and materials. They've each created their own spin on a mermaid. Lemon's costume is a green velvet skirt with a fishtail linking from the back to her wrist, paired with a green tank top that looks amazing with her fire-red hair. Kiko's is a jumpsuit of sequins. A million sequins, all blues and greens, starting with a halter top that glides down into wide legs. Jules has on a fitted black T-shirt over a fitted black-and-white-and-purple-and-yellow-striped skirt that fans out at their ankles.

"Nonbinary merperson," they said as they emerged from the bathroom at Lemon's, where we were all getting dressed. We all cheered, said it was perfect, and then I blushed because it seems like all I do around Jules now is blush and grin.

When Jules saw me in my costume, they blushed and grinned too, and then Kiko told us to go make out—which we have definitely not done yet, but which I can't seem to stop thinking about—and then we all helped Peach get into her costume.

A peach mermaid.

Literally. Kiko had made her a full-length dress with a peach pattern all over the white cloth, little peach sequins sparkling up the cotton, ending in little ruffles at her ankles like a mermaid tail.

Now we're all here together at the pier downtown—me and Jules, Lemon and Kiko, Peach and Mama and Claire—golden spyglasses in our hands, ready to embark on a sighting party with about twenty other people.

"You ready, baby?" Mama asks.

She's holding hands with Claire, but she lets go long

enough to take my face in her hands, look right into my eyes so I know she sees me. We just went to our first counseling appointment last week, with a doctor named Britta, who thinks I might have a form of PTSD, post-traumatic stress disorder. But she also said we can treat it. The meeting was hard and I cried a lot. So did Mama. But it was *good*. It's funny, how talking about sadness and hope and fear can feel like it's tearing your heart out while healing it at the same time.

"I'm ready," I tell Mama. She's got on her own mermaid costume, a simple long-sleeved dress of ocean blue. Claire has on green, like Lemon, and I manage to smile at her as Mama takes her hand again. I don't mind. Besides, I've got my own hands to hold.

Jules and Lemon and Kiko. Peach right with me like she's always been, like she always will be. I slip my fingers between Jules's and look up at the *Lonely Rose*, look out at the sea behind it.

I feel that tug in my chest—the sea, Rosemary. Or maybe it's just my own heart, reaching out for all the things in the world it loves.

I step onto the boat, my friends, my family all around me, and sail over the deep blue sea.

Acknowledgments

This book was probably the hardest one I've ever written but the one I needed to write the most. Throughout the ups and downs, the plot changes, title changes, character changes, and publication-date changes, Rebecca Podos, my intrepid agent, cheered me on and tirelessly advocated for what I and this book needed. Infinite thanks belong to her.

Thank you to my editor Nikki Garcia, as well as Alvina Ling, Victoria Stapleton, Michelle Campbell, Christie Michel, Siena Koncsol, and the whole team at LBYR for their patience, their faith, and their support of this book.

And, as always, thank you to my family, Craig and Benjamin and William, for loving me anyway.